About the Author

Klaus Schwamborn was born in Cologne, Germany and has worked as a software engineer on many continents. He now lives with his wife, two children and their grandchildren in Toronto.

LOREN - WHO NEVER LOST FAITH IN ME OR THIS BOOK - DAD KLAUS

Emily

Klaus Schwamborn

Emily

Olympia Publishers
London

www.olympiapublishers.com
OLYMPIA PAPERBACK EDITION

Copyright © Klaus Schwamborn 2018

The right of Klaus Schwamborn to be identified as author of this work has been asserted in accordance with sections 77 and 78 of the Copyright, Designs and Patents Act 1988.

All Rights Reserved

No reproduction, copy or transmission of this publication may be made without written permission. No paragraph of this publication may be reproduced, copied or transmitted save with the written permission of the publisher, or in accordance with the provisions of the Copyright Act 1956 (as amended).

Any person who commits any unauthorised act in relation to this publication may be liable to criminal prosecution and civil claims for damage.

A CIP catalogue record for this title is available from the British Library.

ISBN: 978-1-78830-300-2

This is a work of fiction.
Names, characters, places and incidents originate from the writer's imagination. Any resemblance to actual persons, living or dead, is purely coincidental.

First Published in 2018

Olympia Publishers
60 Cannon Street
London
EC4N 6NP
Printed in Great Britain

Dedication

To Francesca

Prologue
A few years ago

The administrator couldn't believe his luck. The operational schematics that had surreptitiously arrived in his personal mailbox a few days ago had presented a stratagem that, if commissioned successfully, would make him powerful and wealthy beyond measure. He would be in total control of the prices people would be forced to pay for food.

The administrator would, of course, have to replace the existing Director of Operations with someone a little less sharp-minded and perceptive; someone who trusted promises of personal gain and was willing to follow rules without questioning motives.

Another consideration was using the resources of a reasonably well-connected government official. That would be easy. There were more than enough corrupt contenders to choose from. The question was, how much were they willing to sell themselves for? A greedy candidate from the Food and Drug Administration would be ideal, and for that he already had a name in mind.

Lastly, if everything went south, he would need a flunky who would take the rap for everything. For that, he had already decided on one of the dim-witted consultants working in logistics.

The administrator would need to be careful that the three new collaborators in his scheme were closely associated with each other, but far enough removed from himself, in case things didn't culminate quite as expected.

The administrator prided himself on being very prudent with corporate expenses. The director of operations had been with the company for over thirty years. Laying him off would mean a substantial payout, a cost the administrator would not even consider. That left him with two possible choices: fire the director, which would be difficult considering his impeccable track-record and high level of productivity, or make his life so miserable that he would leave of his own accord. The administrator decided on the latter.

Reclining his bullfrog - shaped body comfortably in the high-backed executive leather chair, the administrator lit his second Cuban cigar of the day and gazed out through the windows of his top-floor office in Lower Manhattan. Smoking was strictly forbidden in the building, but he certainly didn't inconvenience himself about that ruling.

Yes, he would show his sceptical investors how real money could be made, and if an entire population suffered as a result, so be it.

Anyhow, America had far too many obese individuals. They could do with a bit of hardship in their snug little lives.

He would need to spend some time at operations. He called in his personal assistant and had her arrange the flight to Missouri on the company-owned Cessna Citation executive jet.

The director of operations was infuriated. He normally welcomed the administrator's occasional visits to operations, but not this time. He had presented a solution to the administrator that would maximize productivity at absolutely no extra cost. More so, their profit margin would be increased by millions almost immediately. He had spent months on this document, which exemplified a total overhaul of their existing distribution system, such that delivery could be achieved in almost half the time. His proposal clearly outlined how all inefficiencies in the current operation could be removed. Best of all, nobody needed to be laid off; they would simply be doing the same job, but in a different way.

The administrator glanced at the document, briefly considering the director's proposal. After a few moments, he looked up and rejected it outright. His reasoning – it wasn't feasible at this time.

A short time later the administrator presented the director's proposition to the board as his own work. They approved it immediately and awarded him a healthy financial bonus for his dedication, hard work and far-sightedness.

The director couldn't understand what game the administrator was playing. Certainly, credit had been taken for other things he had done in the past, but they were minor and offered no more than an irritation.

Since his arrival, the administrator had openly challenged the director over the way the department was being managed. He had taken it upon himself to oversee the most mundane areas of operation, such as the number of breaks workers were taking at the water cooler. He seemed to be on some personal quest to micro-manage every part of the director's domain.

Over several days, the director became acutely aware of underhanded suppression of all the decision-making authority that he had once enjoyed. He now felt like nothing more than a dancing marionette, suspended by the administrator's controlling strings.

Ideas about operational improvements for which the director was formally praised were now tied up in a multitude of committee-run approval processes which brought output to a standstill. The director was then accused of not meeting deadlines; not surprisingly, considering that his once-productive department was now subject to bureaucratic policies.

The administrator rejected all of the director's arguments as to why policy should never rule over productivity. He was duly informed that the company had a strict process which everyone was required to follow. The director needed to get with the program and put his house in order. It seemed to the director that this so called *process* only applied to himself and not to any of the administrator's other senior staff members.

Always mindful that he was managing an efficient department, the director found the administrator's actions beyond frustrating. Why this sudden oversight? His managers and operators were hard-working and loyal simply because he treated them with respect. He knew each one by name and regularly enquired about their families and home life in general. His management style was such that his team had a sense of belonging.

The administrator pointed out the smallest mistakes, blowing them completely out of proportion. Certainly, operational slip-ups did occur, but these were extremely rare; efficiency and innovation prevailed by far.

Worst of all, the administrator had informed the director that he would need to move out of his office in the executive suite and down to the cold and uncomfortable workspace overlooking operations. His own office in the admin block had been designated to one of the administrator's yes-men, a low-key manager of nowhere near the same level of seniority as the director.

That was the final straw.

Although not completely prepared for such a life-changing event, the director decided that early retirement was his best option. If he stuck around here any longer, he would likely do some serious damage to someone, go completely crazy, or spend the next few years dwelling in hatred. Financially secure, he concluded that retirement was a viable alternative to seeking other employment where his age was against him in today's world of young self-absorbed executives. Vengeance against the administrator would certainly be sweet, but that wasn't in his nature.

Or was it?

The administrator smiled with satisfaction as he read the director of operations' letter of resignation; it was effective immediately. That was faster than he had thought.

He would now line up his new lackeys and put the rest of his plan into motion. He was still puzzled as to who had sent him the operational schematic.

And why?

It certainly wasn't the director; he would have at least put his name to the document. As resourceful as he was, the director would never have concocted something quite so devious or ambitious. Well, no matter, the administrator reasoned, there was no way that this could possibly fail.

Three months later, the entire scheme was exposed to the media by an anonymous source. Investors lost confidence and stock prices plummeted.

Shareholders had seriously underestimated the administrator's tenacity.

Chapter One
Present day

"Stop it," uttered Emily Hurst quietly to her naked reflection in the bathroom vanity mirror. Frustration with the media's constantly swaying people's thoughts and opinions as to what women and men should look like had been playing on her mind for far too long now. The majority of people simply weren't hard-bodies in their twenties with perfectly formed physiques, unblemished skin and brilliant white smiles.

In her late forties, Emily saw nothing wrong with her teeth and was proud of the fact that they were all her own, a result of having avoided dentists her entire life. The noticeable wrinkles on either side of her brown eyes weren't that pronounced, and, besides, she had earned all of them and liked to think of them as her laughter-lines. Not that she had done too much of that lately.

She pondered on her two failed marriages that had left her with two loving children, both by Daniel, her second husband. He was quite comfortable letting Emily bring up Matthew, whom everyone called Matt, and Eleanor, who favoured Elle, but when some of the responsibility for raising the toddlers fell on Daniel, he just upped and left.

Neither Matt nor Elle knew much of their father, having been without him for most of their lives.

She always wondered why kids had to shorten their names, but concluded that it was a trivial matter. They were after all individuals with their own choices, and, thankfully, were really good kids.

Their two-year age difference, Matt being the older, made it a little easier for Emily to raise them to the responsible and carefree lives they now enjoyed as young adults. Unlike Matt, Elle had always exhibited mental maturity beyond her years. With very little sibling rivalry, Emily was thankful that neither of them had gone through their early childhood in such a way that everything was *unfair* when the other had the advantage.

Both survived their teenage years without too many traumas, and, thankfully, so did Emily. As a single parent, she often doubted whether she had made the right choices or had given sound advice. Not that teenagers asked for advice, she mused, because at that age they already knew it all and were right about everything.

She caught the reflected smile on her face thinking of some of the more memorable events typical to every parent nurturing children through those exasperating early teens. There was absolutely nothing Matt could do or say to pretend that he wasn't doing anything when Emily had walked unannounced into his bedroom one evening, witnessing him in the process of a vigorous masturbation session.

All attempts at covering himself with whatever his hands could grab, failed. Clothing, bed-cover, pillow, just nothing moved fast enough, and his trying to conceal his erect state with his legs was an even funnier sight. If a sink-hole had swallowed him there and then, he would have been quite thankful. Fourteen-year-old boys do blush so very well. Emily found it difficult to keep a serious expression, but didn't make an issue of it.

"Dinner will be ready soon," Emily said matter of fact as if everything was quite normal and walked out the bedroom, closing the door behind her.

Matt, very sheepish for a few days afterwards, avoided looking at Emily directly. Elle knew nothing of the situation, but did make life difficult for Matt by continuously badgering him as to why he was acting so weird all of a sudden. Younger sisters can often do their job too well.

In retrospect, Emily knew that she should have confronted the situation shortly afterward, assuring Matt that it was okay, and that all young men pleasure themselves. In fact, it wasn't only young men, she thought. Men of all ages do it, throughout their entire lives.

Emily found little comfort in the fact that she had actually enjoyed what she saw. The image was still planted firmly in her mind to this day. Her face always reddened slightly at such forbidden thoughts.

She knew that he had started his pleasurable self-indulgences about a year before that, and figured that that was about the age when the angel of erotic dreams visited all young males. What made it evident, though, was his insistence on washing his own sheets. Males are so obvious about their actions, even at a young age; they just don't realize it. Did Matt honestly think that his mom never swept under his bed, where he was convinced his centrefolds were strategically hidden?

Some years later, while Elle had been out with friends one evening, Emily decided that it would be a perfect opportunity to give her daughter's room a good clean. Under a bunch of old clothes which were way beyond their expiry date and should have been chucked out, she discovered a battery-operated dildo. A little disturbed at the size of the thing, Emily hurriedly put it back.

She recalled that her own virginity had been broken not by a man, but by a spare, hopefully unused dildo that Madelaine Porte Burnside, her Barbie-Doll look-alike high-school friend, had insisted she try out – in private, of course. Emily had no idea what to do, except where to insert it.

Her first attempt left a very painful memory. She didn't have the expected excited swelling, nor did her body produce any natural lubricant. It was a dry and very uncomfortable experience that she didn't try again until many months later, having discovered that all pharmacies sell cheap artificial lubricants over the counter.

At the time however, Emily wasn't going to embarrass herself by asking Madelaine, and there was no World Wide Web to draw knowledge from. She did finally figure it out and experimented in a number of ways. It was fun, but it took some months before she experienced her first climax. She discovered that the real technique with the dildo, inserted as high as it would comfortably go, was simultaneously massaging her clitoris. The middle finger was always best.

So this was what everyone was talking about.

Emily purchased a brand new model more to her liking, but nowhere near the size of what she found in Elle's cupboard. Her latest toy, the new Climax SX-6000 Ultra, was, of course, made in China. She wondered what the 5,999 previous models had looked like.

Wrapped in several brown paper bags and sealed with voluminous layers of duct tape, she discarded her old dildo. How embarrassing that would be if her parents accidentally discovered what she did for pleasure. And she certainly didn't want the neighbour's dog digging through the trash and running down the street with it.

Emily had lost touch with Madelaine when each had gone their separate ways after high school. Madelaine had probably gone on to become a super-model, or, most likely, a waitress between acting assignments.

Both Matt and Elle, working in their respective jobs, still lived at home. This suited Emily quite well, since she had an almost non-existent social life. The last fifteen years granted her an agreeable salary as an executive assistant to James Clark, CEO of SkyTech, an aeronautics technology think-tank company.

Well versed in the use of computers, she prided herself in knowing more than her children; a rare situation in today's world of tech-savvy kids who are Internet gurus by the time they're five. Emily spent a lot of her spare time at home dabbling with multi-media software, and in particular with imaging techniques.

Her marriage to Ryan Hurst, Emily's first husband, whose surname she kept, had lasted only two years. He wasn't particularly good-looking, of slight build and a noticeably weak chin that he tried unsuccessfully to cover up with a beard; but she was young and in love. It didn't take too long to recognize that Ryan's ambitions in life were somewhat misdirected and often irresponsible. It was almost as if he needed to prove worth beyond his measure either to himself or to others. He wanted children immediately, but when Emily failed to get pregnant, he had assumed that there must be something wrong with her.

A few years after their divorce, Ryan, much to his disbelief, was informed by a specialist that he was infertile. He moved to St. Louis in Missouri to work as a logistics consultant for some agricultural research company that Emily had never heard of. She had no ill wishes towards Ryan at that time and sincerely hoped he would, some day, find what he was looking for.

Over the years, Emily's memory of their marriage had faded into obscurity - until three months previously. Out of the blue, Ryan had contacted her, and after a few short and awkward pleasantries, had asked if she would join him for lunch. He wanted to bounce a few questions off her about SkyTech. Curiosity, more than anything else, compelled her to agree, so they had settled on a time and place for the following day. How Ryan had found out where she worked didn't particularly bother Emily, but she did wonder what he was up to. He certainly sounded more confident on the phone than he had used to, from what she remembered of him.

Although Emily had very little past experience for comparison, it was obvious that both Daniel and Ryan were very selfish lovers, regarding her as nothing more than a convenient receptacle for their use and pleasure. Daniel was totally insensitive to her needs, satisfying himself, rolling over and going to sleep. Mostly, their so-called love making didn't last longer than two minutes, leaving her frustrated and having to satisfy herself the next morning after a very restless and wearisome night's sleep.

Ryan wasn't much better, but at least he tried in his own misguided way to put a bit of passion into their sex life. He was also a bit of a bigot. Emily recalled a joke he had shared with one of his friends during a social event they had attended in their first year of marriage. "Want to know the difference between a good shit and a good fuck? You don't have to cuddle a good shit for twenty minutes afterwards!"

Emily's mind came back to the present, thinking that some men could be such egotistical pricks. Women were entitled to as much enjoyment out of sex as were men. Was it really her job to just lie there complacently while the man satisfied himself at her expense, and if she occasionally got some pleasure out of it, then it was an accidental bonus?

Weren't women also allowed some self-indulgence? Emily's desires depended largely on what mood she was in, but she would never admit to how she wanted sex. Expressing enjoyment or spoiling herself in some sexual creativity with a man was completely out of the question. She'd be considered no better than a hooker.

Deep down, Emily knew that she needed to get over this imprudent fear. The few encounters which she had had following her second divorce had amounted to nothing more than brief flings. Emily's negative opinion of men, and to some extent of herself, had created too much cynicism in her mind.

Emily had even tried a few internet dating sites, but had given that up almost immediately. Like any other business, they were simply there to sell you something. She couldn't believe the number of delinquents who reached out to her. Wasn't the point of an online questionnaire to match you up with others who shared similar interests and preferences? Which in her case were most definitely not lesbians or she-males. And certainly not psychos who sent photographs of their penises. Men were so juvenile. Didn't they fathom that women started a relationship at an emotional level, one of mutual respect, discovery and understanding?

The loneliness which Emily had tolerated over the previous few years, however, had fostered a sense of longing for an enduring relationship, but at what cost? She had no intentions of pursuing anything doomed to failure, and another marriage was completely out of the question.

Emily picked up her favourite nylon paddle brush from the vanity and tidied up her light brown hair. It was slightly wavy and very easy to manage; she preferred keeping it at a medium length. Signs of grey were kept in check with henna, something that she had been applying regularly, and reluctantly, for the last ten years.

She looked at her small turned-up nose with approval, but was a little thwarted by the slight vertical wrinkle forming over the left side of her upper lip. Her mouth, small and narrow, was a little lopsided from her lifelong habit of chewing the right side of her bottom lip when she was nervous. She knew that over the next few years the wrinkle would grow more pronounced, and others were sure to follow.

Good thing that two of the six lights around the vanity mirror weren't working! If the light had been brighter, she might have found any number of unwanted blemishes she hadn't known about before. Standing away from the mirror, Emily looked at her upper body and assured herself that she was still in remarkably decent shape.

Although not a health nut, Emily did discipline herself in using the Stair-Master twice a week for twenty minutes. It was the only exercise equipment she had ever purchased and had no illusions at the time that it would be used regularly. With so many people she knew, their equipment was duly packed away, out of sight and mind, after a few short months.

Her tummy exhibited a slight bulge, but that was quite normal for someone her age. Her breasts were smaller than average, something she was thankful for because they were still high and did not droop too much after having breast-fed Matt and Elle.

Emily looked down at her legs, which she considered her best asset: almost no fat, and, thanks to her faithful Stair-Master, firm and shapely. She was quite comfortable wearing tight jeans or skirts a few inches above the knee.

All in all though, Emily reluctantly admitted to herself that there was really nothing that projected sex appeal. Well, certainly not according to what the media claimed as acceptable standards.

In Emily's mind, today's women were looking more and more masculine and men were somewhat more feminine, a trend she had absolutely no intention to becoming a part of. It was slightly daunting, however, that almost everything about her was just so very average. There was really nothing she could see in herself that would make men look twice and her five-foot-nothing frame, even wearing heels, didn't help.

Her hands were small, with fingers a little shorter and stubbier than she would have preferred, but she took pride in keeping her fingernails well- manicured and always neatly trimmed to the same length. She knew that men didn't pay any attention to what type of nail polish women donned, but it always made her feel more confident facing the world outside to have applied a new colour or fresh coat.

It was the same on days when she wore her lacy black bra and panties; they changed nothing that could be seen on the outside, but they certainly made her feel more desirable inside.

Emily walked out of the en-suite bathroom and sat on the edge of her unmade queen-sized bed, deciding that today she would slip into particularly delicate and skimpy undergarments - just because.

The early morning sun, filtering through the net curtains of her raised east-facing windows, warmed her naked body. Being high, the windows offered privacy from anyone looking into her bedroom from the street three floors below. Being shorter than most people also helped, and the most anyone could see, even from the sidewalk on the opposite side of the street, was the top of her head.

With her bedroom door closed, Matt and Elle knew not to walk in. Not that it mattered much to Emily if they did, as she really had nothing to hide.

Applying moisturizer to her hands and heels, she glanced idly around her small, cozy bedroom. Her bedside table had a modern fluted-glass reading lamp and she reminded herself that the lampshade needed a good dusting.

Her latest romance novel was lying face down on the pages she had been at before drifting off to sleep last night. Why she bothered with such mundane stories remained a little bit of a mystery. The situations were always predictable and in most cases unrealistic: "... as he thrust his pulsating masculinity against her warm and eager womanhood." She had to smile at some of the metaphors, but reasoned that the books were light reading, and, in some cases, described scenarios that sparked her own fantasies.

There was of course nothing wrong with a little self-help when the occasion called for it, but only at times when Emily knew, or hoped, that Matt and Elle were already asleep, or during weekends when they were out and wouldn't be home until after midnight.

Emily refused to own a TV in the bedroom. There was simply too much drivel shown, and the news just made her thoughts run overtime. She preferred, rather, to drift off to sleep reading a book or perusing a magazine. It certainly helped her forget about the emptiness of not having someone to cuddle up to.

Emily always felt totally relaxed in her private domain and allowed herself the liberty of being unclothed as often as possible. She didn't own any sleepwear or nightgowns and very rarely slept wearing a loose T-shirt, preferring rather to sleep nude, and, during warm summer nights, on top of the blankets. Feeling a little more vulnerable than she would in her bedroom, Emily never walked around the apartment naked, even when she was completely alone.

Chapter Two

Suitably dressed in a cross-over V-neck white blouse, which she hoped wasn't too transparent, light-brown slacks and medium heels; Emily clipped on her favorite hoop earrings and walked through the combined family-dining room into the kitchen.

"Morning, kids," she said, looking over at Matt and Elle sitting opposite each other at the small four-seater kitchen table. Both were engrossed in their coffee, toast and morning texting rituals.

Apart from one corner where Emily kept her laptop, the dining room table, which could seat six at a squeeze, was never used except to hold clutter. This was where Emily spent most of her time in the evenings, while Matt and Elle sat on the corner settee in the family room, feet up on the lounge table, watching TV or occupying themselves with their iPads. They had a good social life outside of the home and often invited friends over, but neither had a serious relationship that Emily was currently aware of.

"Hey, mom," Matt said, without looking up.

"Morning, mom," Elle replied, momentarily redirecting her attention from her phone to Emily. "Sleep well? Macy's is having a sale on clothes this week if you're interested."

"What, you don't like the way I dress?"

"Oh mom, you look great. Just thought you'd like to see what's available. You can take me with if you like," Elle prompted with a smile.

"Sure," Emily responded with a frown. "Just remember to bring your own credit card this time."

"So, are we going?" Elle asked.

Emily repeated the timeless mantra of all mothers. "We'll see."

She walked over to the coffee maker, set on the grey dappled veneer counter top, and prepared a fresh brew of medium-roast. As usual, her children made only enough for themselves, but she figured that that was a small price to pay, considering that they were generally tidy and always washed, dried and put away their own dishes.

On rare occasions, Emily would treat herself to a cup of Blue Mountain coffee from Jamaica; it was reputedly the best on Earth, which she agreed with, but also the most expensive.

Emily sat down for a few minutes while the coffee brewed. Conversation was light around the breakfast table, where they typically exchanged news topics, plans for the evening and more banter. Matt would be on his way to work in the next ten minutes, and Elle a few minutes afterwards.

Emily's modern kitchen, with stainless-steel refrigerator, dishwasher and gas stove, was well designed, spacious and practical. She would have preferred enamelled white appliances, but the stainless made it very easy to keep clean. The only problem was the small window over the double sink. She would have preferred it a little larger, to offer more natural light.

Emily's modest third-floor rental apartment on 64th Avenue and 108th Street in Queens was well situated near her hair salon, a mini-mart, the bank, and her favourite of all local retailers, the 99-Cent Store. Not that there was ever anything under $3, but she enjoyed popping in regularly, regardless of whether she needed or wanted anything.

Every few weeks, Emily took Matt and Elle to dinner at the local grill, where they enjoyed good food and a few hours of quality family time.

The narrow residential tree-lined streets surrounding the apartment block were well maintained and always clean. Benches and trash receptacles were well-spaced along the sidewalks. Matt had found the hiding-place of the rooftop access keys used by building maintenance, and often sat with Elle on top of their six-storey complex enjoying the sun.

Looking north, they were able to see parts of Flushing Meadows Corona Park and the tip of the Unisphere, a twelve-storey globe sculpture constructed for the 1964 World's Fair. The park also hosted the annual U.S. Open tennis tournament, and was well known for the building-for-building model of New York City in the Queens Museum. Citi Field, home of the pro baseball team, the Mets, was nearby.

Matt and Elle had both graduated from Forest Hills High School, a two-minute walk from their apartment, but neither had gone on to higher education, preferring rather to get out into the working world as soon as possible.

Emily often spent warm weekends strolling along the paths surrounding Meadow Lake, within walking distance from home. A convenient pedestrian walkway allowed safe access over Grand Central Parkway.

Her rent was probably a little above her financial means, but she loved the quiet and safe neighbourhood. Her needs weren't extravagant, and she felt no jealousy towards those lucky enough to be walking out of exclusive Park Avenue department stores with bags full of clothing and jewellery which they would probably never wear.

Shortly after Matt and Elle had left for work, Emily sat down in her usual spot at the dining room table. Relishing a bagel with her fresh coffee, she responded to a few personal emails and cleaned out the regular daily marketing spam sitting in her junk folder. Finalizing one other item that required attention, she readied herself for another day at the office.

Emily Hurst worked at SkyTech Tower, located on East 72nd Street in Manhattan. Taking a casual stroll from the 72nd Street subway, she could usually get to the office in five minutes. On warm summer days like today, the only hazard was all those young adults walking with their faces down, texting, and the cyclists, whom she occasionally had to dodge when crossing the 2nd Avenue intersection.

On her way to the office, Emily passed a few refurbished brownstone tenements over variety stores, popular Bar and Grill establishments and a convenient grocery store where she regularly picked up a few essentials on her way home. Far too many consumables these days seem to be rebranded as *New and Improved.* And the only things that were new were the escalating prices and diminished content. Does this mean I've been eating *old and inferior* all this time, she mused to herself?

The store also stocked a variety of non-prescription drugs.

Emily's purchases consisted of no more than the occasional bottle of cold and 'flu medication at the start of winter.

Were her eyes really deteriorating that much with age, or had the writing on the drug labels just become smaller? Not that these labels ever specified anything useful. They were there to protect the pharmaceuticals from liabilities. In some cases, the listed side-effects indicated conditions which the medication was supposed to relieve. She could only chuckle quietly to herself at the stupidity.

***

James Clark, or more accurately, as the grandiose bronzed nameplate on his oak panelled office door indicated, *James Worthington Clark III - CEO SkyTech*, was livid. This was now the third time in a month that his private computer files had been scanned by an unknown outside source.

Not wanting to wait for Emily, his executive assistant who would be arriving to work in about five minutes, James Clark walked directly to the Information Technology department, flashed his key-card to the optical security door scanner and stormed inside.

"Nate, where are you?" James bellowed.

Nathan McIntosh, or Nate, as everyone called him—at least it wasn't "Mac"—came out of the computer enclosure with the full report that he knew JW would want to see immediately. Nathan had become aware of the intrusion just moments before James discovered it on his own computer.

"I could only route it back through the last four anonymous service providers situated across the globe," Nathan explained, looking down at the report held loosely in his right hand. "Where was the last point?" James asked, frowning.

"Canberra in Australia," Nathan said, directing James' attention to the bottom line of the report. "Follow me. If there's additional info, we can see it directly on the monitor."

Nathan presented his key-card to the workstation scanner, also optical, to re-activate it. After ten minutes of idle time on the monitor, keyboard or touch-pad, it automatically locked itself as a security measure. Nathan spent almost his entire day working at this station. Having it lock on him was a rare event.

Besides being a programming prodigy, Nathan created applications specific to "what-if" scenarios, as well as a number of very sophisticated tracer programs that could back-track any unwanted attempts to get into SkyTech's computer systems, and subsequently into individual workstations. This week alone, his latest tracer, which he fondly named 'SnagIt', had been responsible for locating the source of over fifty attempted hacks.

It was a remarkably simple algorithm that broadcast a message on the internet suggesting that their data servers were not secured by any firewalls. Hackers who were ensnared by this false claim used rudimentary intrusion software to get in, convinced that they needed nothing very complex. SkyTech's internet facing server collected those unwanted intrusions. It had limited processing power but many terabytes of data consisting of blueprints, formulas and construction models.

Unknown to stalkers, this goldmine of seemingly valuable information, which they believed could be sold to the highest bidder, was developed with a deliberate flaw; none of it actually worked, or it was based on technologies that had yet to be invented.

Regardless of the data, each file had also been encoded with SkyTech's trademark. Not only did you need to know how to decrypt the trademark, you also needed to know where it was. This guaranteed proof of theft in the event someone claimed it as their own technology.

The network server also administered SkyTech's incoming and outgoing email traffic. Messages received were directed to a secured system which inspected the mail, and, if it was free from any malicious code, passed it on to the recipient. The bogus server acted as a deterrent against hackers trying to get into SkyTech's primary systems, where all their authentic proprietary information was warehoused.

Embedded within an email were far more details than those presented to the receiver, some of which were the hardware and software characteristics of the originating computer.

Behind the scene, all emails exchanged two-way traffic asynchronously between the sending and receiving mail providers. They acknowledged successful receipt or notified any failures, such as an unknown email address, or the fact that a destination server was unreachable. In the latter, the mail provider attempted to send a few more times before logging the events and finally giving up.

Along with the message context, detailed email activity was recorded on all mail servers, regardless of whether the exchange had succeeded or failed.

Most people assumed incorrectly that all evidence of their private and possibly incriminating mails would be successfully wiped out by clearing their 'In-Box', 'Sent' and 'Deleted' folders, or with such extreme measures as reformatting their computer's entire hard- drive. They didn't consider that emails were replicated and stored for an almost indefinite period on every provider they passed through.

Back-tracing a malicious email, even if it had come through a multitude of anonymous servers, presented nothing more than a mild inconvenience to an experienced programmer.

SkyTech had a contract with the government to provide hacking data, and using SnagIt, it could trace the large majority of this mischievous activity back to its source. Mostly, this activity came from students working out of college computer centers.

The government had a vested interest in prosecuting hackers and advertised the fact constantly. Their interest was of course for the benefit of themselves and not the private individual.

The revenue accrued by SkyTech for this service to the government was a reliable and steady source of income.

"This particular hack is somewhat unique," Nathan explained, as they examined the real-time global trace image. "It shows Canberra as the last point, Fairbanks in Alaska prior to that and Lagos in Nigeria before that." He followed the connecting lines with his finger along the digital map displayed on his monitor.

"Have a look at this," Nathan said, punching a query into the keyboard. "As soon as I try and reroute the signal backward from Canberra, the IP, or Internet Protocol address in Fairbanks, no longer exists."

James was taken aback. "How's that possible?"

"Using anonymous internet service providers comes with a small cost, but if you need a few more features, they will gladly deliver, with additional charges of course," Nathan clarified. "They call themselves anonymous for very good reason, and pride themselves on total confidentiality, but nothing is foolproof."

Nathan understood the concepts used by these providers, having written and sold many of the technologies now in use. He had very little trouble getting through the so called privacy that hackers thought they were enjoying, and paying for, but this repetitive hack into JW's personal computer was proving to be quite a challenge.

Nathan received alerts of intrusions immediately, both on his monitor or through Instant Messaging which he picked up on his phone when he was away from one of his workstations.

Each personal computer within SkyTech logged unauthorized access to its programs and data files, but that wasn't the only indication which James had had that his files had been accessed. To the best of Nathan's knowledge, the unwanted digital intruder never corrupted anything in the way a virus would do. It just grabbed what it wanted, terminated its own existence and disappeared without trace.

But it also left a calling card.

That was another dilemma Nathan pondered on: a simple image, about four inches square when displayed on a monitor, and plain grey in colour. Nothing that resembled a picture or text message was apparent. Photoshop manipulation, a quick search for embedded program code, or any of the other techniques commonly used, didn't yield any immediate and obvious results. It was a standard JPG image. Nathan wondered why a hacker would leave a plain grey calling card behind, yet instincts, fed by years of experience, convinced him there was more to this - something about these calling cards that he just didn't see.

An essential part of any computer file's metadata was the date and time the file was created, updated or read along with a user identity. In the case of James's computer, the intrusions were on emails only, and the metadata was updated with the same user identifier as with the calling card, namely *Anonymous*.

James was brilliant when it came to aerospace technologies, having two master's degrees from MIT and a communications doctorate in subjects that very few people could even pronounce. He was well versed in multi-media, imaging algorithms being one of his specialities, but networks and the internet remained a perpetual mystery. That was for people like Nathan and his team of developers. His concern was not so much the intrusion, but rather the information being looked at: email communications that could very well put James W. Clark behind bars for a very long time.

The National Security Agency, or NSA, claimed for years that they did not have secret underground computer labs intended to monitor global communication - the privacy act always being hot on everyone's agenda. As much as nobody believed these claims, in this they were telling the truth.

Up to a point.

Operating as an autonomous division of the United States Department of Defence, they certainly collected and stored unbelievably large volumes of digital data, but never actually did any analysis on it. This level of non-ethical surveillance lay within the domain of companies like SkyTech who were contracted out.

SkyTech had all the computing resources available to probe into telephone communications, email, texting or any other form of digital data transfer. The government, besides securing itself with plausible deniability, paid handsomely for this service. Encrypted or compressed data was decoded and examined by very sophisticated software, able to analyse potential threats not only with individual words or expressions, but also in the context of a sentence or paragraph.

The software could decipher messages or program code hidden within audio or image files, and was able to accurately analyse over eighty different languages and dialects. Its algorithms self-adjusted according to the mood of the population. People expressed themselves differently during times of stress, such as a devastating earthquake or another Middle-East conflict, than they would when times were relatively peaceful.

Communications analysis on behalf of the National Security Agency was another lucrative source of revenue for SkyTech.

It always amused Nathan McIntosh to think of the endless money which all governments had readily available in the interests of national security. Of course, it was only for the protection of the self- serving politicians, not that of the people whom they claimed to be protecting.

Along with digital data, the National Security Agency provided all the encryption software used by SkyTech. Although Nathan had contributed much to the sophistication of this, lending his expertise to the agency, at a price of course, any program using a new encryption technique could not end up in the public domain without vetting and approval by the NSA. This guaranteed that nobody used anything the agency didn't know about. SkyTech was also under a contractual clause that prohibited modification of any software provided by the NSA, penalties being so severe that no company would even consider crossing such a legal boundary. This didn't mean that SkyTech couldn't enhance the stream of processes with some of their own functionality.

And that was exactly what James Clark instructed Nathan to do.

Communications were examined by the National Security Agency's code stream and reported back by SkyTech if deemed a potential threat. Anything else was simply stored for an indefinite period of time, in case proof on a legal matter was ever required, or, more accurately, in the event that the government needed a hold over someone.

Data provided to SkyTech for analysis could not be modified or deleted without approval by the NSA. Regular audits comparing SkyTech's files with their original NSA counterparts ensured this. Nathan was perplexed at the sheer volume of digital data which they were required to keep. He could understand phone conversations, emails and even text messages, but most of the other stuff made no sense at all, especially video feeds with no sound, like those recorded by security or traffic cameras.

SkyTech only received a very small portion of data collected by the NSA. Any communications between other intelligence agencies like the FBI, CIA and Homeland Security, along with rival political parties, they kept to themselves. Clandestine surveillance between government departments remained a national pastime, each trying to hold power over the others. Nathan couldn't understand why they didn't just work together.

Internet providers keep a history of all data that passes through their servers, even if the provider only acts as a transient service between sender and receiver. Whether visible to the account holder or not, social media sites store everything, including that which is removed by the client. Deleted accounts and all content are never expunged, just deactivated.

Photos make up the largest volume of data on social media, especially from teenagers and young adults. Selfies now outweigh vacation snaps by a ratio of fifty-to-one - an entire global population declaring *look at me.*

The volume of worldwide digital information is beyond calculation, making the internet the single largest electronic data storage and retrieval mechanism on the planet. Web searches, text messages, images, music, digital phone calls and web-casts; if it's transmitted across the web, it's there indefinitely. Anyone who knows how, can access it. And that includes the NSA.

Nathan McIntosh introduced a new program into the process stream and slotted it in just prior to the NSA's data being stored. It was designed to scrutinise any communication that involved a medical term or discussion on nutrition and then to replicate that information on a discrete database.

James knew that this would be a reasonably involved task, confident that Nathan would be more captivated with the challenge of the job than with how the information would be used.

"I want you to keep this very low-key, Nate," James had instructed him. He didn't want this modification to the NSA's spyware to become common knowledge at SkyTech, as it would no doubt raise awkward questions.

Although SkyTech's addition of a snooping program to the NSA's process stream was technically illegal, there would be absolutely nothing the government could do about it without also exposing themselves to the truth of their eavesdropping practices.

Nathan designed the new program architecture and passed it over to his small team of developers. Each wrote a small functional part that, on its own, could not expose the true purpose of the end result. Only Nathan knew how the individual parts would be pieced together, and in what order. He included some deliberately misleading instructions in the technical specifications, as a precaution against the developers discussing their work amongst themselves or with others. He would take the superfluous code out before final assembly.

Nathan underestimated his development team's curiosity.

Chapter Three

"Stay on top of this hack, Nate," James said, motioning with the printout. "And let me know the minute you find something new." Contempt on his face, he marched briskly out of Info Tech back to his office.

"Good morning," Emily Hurst greeted James with a smile as he walked by her anteroom. "You seem to be deep in thought."

Emily was one of the few at SkyTech who didn't call him JW.

She had just arrived at work and was dumping her oversized black imitation leather handbag on top of the four-drawer filing cabinet next to her L-shaped mahogany reception desk. It was always a bit of a stretch, but the cabinet proved a convenient locality.

"Oh, morning, Em," James replied, as he lifted his perceptive grey eyes from the printout and looked towards her.

Emily, my name is Emily, she thought in mild amusement. Not Em or Emi. Just Emily. What is it with everyone these days?

James Clark was a strikingly handsome man. He fitted perfectly the model of today's expectations when it came to appearance. His midnight-blue suit, tailored perfectly to his six-foot-tall physique, projected an aura of business professionalism which he proudly upheld. James's dress sense was very conservative. His ties, always a darker shade than that of his shirts, were styled in a half- Windsor knot; and typically rested between the top and middle of his belt line. The colour of his thin belts, black or brown, always matched that of his lace-up, Italian leather shoes.

When James walked into a room he owned it. His quick appraising eyes saw everyone and everything all at once. Emily regarded him as a respectable and courteous boss who knew what he wanted, with the ability to make the right decisions at the right time. He was always considerate towards Emily, and the only irritation she had was the occasional *Do you have a minute?* when she wished him a good night. More often than not, the minute turned into an hour, but Emily resigned herself to the fact that it was really nothing more than a mild annoyance. Where did she have to rush off to anyway?

James very rarely closed his office door, even when he changed into sports gear for his weekly squash game on Thursday afternoons. Although he undressed down to his underwear nearer the corner of his immense yet functional office, and out of sight of the general workplace, Emily always had a clear view.

He was broad- shouldered, with a well-formed chest and arms, along with a hard, flat stomach. His tight slim-line underpants revealed his well hung manhood, and amplified his flawlessly-rounded buttocks. He upheld a respectable appearance in suits or sports gear, and ensured that he was always clean-shaven and that his hands were perfectly manicured. His dark brown hair, parted on the left and with greying temples, was kept short and tidy.

Emily was sure that he was all natural and doubted whether he ever had cosmetic surgery, something now as popular with men as with women. In the US alone, over ten trillion dollars were spent in 2015 on face-lifts, skin stretches, implants, bone-restructure and any other sort of bodily augmentation imaginable. Cosmetic surgery was not restricted to aging actors and actresses trying to keep their youth, but was becoming progressively more popular among teenagers with well-to-do parents. Tanning salons had apparently lost their appeal in today's world, where appearance held dominance.

Emily often imagined what this man could do to her in bed. Anything he wanted, she mused. Emily smiled to herself thinking that, with his masculine perfection and her feminine plainness, they would appear as a truly odd couple. Not that she ever made any suggestion about her thoughts, nor was there a need.

James Worthington Clark was gay.

Emily tilted her head slightly in a questioning manner as James walked by her desk. "Is there anything wrong? You look like you're in another world."

"Yes," he replied after a stilted pause. "My computer was hacked."

"On no, not again!" Emily said, a little apprehensively. "This is what, the third or fourth time this month?"

"Third," James replied, walking into his office and sitting down behind his Victorian-styled nineteenth-century rosewood desk. The adjoining Bordeaux marble- topped credenza, on which he had placed his Stanford briefcase earlier, imparted a sense of grandeur to the office.

Emily followed. "Is anything missing or corrupted?"

"Nate is looking into it now. And if you could please close the door on your way out?" James said, abruptly dismissing her.

"Well, if you need anything, just let me know." Emily closed the door and walked back to her private reception area. Nathan would probably mention it to her during their regular lunch session later today.

Emily sat down on her swivel chair and powered up her computer. She couldn't understand why she had to re-adjust the chair's height every day. It was not like anyone else used it.

She looked at the framed photo next to her four-line telephone console, with fond memories of last year's vacation to Florida: Matt, Elle and Emily waving enthusiastically at the camera in the hands of an obliging tourist.

Emily did not get an annual bonus like most of the managers. Instead, James paid for an all-inclusive two-week holiday once a year for her and her kids. A bonus would have all ended up with the IRS anyway, so this arrangement suited her perfectly.

The office area started livening up, as employees, greeting each other, walked briskly out of the elevators into the foyer and through the glass doors facing Emily.

Most of the administrative work-stations on her left were open-plan. Beyond that were facilities with a small kitchen, restrooms, storage and the closed security doors leading into Info Tech. To the right of reception were the spacious client seating areas, manager's offices and two conference rooms. Plush tan carpeting covered the entire floor.

Along with the basement, located below the underground parking levels, SkyTech occupied the topmost seven floors. The rest were rented out to a variety of businesses, ranging from lawyers' offices to travel agencies. The ground level had an assortment of high-class fashion retailers which were beyond Emily's income. She did enjoy browsing, but purchasing anything, even the cheapest of items, was totally out of the question. Not that she could ever see herself in any of the designs, some being quite hideous with sharp contrasting colours; they were just not styled for women of Emily's short stature.

Chapter Four

James Clark had been contacted two years previously by Adrian Bowers, a member of the board of directors for the Food and Drug Administration. They had agreed to meet for dinner that evening at Donatello's, an upscale family-friendly restaurant, located a city block from SkyTech.

James felt instant relief from the oppressive warm and humid air as he entered the climate-controlled establishment. Walking towards several people gathered around the hostess' podium, he recognized the face matching that on the electronic business card which Adrian Bowers had emailed him earlier that day. Adrian raised his hand in acknowledgment and smiled broadly - his teeth were too straight and white to be real.

Adrian was a large, overweight man who perfectly matched what James had envisaged from his booming voice when they first spoke on the phone. After greeting each other, exchanging pleasantries and comparing power ties, they were escorted to a private booth at the rear of the restaurant and away from the tedious piped music, for which James was thankful. He never understood the need for swanky restaurants to try and lull their clientele to sleep with wearisome chamber music.

A few single men, typically looking for a bit of action, occupied the expansive bar area on the right. Their numbers would increase as the evening progressed. Most of the white linen-covered tables were taken by families enjoying a night out, or businessmen discussing golf.

Lights hidden in deep recesses of Adrian and James' cubicle provided a warm ambience and were just bright enough so that miner's lamps weren't required to read the menu. After they were comfortably seated and had ordered their drinks, Adrian, with his inflated sense of self-importance, came directly to the point. As he had explained in the phone call, the FDA, whom Adrian represented, had a business proposition that would be very profitable for SkyTech.

"I know the National Security Agency isn't exactly vocal about it, but we at the Food and Drug Administration are well aware that they use companies like yours to snoop on global communications," Adrian stated as a matter of fact.

Not taken aback, or even overly surprised, James replied with caution. "I don't know where you get your information, but how is an aerospace technology company of any use to you or the FDA? We are hardly in the same line of business."

"It's not the business so much as it is the information you process on behalf of the National Security Agency," Adrian continued, undaunted. "Look, the NSA and FDA are just subdivisions of the same government. The fact that we don't speak doesn't mean we're ignorant about what the other is doing."

Adrian paused a moment as the attendant placed their drinks on the table; a calorie-free "Old-Fashioned" for himself and a club-soda for James.

"The FDA has a bit of a bad reputation and much of our research into food is outdated," Adrian said. "As you well know, half the planet's first-world population is either totally obese, or has a life-long medical condition like diabetes. We know the long-term effects of genetically modified or highly refined foods, but what we don't know is why so many people now have allergies to natural products like peanuts. Similarly, why do people have allergic reaction to gluten or dairy products? What was extremely rare twenty years ago is now commonplace."

Adrian took a sip of his Bourbon, and caught the attention of their server. "Are you ready to order?" he asked, looking towards James.

"No starter for me. I'll just have the Steak Neptune, medium- rare, with a Village Salad on the side," James said to the server. "And if you could please bring me another club-soda."

James had never acquired a taste for alcohol. All it did was make his head spin; it would likely contribute to a bad liver as he got older.

"No starter for me either," Adrian said. "I will have the sixteen-ounce Porterhouse, very rare, baked potato with extra sour cream and a Greek salad, but without the olives."

The server thanked them and hurried away.

"One of many conditions we see now is an overwhelming number of people developing Alzheimer's and dementia,"

Adrian continued. "These are no longer rare ailments restricted to the very old, but in the last ten years it's become apparent in people in their fifties. Same with Parkinson's. We now see it in people as young as twenty-five."

James Clark knew the truth of what Adrian Bowers was telling him. "Go on," he prompted.

"People have lost trust in their physicians," Adrian explained, "and we see a backward move towards more traditional cures provided by herbalists. What the FDA wants to know is what people are speaking about. How are herbalists and nutritionists able to cure diseases that remain elusive to modern sciences and technologies?"

James was a little confused. "Adrian, isn't it obvious? Today's medical practices are to keep the pharmaceuticals in business; in my opinion, they are the biggest drug pushers on the planet."

"Yes, yes," Adrian replied quickly. "You're just a little ahead of what I was saying. It's true that doctors have no interest at all in curing people and they are certainly in the pockets of big pharma. You wouldn't believe the way they compensate medical professionals for prescribing their drugs. It's never money or royalties, but rewards like two-week cruises in first-class cabins for the entire family, new cars, and I know of three cases where doctors were rewarded with fully-furnished luxury homes. On top of that, doctors don't want any liability, so bounce individuals from one specialist to another. It's an excellent way to generate money all around, but does nothing for those who want their health restored."

James considered this as their entrées were served. His Steak Neptune, an eight-ounce filet mignon topped with crab meat, asparagus spears, and hollandaise sauce, was butter-fried to perfection. The Village Salad included the regular mix of vine-ripened tomatoes, thinly-sliced cucumbers, red onions, kalamata olives and feta cheese, all tossed with extra-virgin olive oil.

Adrian Bowers beamed as his mouth-watering Porterhouse, sizzling in its wood-based cast-iron platter, was placed in front of him. The size of the steak matched his considerable ego. The baked potato was large and smothered with sour cream. Just the way he liked it. The Greek salad was a generous serving of romaine lettuce, feta cheese, black olives, ripened tomatoes, small chunks of cucumber, and red onions. The server had obviously forgotten to make a note that Adrian didn't want olives, so he put them aside without further thought.

"Will you join me in silent prayer?" Adrian asked James as he folded his hands. "We should give thanks for our food."

"Er, please go ahead," James said, with mild amusement. "I hold no religious beliefs. I find it all a little contradictory."

"How so?"

"Too many people killing each other and dying needlessly over what I see as exactly the same belief, just with different doctrines," James replied.

"Obviously it's part of God's plan for humanity."

"But He or She, whatever the modern politically correct term nowadays, is supposed to be all loving and giving. Why, for example, take children away from their parents?" James argued. "Isn't that a little mean and vindictive?"

"Ah, but you see, God is simply testing their faith."

As if James had never heard that before: he hoped Adrian wasn't about to recite quotations from the *Book of Job*.

Adrian went on. "Their children are now living an eternity of carefree existence in the Kingdom of Heaven."

"Then what about armed conflict?"

"What do you mean?" Adrian asked.

"Each side proclaiming that God is supporting their cause and not that of their enemy."

"Our Lord truly works in mysterious ways, but ultimately supports the righteous," Adrian stated, as if it were obvious.

Maybe your *Lord*, thought James. Certainly not mine.

Adrian bowed his head and closed his eyes for a few moments.

James watched him briefly in bewilderment and then diverted his eyes to his food, waiting politely for Adrian to conclude his dialogue with God.

"Shall we?" Adrian Bowers said abruptly, as he reached to his right and rolled the silverware out from his linen napkin. "Let's get stuck in. Don't want the food to get cold, do we?"

Reassured that he wasn't about to be converted, James continued where they had left off before Adrian's brief spiritual interlude. "So, how would you use communications on nutritional foods and traditional cures? Assuming, of course, that we would be able to provide what you're asking for."

"Research, mostly," Adrian answered. "If we can prove beyond doubt that readily available natural products are safe to use in a controlled environment, we would endorse them. Take the eucalyptus leaf, for example. Correctly prepared, it can cure a severe cough in a few days, and it's perfectly safe. Prescription drugs do nothing but cover up the symptoms. They are not designed to cure."

James savoured every bite of his steak. "I must confess," he said, "I'm surprised to hear this from an FDA representative."

"Here's the thing," Adrian admitted between mouthfuls. "Most people assume that the Food and Drug Administration not only supports these unethical practices, but are the instigators. We're nothing more than a typical government-controlled entity with a limited budget, but are accountable every time someone eats something bad or overdoses on a prescription drug."

James understood very well how government budgets worked, and certainly concurred with Adrian's point of view.

Throughout the remaining conversation, while they finished their meals, James debated a few points, but was in total agreement that it was time big pharma's immense profits were redirected back to where they belonged: curing sickness.

The server noticed the olives put aside as he came to collect the dishes at the end of James and Adrian's meal. "I'm terribly sorry, sir; I should have reminded the cook to exclude the olives. I will have the salad removed from your bill immediately."

"Don't worry," Adrian assured the uneasy server. "An honest mistake, I'm sure."

"I don't want your answer immediately," Adrian said to James, as he took care of the bill, along with a generous tip. "Give it some thought and let's get in touch next week." He scribbled something on the back of his copy of the receipt and handed it to James. "This is what we had in mind as a monthly imbursement, if you provide the service we require."

James Clark was used to boardroom games, but had never quite perfected his poker face. The FDA's budget was obviously not as limited as Adrian had implied.

Adrian smiled openly to James. "As you can see, we are serious about this."

After a few polite exchanges about the hot weather and deteriorating traffic conditions in Manhattan, Adrian and James bid each other a good night and agreed to a further discussion in a few days.

Stepping out of Donatello's on to the sidewalk, James considered his options. The proposition appeared legitimate enough and Adrian seemed to be sincere. He was certainly a devout Christian, but something just didn't feel right to James, something he couldn't quite put his finger on. He brushed it off as nothing more than the anxiety which he often felt negotiating new business ventures. Or maybe it was simple cynicism towards the self-righteous? By the time he reached the garage where his Bentley Continental waited in its reserved bay underneath SkyTech Tower, he had concluded that he'd go ahead with the deal.

Sitting alone in the cubicle, Adrian picked up his phone and dialled a number. "We have him," he said and hung up.

***

Walking towards the exit of Magentis International GMP's corporate offices in downtown St. Louis, Missouri, Ryan Hurst smiled as he disconnected the call from Adrian Bowers. He had expected nothing less and felt a certain sense of importance at being kept in the loop by such a highly placed FDA official. Outside, he hailed a cab to take him to Lambert International, from where he would catch his eleven-hour flight to Oslo in Norway. From there it was another two hours' flight to Svalbard Lufthavn.

***

A week later, agreement was reached between James Clark and Adrian Bowers. Contracts were drawn up, and SkyTech's profits were guaranteed for the next five years, and perhaps even longer. It took Nathan McIntosh and his team of software developers just under five months to have the required application in place. The month after program deployment was a period of quality assurance, bug fixes and refinement.

It was incredible what people spoke about when it came to their health, and how many natural and freely available herbs and foodstuffs worked. One of the biggest surprises was the number of young people who were taking their health and nutrition seriously.

Most of the software refinements were to filter out communications between people who were convinced that some or other cure which they read about on their favorite wiki provided the solution to all their ailments. These were deemed useless and simply discarded, as were the bulk of text messages between people. The most reliable sources of information were still phone and email conversations.

Now, two years later, James Clark sat behind his desk, reclined slightly in his high-backed leather chair and looked out through his South-West facing corner windows at the city traffic, thirty-one floors below.

His office included a small bar which he rarely used, a conference area, two occasional chairs with side tables, and, opposite a low rectangular coffee table, a three-seater Chesterfield. Opulently framed portraits of space shuttles, Saturn-5 rockets and military jets were displayed proudly along the office's North wall.

James was particularly fond of an artist's rendition of an F/A-18F Super Hornet fighter jet in a steeply-inclined manoeuvre. Capable of vertical ascent, and of reaching fifty-thousand feet in just over one minute, the Hornet could destroy an orbiting satellite with one of its wing-mounted guided missiles. A fourteen-inch model of a Grumman F-14 Tomcat was exhibited on the topmost shelf above the bar.

In the opposite corner, an ornate grandfather clock, given to James on his thirty-fifth birthday by his dad, ticked unobtrusively in tempo with its brass pendulum.

Still with the printout in hand, James deliberated at how quickly things had gotten out of hand and what he was going to do about it. Had he really been that blinded by profit as to be so easily entrapped by Adrian Bowers from the Food and Drug Administration?

Chapter Five

Walking out of his Info Tech office, Nathan McIntosh considered the security measures which they had employed to protect their primary computer system. The multi-layered firewalls and intrusion prevention applications were all software-related, but the actual hardware and its vulnerability to physical attack presented different challenges.

Securely located three levels below SkyTech's office tower, an IBM Sequoia super-computer processed incoming data at over sixteen petaflops. Super-computer speeds were measured in how many mathematical floating point operations they could process every second, simply known as *flops*, and *peta* being a representation of ten to the power of fifteen, or a thousand trillion. Governments made prominent use of companies with such processing power.

Housed in an environmentally-controlled cube constructed of three-foot-thick reinforced concrete, the IBM Sequoia, oblivious of purpose or existence, assembled intelligible information ingested from raw data at phenomenal processing speeds. Data replication and backups were transmitted along a fibre-optic cable to a secure off-site data center. Fibre-optics ensured freedom from magnetic and electrical interference.

Located behind Info Tech's security doors on the top floor, a high-speed elevator, custom-built by ThyssenKrupp, provided the only means to descend into the IBM's domain. Access required that a valid pass-code be entered into an attendant alpha-numeric keypad, as well as optical key-card recognition. Once inside the elevator, a subsequent retina scan was needed, but only when descending to the basement level. There were no controls to select a destination and no intermittent stops. The elevator could not be summoned from the thirty-first floor if someone had taken it to the basement.

When not in use the elevator randomly positioned itself somewhere between the twenty-fourth and thirtieth floors. Nobody ever knew exactly where it came to rest. Forcing open the top floor elevator door usually exposed a dark, seemingly bottomless pit. Without ceiling access into the elevator car, any attempt to rappel down the shaft proved futile. The elevator ran on two fail-safe systems through independent power supplies, each backed by emergency diesel generators, housed securely in a well-ventilated corner of the lower parking level.

"Ready for some lunch, Em?" Nathan McIntosh asked, popping his head around the partition surrounding the executive suite of offices.

"Hi, Nate," Emily replied. "Just give me a moment. I must quickly pass by the little ladies' room."

Nathan watched Emily proceed towards the washroom. She had great legs, and, being somewhat shorter than most women, was cute. Her way of walking projected subtle sex appeal that she was apparently unaware of. He had always been attracted to women like Emily. Mature in body and mind, no pretence, and feet firmly planted on the ground. Unfortunately, Nathan's relationships were few and far between and he had never married.

If Emily Hurst disagreed on something, she said so, and her contradictory points of view always made for animated and interesting dialogue. He was extremely fond of her, and had discovered a few years previously, during their varied lunchtime discussion topics, how easy she was to talk to; most surprisingly, she understood most of the computer lingo he so often used.

He also liked her intelligent and inquisitive eyes. Emily never paid much attention to him in ways he hoped, so Nathan automatically assumed that she had no interest in pursuing a relationship. She had certainly never hinted at any such thing.

Nathan was usually deep in thought on one or another of his software-related challenges. It didn't help that he regularly carried a somewhat confused expression on his face, not the best for inviting open or casual conversation from others. Most people gave no attention to this and simply regarded him as "Nate, existing in his own little world of binary ones and zeros." He figured that Emily thought much the same.

As far back as his late teens, Nathan's encounters with women had usually resulted in their standpoint of *let's just be friends*. Having finally accepted that his personality or appearance obviously weren't getting him into the type of physical and emotional relationships for which he longed, Nathan engrossed himself deeper into his career and passion for technology. He was already friends with Emily, good friends. He just didn't want to hear her repeat what he had heard from others so often in the past.

A few minutes later Emily and Nathan entered the ultra-clean, almost clinical, staff cafeteria one floor below. They placed their order and sat down in their usual spot by the south-facing windows away from the long tables that buzzed with people engrossed in animated conversation. It didn't take long for the ready-made meals to arrive. Emily had her usual tossed salad and juice; Nathan, a large cheeseburger, fries and coffee.

"Did you manage to find anything more on the intrusion into James's computer?" Emily asked, adjusting her chair closer to the table.

"Just spoke with him an hour ago," he replied. "My best guess on how they got in was through a *phishing* email." Nathan took a huge bite of his burger and followed it with a gulp of coffee. "Made to look exactly like one of his regular profit and loss reports, the email probably had embedded code that activated as soon as it was opened. Its function would be to get into the computer's internal registry, turn off his anti-virus protection and notify the sender through an anonymous address that the computer was open to intrusion."

"And if it wasn't incoming mail?" Emily asked.

"I still have more digging to do, but it was either that or an automated malicious software patch. One thing is certain: with JW's computer open to the world, the sender directed a request to scan JW's email inbox, extract specific content and reactivate the anti- virus."

"What was it looking for?" she asked, a little too casually.

"Just about anything related to the FDA," he cautiously replied, remembering JW's instruction not to make the addition of his snooping program public knowledge. "But that's not what bugs me," Nathan went on, chewing between sentences. "How did the intrusion know to work its way directly into JW's computer, and not someone else's?" He shook his head and stuffed a few fries into his mouth. "And why only emails between SkyTech and the Food and Drug Administration?"

Nathan couldn't work out exactly what the agency's angle was, or whether the NSA was somehow tied directly into this, but why had a devious third party now become a troublesome player?

"Have you looked at any of the emails that were scanned?" She reached over and helped herself to a few of Nathan's fries.

"I like the new nail colour you're wearing today," Nathan remarked offhandedly.

Emily was surprised and a little flattered at his observation.

"I think you have very nice hands," he continued nonchalantly. He considered reaching out and stroking her fingers, but quickly reverted his thoughts back to the conversation. He valued their association and she was the only person in the office he considered more than just a work colleague. He always felt comfortable in her presence and didn't want to ruin that side of a solid relationship.

Anyway, he wasn't daring enough for such a bold move and certainly didn't want to get slapped.

"Well, the email contexts are nothing more irregular than requests for various updates on a business proposition that JW is working on," he said. "I've asked Sven to do some research on the sender. Maybe he can find something more specific that I've missed?"

Emily nodded without comment.

Sven Labrowski, Nathan's top software engineer, was born of a Swedish mother and Polish father. Nathan regarded him as the most talented of his team. A little outspoken at times, and often insolent, Sven had absolutely no regard for authority. Nathan probably gave him a little more slack than the rest of his team, because of his uncanny knack for trouble-shooting the most difficult problems.

What Nathan didn't know, and knowledge that Sven Labrowski kept passionately to himself, was his involvement with an elite community that considered him as one of the world's top hackers. Known only within this elusive group as "Trinity," Sven made a small fortune on money transfers, acquiring information or disrupting services for anyone who needed it.

Conspiracy blogs often credited Trinity for redirecting charitable funds out of the hands of so-called administrators, to where they should have gone in the first place: providing food and shelter to the needy.

Emily Hurst had finished her salad, and, pushing her plate aside, watched Nathan as he downed the last of his coffee. As usual, his reading glasses were balanced on the tip of his nose, and when he wasn't frowning, as he was now, he had a friendly and sincere smile.

Nathan McIntosh's pale grey-green eyes were soft, warm and kind. His brown hair pigment had resigned their commission years ago, leaving him with a wayward grey mop on his head. Reasonably long and wavy, it fell just short of his shirt collar.

Emily often thought that with a cowboy hat he would look like Sam Elliot, but without the moustache and not quite as tall. Besides her attraction to Nathan, she respected him. He never spoke to her in a condescending way, and certainly never treated her like a fool. Yes, she could very easily get intimately involved with him. Pity that he never showed any interest.

Lunchtime discussions between Emily and Nathan were usually work-related or about some item that made the news headlines. Occasionally Nathan would inquire about how Emily's children Matt and Elle were doing, or ask about her weekend plans. Emily reasoned that very few men would be interested in a twice-divorced woman with grown-up kids. Why would she expect Nathan to be any different? She diverted her eyes slightly as Nathan looked up over his glasses from the empty coffee mug.

"James looked really worried when I spoke to him earlier today," Emily said, after a brief pause. "I'm not sure if he was more concerned about the emails, or about a hack getting through our firewalls."

"Emails, most likely," Nathan replied. "You know that he takes security very seriously, but not to the extent where there are so many protection mechanisms installed that we bring ourselves to a standstill."

Nathan wiped his mouth with a paper napkin, crumpled it up and tossed it on his empty plate. "Ready to get back to work?" he asked. "I need to see if Sven has unearthed anything new."

They walked up the stairs and returned to their individual workplaces on the top floor. Emily couldn't understand people who were always rushed, but were prepared to wait two minutes for an elevator to take them up or down one flight when stairs would obviously be faster. Just another excuse to catch up on some texting, she figured.

***

With his tall, thin frame reclining comfortably in his workstation chair, Sven Labrowski ran long fingers through his unruly blond hair. He quickly reviewed JW's emails, which Nathan had brought to his attention. Not that there were any surprises, as Sven knew exactly what they were about. He had been prying into James's files and emails for quite some time, but had had to be careful what findings he reported back. Unlike his other probes, this investigation was officially above board.

It never failed to surprise Sven just how ignorant most people were about their computer security measures. If a computer was Wi- Fi enabled or plugged into any kind of internet-facing network, its data was accessible to anyone who knew how.

Most companies had policies that required a password be changed every two or three months. Strict rules enforced by the computer's operating system ensured that a password hadn't been used previously and that it didn't consist of a name, birthdate or any other obvious information about the individual.

Complexity rules were such that most people created arbitrary and meaningless sequences of characters and numbers just to comply with these rules. Their new password was then jotted down in a convenient place because they were sure to forget it. People like Sven Labrowski didn't ingeniously guess someone's password within three attempts the way Hollywood suggests. No, there were much easier ways.

To ensure that computers are protected from the latest trojans, spyware, malware, bots or any of the multitudes of unwanted intrusions, anti-virus software allows updating of itself. It's essentially self-maintaining and at pre-determined intervals, usually every twelve or twenty-four hours, sends a request for the latest update, patch or bug-fix. If available, the software provider delivers the applicable file through the computer's network, and it self-installs. This happens automatically in the background, without any human intervention or awareness.

Computer users don't care how their systems are protected or what updates are applied; they just want peace of mind that their data is safe.

Sven Labrowski's traditional method of hacking was a straightforward trojan disguised as an anti-virus security patch – self-installing and without any further interference from the computer.

The information collected, modified, corrupted or destroyed by Sven's hacks, along with the cost, varied according to customer needs. Method of payment was by electronic bank transfer to one of his many off-shore accounts, each registered under a fictitious name. The customer had thirty-six hours to make the deposit, failure resulting in the local authorities receiving an anonymous tip about illegal activity.

Nothing could ever be traced back to Sven Labrowski.

Six months previously, he had been contacted through his Trinity internet-persona by an Argentinian investment banker who wanted ransomware installed on one of Chase Manhattan's New York based computer centers.

The malware Sven installed was essentially a worm designed to corrupt data, and, much like a biological worm, it was singular in its purpose: eat data, shit out garbage, slither forward. It was scheduled to activate within the applicable time period unless five million bitcoins were deposited through an anonymous provider to an internet account. Confirmation of the transfer ensured that the worm was destroyed without causing any harm. Sven's fee for his services to the investment banker was a modest fifteen percent.

Banks were hacked regularly, but never made it public knowledge, for fear that wealthy investors would lose trust and sever their business ties. All the video surveillance imaginable was defenceless against modern bank robbery practices. Banks simply accepted it as a fact in today's world of electronic blackmail, and recovered their money in the usual way by increasing banking fees on low- and middle-income account holders.

***

James Clark followed Nathan McIntosh through Info Tech's security door and threaded his way around the various printers and hardware components scattered everywhere. They made their way to Nathan's small office, adjacent to the four open-plan developer workstations.

"It's quiet here," James observed.

"Everyone's probably still on lunch," Nathan responded.

"Good, because I want to discuss something with you that's extremely sensitive," James said, lowering his voice slightly. "Hope you don't mind that we use your office."

James was well aware of the discomfort Nathan felt sitting opposite his large and ornate desk. Nathan loathed any environment that brandished authority and control. What James had to say needed to be on Nathan's home turf.

"There's been a very disturbing turn of events following the deal I reached with Adrian Bowers from the

FDA," James said. "Apparently, the data we're collecting for his so-called research into nutrition and herbal cures was only part of his agenda. Bowers is now blackmailing SkyTech, and if I don't comply with his wishes, we have a very good chance of losing the business. I will undoubtedly end up in prison."

Nathan looked directly at James in bewilderment and uncertainty. "Are you sure this is something you want to discuss with me?"

"Yes," James replied, "and I'm going to need every bit of help that you can provide."

James spoke freely now, recalling the sequence of events that had started three months ago. He had agreed to meet with Adrian at Donatello's, but just for a drink.

In a secluded corner booth away from prying ears, Adrian Bowers made his demands. "What I need from you James is to create a piece of secure software that can listen in on Smartphones. I know you have the expertise to do this."

James was outraged. "Are you seriously suggesting I go along with this?"

James was well aware of just how easy it was to listen in from anybody's phone, even if it appeared to be off. Smartphones were never truly powered down unless the battery was removed, something no longer possible with many of the newer models manufactured without a detachable back cover.

GPS, Maps, Camera and many other applications sent and received data continuously, as well as using other features of the phone. It made sense that the Camera app would need access to GPS and Clock if the photo were to include location and time information. Other apps were less ethical, using GPS to track and record the owner's location for the purposes of marketing and advertising.

Some apps were designed to *listen in*. Depending on the choice of phone, by simply saying "Siri" or "OK, Google," the device answered almost immediately.

Nathan had recently cautioned SkyTech personnel to be vigilant when downloading applications, and to note what access rights those apps required, especially the free ones. Some were questionable, others totally absurd. Did the Flashlight app really need access to Contacts in order to work?

Adrian went on as if James hadn't said a word. "I want you to create a digital replication of all the SIM Cards for the phone numbers I will provide. I then need a secure link into that data with the ability to replicate the SIM on my phone."

"And have you considered the legal implications of such an absurd request?" James pointed out.

"Legally, SkyTech would be held accountable. You are under agreement not to modify data or programs provided by the National Security Agency. Even though you didn't make any direct code changes, I would provide a leak that you did change their process stream by introducing programs of your own. The lawyers would fight it out in the Supreme Court, and the agency's argument would be that you were sub-contracted to test their programs on the plausibility of undesirable regimes using spyware applications."

James felt his blood pressure mounting.

"What you are doing," Adrian continued, "would be considered as theft of classified government property. Legally, it's a grey area, but the courts would side with the NSA. Case closed! You go to jail." Adrian looked James menacingly in the eyes. "The Food and Drug Administration would of course deny all involvement."

Sanctimonious prick! James ordered a double shot of whisky and downed it in a single gulp. He ignored the burning sensation in his throat.

"You will do this," Adrian stated, obviously enjoying the moment, "otherwise National Security will be hearing from me indirectly. You have six months to complete the development, and I expect regular updates on progress."

Stunned at what he had just heard, Nathan McIntosh looked sympathetically at James as he concluded his story.

"That doesn't leave much time," Nathan said. "Unless you have any alternative suggestions, I can start on the work almost immediately."

James looked at Nathan thoughtfully. "I've been stalling on providing any useful information to Bowers, but he's becoming restless and his last few emails have a very threatening undertone."

Nathan sat silent, sensing that James had more to say.

"Nate, think about it," James said. "These are precisely the emails and my responses that are being scanned by the intrusion hack into my computer. There's something else, and one of the reasons I haven't said anything to you before now. I have a suspicion that the source of the intrusions may be within SkyTech itself."

Nathan drew back with a start. If that were true, there were grave consequences on how their internal and external security controls were being managed.

There was a strained silence between the two, each momentarily consumed in his own thoughts.

Nathan looked up. "I have an idea."

Sitting inconspicuously behind his workstation partition, Sven Labrowski, expert software engineer and notorious hacker, had heard the entire conversation.

Chapter Six

Located four hundred feet inside a remote island mountain in the Svalbard archipelago, situated between Norway and the North Pole, lies the Svalbard Global Seed Vault, more commonly referred to as *The Doomsday Vault*. Built and paid for by the Norwegian government, the vault represents the world's largest collection of crop diversity. It has the capacity to store over two billion seeds that make up a variety approaching almost a million samples.

The vault is managed by the Crop Trust Organization, regulated under international law, and funded largely by participating governments along with generous contributions from companies like Magentis GMP.

Svalbard's vault is one of the most secure and heavily protected structures on the planet. It remains closed for three hundred and fifty days of the year. The archipelago is politically stable and military activity is strictly forbidden. Any country or organization can store seed in the vault, and there are no governmental or diplomatic requirements. There are roughly seven thousand five hundred gene banks, situated in almost every country across the globe. Svalbard provides a secure backup for over fifteen hundred of these independently run facilities.

With geological stability, low humidity levels, permafrost that offers natural cost-effective freezing and its location well above sea level, the vault is designed to withstand natural and man-made disasters. The low temperature and moisture levels inside ensure passive metabolic activity, keeping the seeds sustainable for many years.

Magentis GMP logistics consultant Ryan Hurst drove the company owned Volvo T6 SUV along the icy road to the vault's entrance, less than two minutes from Svalbard Lufthavn, the archipelago's international airport. The car was provided by his company's newly established provincial office in Longyearbyen, a small commercial center nearby. Adjacent port facilities at Gammelkaia managed the transport of seed and other commercial produce to Svalbard.

Ryan's overnight flight aboard the massive Lufthansa A-380 from St. Louis was smooth and uneventful. He had slept most of the way. Crossing seven time zones, he arrived in Oslo, Norway, to a late continental breakfast, which he consumed waiting for the two-hour transfer flight to Svalbard.

Briefcase in hand, Ryan leapt out of the car and quickly tugged the hood of his bright red Brookvale jacket over his head, to protect himself from the frigid, minus-twenty-degrees centigrade temperature. One thing about Canadians, they knew how to make good winter clothing! He had ordered this one from the Montreal-based company prior to his first visit to the archipelago two years earlier. The jacket was expensive, but well worth the price.

The bright piercing sun, hovering a few degrees above the south-eastern horizon, offered no noticeable warmth. Small, rocky protrusions cast elongated shadows along the snowy terrain. Walking the few steps across the railed metal walkway towards the vault's eight-foot tall steel entrance door, Ryan raised his hand to greet his colleague. "Henrik, how are you?"

"Come on inside where it's warmer," Henrik Torbjon replied with a broad smile, as he turned to unlock the door.

They hurried in, but Ryan didn't feel any warmer at all. At least there was no frosty wind once the door sealed shut behind them.

"Good thing it's summer, ya," Henrik stated in his distinctive Norwegian accent. "So how are you, my friend?"

Henrik Torbjon, tall, with long blond hair and bushy beard, worked for NordGen, the company overseeing seed deliveries. Countries that stored seeds from their gene banks had no direct access to the contents in Svalbard's vault, other than to their own reserves. When samples arrived at Gammelkaia, the boxes were X-ray scanned, to ensure that only seeds were being deposited into the Vault. NordGen personnel transported these boxes directly to the Vault for storage.

"I'm glad to be out of the wind," Ryan replied, walking towards the regulatory safety equipment lining the right side of the entrance hall. Above the equipment, a rack of overcoats in numerous sizes were available to provide visitors with additional warmth if needed.

Henrik Torbjon punched the required code into the security access panel located just inside the entrance.

"It's good to see you," Ryan said. "How is Grete? Your five boys still keeping you busy?"

"Five? We now have six," Henrik boasted, proudly. "You will obviously join us for dinner tonight. Grete will be delighted to see you again."

With clearance into the facility electronically authorized, the panel activated the power providing light and ventilation to the seed vault. After they had equipped themselves with helmets, boots and gloves, Henrik Torbjon led Ryan Hurst alongside the utility access stairs, toward the doors opening into the main tunnel.

Ryan was impressed with the state-of-the-art security systems visible everywhere. He had no doubts that there were many other sensors and devices, not quite so obvious or visible. Although Ryan had been to the vault twice before, he had never gone beyond the main entrance. Prior visits had been to oversee delivery of seed shipped from Magentis GMP. This appointment was to take full inventory along with inspecting seed quality, and to ensure that sustainability was being maintained.

Unlike the cubic configuration of the entrance hall, the main tunnel was of circular construction. Fourteen feet in diameter, it penetrated four hundred feet into the mountain. Crenellated steel sheets lined the reinforced concrete passageway. Although on a much smaller scale, it was similar in appearance to most of the road and railway tunnels throughout Europe.

Power cables and ventilation pipes, suspended from the apex of the tunnel, coursed the entire length. Ryan hesitated a moment, before following Henrik through the channel's ingress. They strode briskly along the gently descending concrete walkway towards the main section deep within the heart of the mountain, footfalls echoing ominously in the chilling air. Fluorescent strip lights equipped with motion sensors illuminated above and ahead of them and extinguished themselves behind, giving Ryan a bit of an unnerving feeling.

"Do you ever have power failures?" Ryan asked.

"Oh, all the time," Henrik replied, looking over his shoulder at Ryan with a sideways grin.

Ryan felt it getting colder as they neared the end of the tunnel.

"What happens then?"

"It becomes totally dark," Henrik joked, sensing Ryan's nervousness. "But don't worry! We are all required to carry one of these."

Henrik moved his coat aside, reached into his pocket and pulled out a small but powerful LED flashlight which he displayed to Ryan. Also visible was a German manufactured Mauser C96 pistol fastened securely in its holster hanging off Henrik Torbjon's belt.

"Loss of power is not a major concern for us," Henrik explained. "The Arctic permafrost and insulation properties of the mountain maintain a constant climate in the vault. We've only had to turn on the cooling units once in our twelve years of operation."

Ryan couldn't imagine a place like this ever warming up enough to have to be cooled.

"Ventilation only runs when the vault is occupied," Henrik explained. "You may have seen that small grey utility building on the side of the road from the airport. That houses the backup power generator, which is serviced and tested twice a year. We have contingency plans for unlikely events."

Reaching the end of the long passage, where a huge control panel dominated the right wall, Henrik pulled out another set of keys from his trouser pocket to unlock the doors leading into the main chamber.

"From this panel every feature of the vault can be monitored and controlled," Henrik explained, waving his hand towards the panel. "We have a similar but larger unit at our control center in the town, from where the vault's environment is closely monitored twenty-four hours a day."

Ryan was captivated by the multitude of levers, rotary controls, dials and digital gauges mounted floor to ceiling in the twelve-foot wide unit.

"Everything has redundancy built in, so any device that fails is automatically switched to its backup counterpart," Henrik said, when he saw the enquiring look on Ryan's face. "The panel runs on its own power supply, which, in turn, also has redundancy built in."

Henrik selected a hand-held scanner-keyboard from the charging station flanking the panel and led Ryan into the receiving area. Unlike the entrance hall and the tunnel, this chamber had no concrete lining or support pillars anywhere.

It was carved directly out of the mountain's core, as were the vaults themselves.

To ensure efficient use of available artificial light, the walls and roof were painted white. Only the floor remained, with its natural dark grey granite hue. Running perpendicular to the tunnel, the main chamber was just over seventy feet wide, and roughly twenty feet deep. The steel doors into the three vaults on the opposite wall were spaced thirty feet apart. Ryan noticed thin layers of reflective ice covering the doors.

"The only area of the vault that is above freezing, but only just, is through that small door," Henrik said.

Ryan's eyes followed to where Henrik was pointing and regarded the door clearly marked WC. "Ah, the ever-important washroom." Toilets and restrooms throughout Europe were referred to as *water closets*.

Henrik prompted Ryan toward the central vault, where he presented a security clearance card to the responsive electronic scanner. He unlocked the door with an oversized key.

"Only the middle vault is currently in use," Henrik explained.

Fifteen feet beyond the central vault's final security gate, Ryan appraised the eight aisles of heavy-duty blue and grey rack-wired steel shelves running eighty feet further into the mountain's core. The shelves held numbered seed boxes, stacked nine high and partitioned in sets of three.

Each container had a capacity of two cubic feet and housed individual vacuum-sealed silver packets and glass test tubes. Seed batches were labelled with a unique reference number, along with the category-type, gene-group and sub-class using the traditional Latin classification. A bar code represented this information for convenient scanning of the content. Magentis GMP restricted its seed storage to food produce.

"Why are the boxes different colours?" Ryan asked. "I thought they were all dark-blue, like ours."

"That's up to those who send us their seed. The only ruling from NordGen is that they are made of resilient plastic or carbon-fibre, and they must conform to an exact shape and size."

"I can see some of Magentis' boxes halfway down on the left, but they seem to be mixed in with an assortment of others," Ryan remarked.

"We store incoming containers in the next available location," Henrik explained. "The vaults would have to be ten times their size, and largely empty space, if everything was partitioned by organization or country."

Ryan gave a thoughtful nod.

"Also, doing it this way hopefully encourages the idea of international cooperation for the benefit of all human-kind. Do you really think seeds from Palestine care if they are stored next to Israeli seeds?" Henrik asked facetiously.

"Good point," Ryan concurred. "The vault is quite an achievement," he said, changing the subject.

"Digging a hole into the side of a mountain was easy. Even getting the government to pay for it was nothing compared to the real challenge."

"And that was?"

Henrik looked mischievously at Ryan. "We had to develop a rechargeable battery suited to such cold conditions. Now that was a challenge!"

Ryan was impressed. "I wouldn't have even considered something that's so obvious to you. Are the batteries developed in Norway?"

"No, they come from Mutsuka Electronics in Japan. They're not much different from regular lithium types, but all the manufacturer is willing to disclose is that they have introduced a specific combination of solid state electrolytes. At the moment it's a closely guarded secret. The batteries charge in half the time and have a lifespan about three times longer than regular lithium cells."

"Impressive. Are they only used by NordGen?" Ryan asked.

"They've been available to companies like ours in Europe and Asia for almost five years. They're expensive."

Ryan could believe that.

"You Americans," Henrik mocked with a smile. "Always years behind in technology, but seemingly decades ahead with misleading marketing. You won't see innovations like this on your continent until the industry has managed to steal the formula and patent it as their own. Then they will be made as cheaply as possible with parts being provided by the lowest bidder and assembled with built-in obsolescence in some foreign country. They will of course be sold at fifty times the price of the manufacturing cost."

Ryan reluctantly had to admit the truth in Henrik's observation. Was America really so transparent to the rest of the world?

"I'm surprised your manufacturing industry has survived this long without any ethical quality control being enforced," Henrik said, shaking his head.

"Oh, we have quality control," Ryan answered, matter-of-fact. "Our rejects are sold online or shipped to retail outlets in Canada."

Henrik wasn't surprised. "I have the Japanese Mutsuka batteries in my phone as well as the torch and scanner. The phone battery doesn't even need a special charger, just the regular one that was provided with the phone. See if yours works. I'd be surprised if it even turns on."

Ryan hurriedly pulled a Samsung S8 out his pocket and pressed the power button. It flickered to life briefly and shut off again. "That's disturbing," he said with concern.

"Don't look so worried. You won't get a signal down here. Anyway, humanity has successfully communicated for thousands of years without these electronic appendages consuming every moment of our lives."

Henrik plucked his phone out of its leather holster, dialled a number and quickly uttered a few words in a hushed tone.

Not that Ryan could understand Norwegian, but it did spark his curiosity. "You don't seem to have signal problems," he observed.

"I'm connected to the internal Wi-Fi," Henrik replied. "A privilege that I unfortunately cannot grant you. I'm sure you understand."

Ryan nodded, but still felt at a bit agitated being disconnected from the outside world.

"Did you bring a printout of your inventory checklist as requested?"

"Yes," Ryan replied. "But I have it electronically on my tablet..." He didn't finish what he was saying as realization hit him. Like his phone, the tablet wouldn't work under these frigid conditions either. "In a job like this, we tend not to take all our electronic conveniences for granted," Henrik said, smiling at Ryan. "Sometimes pencil and paper still work best."

Ryan was beginning to see that.

"Let's get started," Henrik suggested, handing Ryan one of the clipboards from the rack. "I have the Magentis' box codes listed as MAG-USMIS-2015."

After Ryan confirmed from his own records, which he now attached to the clipboard, Henrik punched the code into the scanner.

A scrollable list of bin locations for each of the containers was instantly displayed. "I have twenty-six boxes listed."

Ryan confirmed and followed Henrik to the first of the boxes in Aisle-C where it was pulled out and placed onto a nearby cart for easier examination. Henrik unlatched and lifted the lid, then carefully removed the contents of several glass vials and five vacuum-sealed bags.

It was impossible to determine visually the type of seed stored. That would be seen on the readout when the barcode was scanned. The audit was to ensure that the holders were sealed and had not deteriorated. In the case of the ampoules, a quick inspection would reveal any seed contamination.

First with the bags, then the vials, each was scanned by Henrik and verified by Ryan against Magentis' inventory list. When handed the first of the glass cylinders labelled *Genus Cibus-Fructus*, *Semen-Pupillam-Rutilus,* Ryan gazed at the little apple seeds with humble reverence. Asking nothing in return, oblivious of existence or purpose, each seed could develop into a tree with fruit that enclosed replicas of the seed itself. With the ability to survive indefinitely under ideal conditions, all it required was soil to germinate, a few simple nutrients, water and light.

Daunted by the thought that he might be holding man's last mechanism of survival from self-destruction, Ryan carefully placed the tube back into the box and checked it off his list.

Although not arduous, the task of auditing each sample was a long and careful process. By early evening, they had inspected eighteen of the twenty-six boxes. They would continue the next morning, and would be finished well before Ryan's afternoon departure to Oslo and subsequent overnight flight back to St. Louis, Missouri.

Chapter Seven

Like many who conducted their business affairs from Longyearbyen, Henrik Torbjon and his family lived in Grumant, twelve miles south along the scenic Svalbard shoreline. Dwellings were a mix of Norwegian and Russian design, left-overs from the abandoned Roussanova Kolsbey mining settlement.

Of birch and spruce construction, with a peaked roof pierced by a pipe stack chimney, the interior of the Torbjon family home was large, modern and welcoming. Ryan Hurst was glad to shrug off his bulky coat and thick woollen gloves. Grete Torbjon, carrying their youngest, embraced Henrik warmly as he and Ryan entered the capacious cluttered family room.

The rest of his boys, aged twelve years and younger, all with prominent Nordic features, greeted Henrik with their usual raucous enthusiasm. Grete, tall, slender and strikingly attractive, welcomed Ryan with a broad smile and firm handshake. Visitors to the household were rare, and one from overseas was an event to be celebrated.

Although heavily accented, all but the two youngest boys spoke English, and, to Ryan's relief, remarkably well. It certainly saved a lot of time having everything translated for the curiosity of the elder boys.

Discussions around the outsized dinner table were animated, and Ryan was captivated at the diversity of topics. He didn't think that small isolated communities led such varied and eventful lives.

While family matters were being debated, Ryan's thoughts drifted from the conversations to that day two years ago which first brought him to this remote archipelago.

"We have him," Adrian Bowers disclosed to Ryan. He had no doubts that Adrian would successfully manoeuvre James Clark into providing the technological resources SkyTech had at its disposal. Data would soon be made available by the FDA, so that Magentis GMP could research the most common natural foods used by traditional herbalists and nutritionists to cure ailments. Magentis ensured that a complete stock of natural seed, uncorrupted by genetic modification, was safely secured at the Svalbard vault in the event of irreversible alteration at the local Missouri gene bank.

Creating better and healthier food products was one area of research; another was to engineer seeds that could be grown in the harshest conditions.

Ryan's association with Adrian Bowers gave him a sense of importance. He was involved in an industry that could well find a solution to global hunger and starvation; an industry that formulated strategies towards making life better for an ever-growing global population.

There was no doubt: Magentis GMP had plans for Ryan Hurst.

Safe transport and storage of the seed was of paramount importance, and Ryan was responsible for overseeing deliveries planned over several years. Access into the vault itself for inventory audits and quality assurance was left to the more senior logistics controllers, a position he now held, two years later.

Ryan felt that he was well on his way towards a very lucrative and financially secure future. Why else had he been entrusted to work directly with Adrian Bowers, who, he knew, was well placed within the FDA's most senior hierarchy?

A few months previously, Ryan had been asked by Adrian to reach out to Emily, his ex-wife, and get some information about SkyTech. Ryan had no idea how they had found out about his marriage to Emily, but no matter. It was also the first that he had heard as to where she worked.

Adrian explained to Ryan about the business relationship which the Food and Drug Administration had with SkyTech. They were moving ahead into new and profitable areas and simply wanted some assurances that SkyTech was still the right company to move forward with.

What the FDA wanted to know seemed harmless enough.

Typically: was SkyTech still a solid company? Were adequate security measures in place? Were their systems stable and up-to-date, with the latest technologies? That sort of thing. Emily Hurst, as a long-term employee of SkyTech, would be able to provide most of the answers in an unbiased way.

Yes, there was no doubt, from the way in which Ryan was involved with some of the decision making, that his career was finally moving ahead.

Or so he had been led to believe.

Smiling inwardly, his thoughts returned to the present as he swallowed the last of his roasted game that, along with *raspeballer*, a minced fish added to potato dough, made up a truly wholesome and satisfying meal. The Norwegian population was reputedly the healthiest on the planet, and diet obviously played a large part.

The feast was concluded with a loaf of *Knekkebrod* and *Flatbrod*, a thin crispy rye bread on which Jarlsberg cheese and the popular brown goat cheese called *Gjetost* were generously layered. Beer and wine were still flowing freely. Ryan had yet to savour his small measure of Akvavit, Norway's famous liquor distilled from fermented potatoes.

"So, where do the boys go to school?" Ryan asked Grete.

"They are on summer vacation now, but the rest of the year they attend the Tromsø public school on the mainland," she explained. "Of course, we fly them back home at least once a month and for long weekends."

Ryan had heard of Tromsø, a commercial hub far north along the ragged Norwegian coastline. He recalled that it was noted not only for the unique design of its wooden buildings and houses, many unchanged over hundreds of years, but also as one of the best places from which to view the northern lights.

"That must get expensive," Ryan commented.

"No. NordGen have daily shuttle flights between Svalbard and the mainland."

Ryan nodded. Shame that American companies didn't look after their employees the way European ones did, he thought. Glancing idly out through the ornate ocean-front bay window, he noticed that the sun had now skirted its way towards the north-western horizon. Sunset would not occur for another two months.

***

By mid-morning of the following day, the remaining seed deposits had been successfully inventoried and inspected for quality.

"Here, my friend, I have something for you," Henrik said, pulling a small, flat rectangular box out of his pocket and handing it to Ryan.

"What's this?" Ryan opened the box with an inquisitive frown. There was no hiding the relieved smile on his face as he recognized the Samsung battery replacement, clearly labelled Mutsuka Electronics.

"But you still won't be able to get a signal in here," Henrik teased. "When I suggested yesterday that you try your phone, I of course knew that it wouldn't power up. I just wanted to see what type of phone you had. The private call I made was to have our office check if they had a compatible battery available, and, as you can see, they did."

Ryan removed his gloves to detach the phone's back cover and exchange batteries. His smile grew even broader as his phone immediately turned on and activated the bright touch-screen.

Walking towards the exit of the main chamber, Ryan couldn't help but notice what appeared to be an arrow mounted horizontally on the left wall just before the chamber's door. It had a dappled arrow head on one side of the shaft but no fletching on the opposite end.

"Why do you have an arrow hanging there?" Ryan asked, pointing to the enigmatic object.

"That's no arrow," Henrik said, with his typical jovial expression. "It's a famous piece of art. Look closer. You may not know this, but the vault is classified as a public structure. Under Norwegian law, all public buildings are required to have artwork."

"That I didn't know," Ryan responded in surprise.

"You will have seen the stainless steel mosaic above the entrance outside the vault. Collages also run along the outside of the short roof covering the entrance hall. It's illuminated by colourful lights at night, and can be seen from the air many miles away. As you know, our nights at Svalbard are six months long."

"That I did know," Ryan laughed. It was not surprising that Henrik and Grete Torbjon had six children.

Created by the Japanese sculptor Mitsuaki Tanabe, the artwork, aptly entitled *The Seed*, had been presented to the vault as a gift. It was a smaller version of the thirty-foot creation donated to the Crop Trust and mounted for public viewing at the United Nations Food and Agriculture Center. The sculptures symbolised the way in which a seed could be the source of life if conserved, and the source of death if left to extinction.

Ryan Hurst, necessary but dispensable, remained an ignorant pawn in Magentis GMP's objective of ensuring that just such an extinction would occur.

Chapter Eight

Emily Hurst had finalized the meeting schedules for the next day, and was locking James's office when Nathan walked through from Info Tech.

"Hey Emily," he said with an awkward smile. "JW already gone to his weekly squash meet?"

"Yeah, he set out about an hour ago, and I'm just about ready to leave myself."

"There's something I wanted to ask you." Nathan stammered, looking a little self-conscious.

"What's up?" she asked hesitantly.

"If you aren't doing anything Saturday night, would you like to come to a small get together I'm having at my condo? It will be around seven o'clock. But only if you want to and haven't anything else planned."

Emily immediately relaxed. She had never seen Nathan blush.

She beamed at him in delight. "I'd love to, Nate. Are you asking me out on a date?" she chided with amusement.

"No, no," he responded quickly. "It's just a small celebration. My brother Daryl and his wife Bronwyn will be there, Bob and Carrie from accounting, and I was sort of hoping you could also make it."

"Nate, loosen up. I said that I'd be delighted to come. What's the occasion?"

"My fiftieth birthday."

***

"Come on in," Nathan McIntosh said with a broad smile, greeting Emily at the door of his condo. "Right on time. You look great." He avoided the desire to have a quick peek down the front of her low, V-line top. Awkwardly taking Emily's left hand, he guided her through the small entrance hall into the comfortably furnished lounge. "No one else has arrived yet, but they should be here in a few minutes," he felt the need to explain. "Hope that's okay?"

"Nice place," Emily said, looking unhurriedly around the room. "Doesn't look like a bachelor pad at all." She heard the easy-going sounds of Bryan Ferry playing in the background and looked over his shoulder to see that it was coming from a corner mounted turn-table next to a forty-inch flat-screen TV. People still have vinyl, she thought to herself.

"God, I love Roxy Music," she said with appreciation. What she didn't admit to was the arousal it sparked inside her. She always considered it the type of music associated with kinky sex, but without any personal experience, couldn't say, so it remained a private fantasy.

"And before I forget." She reached into her small black clutch bag and pulled out an envelope. "A little something for you. Happy Birthday." She hugged him gently, relishing the smell of his masculine aftershave, which she was unable to identify. She couldn't get used to the fact that in today's world of metrosexuals, men seemed to prefer floral scents to the more traditional manly fragrances. She was glad Nate wasn't like that. He accepted the envelope and kissed her tenderly on the cheek.

"You didn't have to bring anything, but let's have a look."

Nathan opened the envelope and pulled out two tickets for next Saturday's ball game at Yankee Stadium.

"This is the Grandstand on the 400 level," Nathan exclaimed in utter disbelief. "How did you get your hands on these?" He hugged her tightly and just as quickly let her go, not wanting to give the wrong impression.

"Let's just say that I have connections," she replied with a mischievous smile. They had been given to James last week by one of his business associates, but, having absolutely no interest in baseball, he always left them for Emily to keep or pass along to someone who would appreciate them. Mostly she gave them to Matt, who was an avid fan. She couldn't figure him out when he was at school; struggling through maths, but able to keep years of baseball statistics readily available in his head. He could also calculate player averages instantly during any game he was watching. Elle had no interest at all and claimed that if she ever had trouble sleeping, she could always watch a ball game.

"Make yourself comfortable," Nathan offered, pointing to an elegant black five-seater corner lounge suite. "What can I get you to drink?"

"White wine if you have it," Emily answered, sitting down on the left side of the couch by one of the small rectangular coffee tables. She crossed her legs and adjusted the hem a little closer to her knees, hoping that her favourite little black dress wasn't too revealing.

"This is very comfortable," Emily said, gently caressing the armrest. Nothing cheap about this furniture, she thought. Genuine leather, too, judging by the scent. Smiling, she perused Nathan's collection of four Salvador Dali prints, tastefully framed on the opposite wall. Surrealistic artwork was well-matched to his personality.

On the center table was a magnum of Champaign cooling in a silver ice bucket. She leaned over and tilted her head slightly to read the note. 'Happy 50th, Nate! Sorry I couldn't make the party.' It was signed "James."

So typically considerate of him, Emily thought. Most CEOs expected their executive assistants to take care of things like this, but when it came to his staff, James did it all himself and was totally sincere about it.

Nathan returned from the kitchenette with Emily's wine, and placed it on the side table. "Pinot Grigio, and if you want something a little less sweet with dinner, I also have Chardonnay."

"This is perfect. Thanks Nate."

"Judging by the noise in the corridor, Daryl and Bronwyn have arrived," Nathan remarked, turning towards the opening door.

His brother and sister-in-law, followed closely by Bob and Carrie from the office, crossed the threshold into the apartment. The boisterous couples haphazardly dumped wrapped gifts along with bottles of beer and wine on the kitchenette counter-top, before enthusiastically descending on Nathan with garrulous greetings and birthday wishes.

"We bumped into Bob and Carrie downstairs," Daryl McIntosh said, embracing his brother with a tight hug. "Happy birthday, bro."

Emily could see the deep affection they shared with each other. Tagging Nathan along by the shoulder, Daryl walked over to her.

"And you must be Emily," Daryl said, then looked to Nathan disapprovingly. "Why have you never invited her over before? She's cute."

Emily looked up at Daryl, smiling modestly. Aside from his eyes, Daryl looked nothing like his brother. A few inches shorter, Daryl was bald and stocky. His solid physique suggested that he spent many hours at the gym.

"Mind if I sit?" It wasn't a question. Daryl made himself comfortable on Emily's right. "Nate speaks very highly of you, and from what I gather, you can actually understand most of the convoluted jargon that comes out of his mouth."

"It's not jargon," Emily replied laughing. "It's fascinating stuff."

"Fascinating to computer geeks, perhaps." He beckoned to Bronwyn. "This is my better half."

Bronwyn McIntosh, long-limbed and athletic, strode over and sat down on the edge of the center table opposite to Emily. She was careful not to bump the ice bucket.

"Your brother is not a geek," Bronwyn challenged, looking sternly at Daryl. "Don't mind him," she said to Emily. "You know what structural engineers are like. Any conversation that doesn't involve steel, bricks or mortar must be jargon."

"At least I work with things that you can touch, and not those elusive ones and zeros," Daryl argued.

"Nothing wrong with ones and zeros," Nathan interrupted. "Or being a geek for that matter. One day we will rule the world."

Daryl laughed. "I would have thought you'd have more fun with hardware than software," he retorted, landing another precision punch-line on his older brother.

Emily caught the double meaning.

Nathan muttered a few colourful expletives. "Come, Daryl. If you're desperate to touch something, Bob has just the job for you."

Even though Bronwyn McIntosh's talk was essentially self-serving and filled with personal flattery, Emily warmed to Bronwyn immediately. Carrie, bringing a bottle of wine, sat down and joined the conversation while the men busied themselves in the kitchen preparing what would certainly be a feast.

***

James Clark swallowed the last of the pizza dinner delivered to his office earlier in the evening. Not his favorite choice of foods, but he needed to get something into his stomach, even if it lacked nutritional value. Being judiciously health-conscious, he avoided take-out and fast foods whenever possible. The only weakness that remained was for gelato, which he light-heartedly considered an essential food group. Hats off to the Italians for inventing it.

He had spent most of Saturday evening digesting Nathan's suggestion of going ahead with Adrian Bowers' demands. Nathan didn't provide any detail, other than to imply that, if carried out successfully, it would turn the tables on Adrian and the Food and Drug Administration. They would discuss it further on Monday.

Technology was James Clark's life, and having his own company used against him, or, worse, shut down, was unthinkable. He realized over the years that his passions were waning. He was now in the business of making money. SkyTech employed over three hundred people, and he had absolutely no intention of seeing them line up for jobs at Burger King.

Aerospace had fascinated him as a young boy, especially man-made satellites and their ability to be controlled by co-ordinated digital communications stations located across the globe – computers talking to computers.

His interest in space had been sparked on his sixth birthday when his father, sole owner of the multi-million dollar Clark Construction conglomerate, had presented him with a small Newtonian Reflector telescope. James's parents supported and encouraged most of his activities and pursuits, but his father was always reminding him that nothing in life was for free. *You have to work, and work hard, for what you want.*

As an only child, he was not raised with a sense of wealth or entitlement, and by his early teens, he understood the value of hard-earned money.

James had been popular with girls at high school, and had been oblivious to his own good looks. He justified his lack of interest in pursuing relationships as simply a question of having more serious things, like his studies and hobbies, to worry about. He had no trouble finding a date for prom-night, and Cyndi Reyes, a bubbly attractive class-mate, gladly accepted his invite, and couldn't wait to show him off.

James was a perfect gentleman, and, much to Cyndi's disappointment, had her home shortly after midnight. Most of the other students had hotel rooms booked for the night. No doubt, James scored highly in her parents' books, but he never saw Cyndi again.

The days of Sputnik, Gemini, Apollo and large IBM mainframes were of his parent's era; his youth being that of the space-shuttle, communications-satellites and the dawn of super-computers.

The advent of the Internet was still a few years away.

College education consisted of reading books and writing things down with pen and paper. Unlike today, *copy* and *paste* were not the accepted method in completing assignments to be handed in the next day. Higher learning, for which most parents had likely taken out a second mortgage, consisted of late nights reading, understanding and remembering the subjects in which you were enrolled.

Although James's parents had had the financial means to further his education in whatever direction he chose, he took his studies very seriously.

James had absolutely no interest in the social life enjoyed by arts students and those with football scholarships. He couldn't understand the need for Doug, his roommate, to plaster centerfolds of nude celebrities along the walls adjacent to his bed. All available space on James' side of the room was taken up by shelves neatly stacked with books that didn't fit on his study table. Doug's table was usually cluttered with foul-smelling laundry and half-empty beer bottles.

Continuous and disruptive noise during his second year in the local residency proved too much, and with the agreement of his parents and those of Warren Ellison, his only close college friend, a small two-bedroom rental unit outside the campus was made available for them to share. It had some items of furniture that would be replaced, and a few scattered piles of magazines left behind by the previous tenants. One, boldly labelled *Muscle*, with a partially revealing cover photo of a steroid-enhanced jock named Troy, had caught his attention.

Paging through to the featured article on Troy ignited an arousal James had never known before. He noticed some areas where the photos had been touched up, probably to remove skin blemishes or wrinkles.

Photoshop was not yet a household word, so photographers and printers used a manual air-brushing technique referred to in the trade as *sandblasting*. Altered or not, Troy was still a remarkable specimen of masculinity. He quickly tucked the magazine into his carry-bag. A sudden awareness of his sexuality was undeniable.

Laden with a few personal items, Warren Ellison backed through the unlocked apartment door, turned and looked at James quizzically. "You look happy."

"Oh... uh, just relieved to be out of residence," James hastily replied.

"Me too. That perpetual noise and commotion. How is anyone expected to learn anything?" Warren was a computer science major and spoke enthusiastically to James about all his latest assignments. Both had an avid interest in photography and amateur astronomy, shared interests that sealed their friendship during the first semester.

Chores around the apartment had been apportioned equally, as were the expenses of refitting the kitchen with new cutlery, crockery and a variety of useful appliances. Neither James nor Warren had any interest in purchasing a TV, radio or turn-table, having agreed that the silence was far preferable to the rowdy environment they had moved away from.

They respected each other's privacy, intuitively aware when the other was deeply engrossed in his studies. Warren motivated James toward a lifestyle of healthy eating and regular workouts. The only exercise James was getting, or so he convinced himself, were his early morning masturbation sessions in the shower, images of Troy and the likes firmly on his mind.

They had been comfortably settled in the apartment for just over two months, during which time a routine had been established: washing dishes, dusting and vacuuming by one, laundry and general tidying up by the other - their individual schedule of chores swapping every week.

James fondly recalled that particular Sunday morning which had changed his life. He had pulled back the shower curtain, and was drying himself when Warren unexpectedly walked in totally naked and fully erect. James' eyes absorbed everything at once. Fit, athletic and desirable, Warren Ellison certainly didn't resemble the appearance of how most people envisaged a computer science major.

Their eyes locked. Awkwardness, perplexity, uncertainty - instantaneous and mutual understanding. No words were necessary. Their bodies embraced with urgent physical and emotional desires.

Chapter Nine

The attraction between James Clark and Warren Ellison, like most gay couples, was one of love, compassion and understanding, not endless lewd and raunchy sex like that manufactured by the media. Emotions, typical with couples of the opposite sex, run just as deeply. Passionate love and respect for the other matured and was nurtured. Jealousy between the two was very rare. Hopes and dreams were shared; their discussions, disputes and quarrels were no different from those of anyone else.

James's closest friend was now his intimate lover. Neither had past experiences to draw from; the physical contact between them was the first for both. They satisfied their needs with instinctive understanding of what the other wanted. Deep-throating and anal sex were sporadic, not because of the current AIDS scare, but rather that neither found it a particularly necessary part of sexual enjoyment. The aftermath of James's first penetration was rather painful, leaving him uncomfortable and tender for a few days after.

Much like their diet and exercise, personal hygiene was important, and additional precautions were always taken. They savoured their intimate evenings on the newly acquired love-seat, sometimes just holding hands, each with his own private thoughts, and at other times excitedly exchanging ideas and opinions. The occasional times they were in briefs or fully naked would almost always start with gently caressing and fondling each other. Passionate kisses and forceful embraces followed. Strong hands delivered demanding orgasms either to themselves or to the other.

In both body and mind, Warren and James projected masculinity, neither having any feminine characteristics in looks, mannerisms or speech; their sexual preferences simply being what they were.

Saturday afternoons, James earned some extra cash working at a local photography shop from which he purchased his first camera, a 35-mm Pentax. It could be set to keep the shutter open as long as required, exactly what James needed for astronomical photography.

His equatorial tripod was equipped with a small battery operated motor and gear mechanism which slowly swivelled the telescope in the opposite direction to that of the earth's rotation. Lined up with the polar axis, the telescope could then be fixed on a selected region of the night sky.

Adapting the camera to the telescope's eyepiece was a simple process, but knowing exactly how long to keep the shutter open, or what film speeds to use, proved a real challenge. After hundreds of wasted photos, James started seeing a few successful results. To a certain degree, they were amateurish and mostly out of focus, but a major achievement, in his mind.

James discovered that monochrome film far outweighed colour for quality. He finally settled on fifteen- to twenty-second exposures, using ISO-400 film speed photographing the moon, and twenty-minute exposures with ISO-800 for the Milky-Way. He had not yet mastered clear photos of planets or deep-sky objects, but then his second-rate equipment was hardly geared towards such optimistic endeavours.

James's intimate relationship with Warren Ellison had lasted through graduation, after which they temporarily parted ways, each understanding that what they shared was behind them, and it was now time to move forward. James furthered his education, and Warren became an intern with Curative Solutions, a medical technology provider in Silicon Valley.

They fostered relationships with others, but their firm friendship remained, as did their mutual interest in photography, a good a reason as any to get together on a regular basis.

As popularity with information sharing across the World Wide Web increased in the late 1980s, digital photography also gained momentum. With the technology still in its infancy, quality and image resolution were unavoidably poor. The maximum colour variations were limited to sixteen shades of grey for monochrome, imaging and 256 for colour. Storing an average-sized digital photo on a computer took megabytes of disc space, considered then as a vast amount of storage realty that could best be used for something else.

In 1987, the internet service provider CompuServe developed the Graphics Interchange Format, or GIF as it was more commonly known, as an ideal format for storing digital images. Able to compress photos down to as little as one-tenth of their original size, GIF gained widespread popularity for its portability across the internet.

Serious-minded photographers, however, were discouraged at having their creations reduced in colour depth and resolution before they could transmit them across the internet. They took the limitations of GIF to heart, and, three years later, the Joint Photographic Experts Group came into being.

The group consisted of photography and software experts from all over the world; James Clark and Warren Ellison were associates. Most proposals put forward by the members involved reduction in quality, as well as putting limitations on the sixteen million colours that scanners and computers were capable of processing. These ideas were discarded outright, as being just another version of GIF. Trials resulted in the hues and rich definitions fading, and the images usually ended up appearing more artificial than real. At that time, true- colour digital cameras were beyond affordable price, but scanning from a 35-mm colour print was considered an acceptable alternative.

James had another idea in mind, and proposed that a photo, instead of being reduced in quality, should be reduced in content. Take out small portions of recognizable shapes and outlines that the human eye automatically fills in. Next, instead of recording every picture element, or pixel, find similar image patterns, store each once, and then replicate accordingly during decompression. This could be done by creating a real-time mathematical formula that would reconstruct the individual patterns back into a viewable image rather than capturing as a bitmap representation, the way digital cameras were originally designed to work. He left the software development aspect of his brainchild in the capable hands of Warren.

James's proposition was considered too far-reaching to be taken seriously, until he demonstrated it six months later. This was the onset of JPEG images, or JPG, the preferred shorter acronym. Royalties paid by entrepreneurs on James's patented formula had financed the birth of SkyTech. Warren had used his share of the money for advanced research into a new and somewhat ambiguous field of technology known as A.I., or Artificial Intelligence.

James lost touch with the Joint Photographers Group shortly afterwards, as he now had a far more interesting and profitable venture on his hands.

Over the next few years, Imaging software improved rapidly, allowing users to choose both the quality and compression intensity according to personal preference. James had no illusions: if a mathematical formula could define a single digital image, movies wouldn't be too far behind in using the same concepts.

In today's electronics market, very few people realize the underlying complexity required to decode at the hundred megabits per second which their Blu-Ray player's purchased for $39.95 at Walmart, were capable of. Consumers simply took the fundamental operations of their latest high-tech devices for granted.

Chapter Ten

"Hope you had a great party on Saturday," James said to Nathan on the following Monday. "Sorry for declining your invite, but, under the present circumstances, I would have been very poor company."

"Well, you were there in spirit, if not in person," Nathan said. "Your magnum of Dom Perignon was enjoyed by all. We really appreciated your thoughtfulness, JW. Thanks."

James smiled. "You're very welcome." Sensing Nathan's discomfort sitting behind closed doors in his office, he continued. "I know you don't particularly like talking in here, but this has to be private. I've instructed Emily to make sure we aren't interrupted."

Nathan, awkwardly hunched forward, rested his crossed arms on the desk. "Adrian Bowers isn't quite as smart as he thinks he is, or he just reads too many spy thrillers. What he's asking is that we replicate SIM cards of the phones, for which he will provide the numbers. It cannot be done by just knowing a phone number. We can of course get specific and personal information from the card, but not enough to make a carbon copy."

James was well aware of smartphone technology. Every phone received every call transmitted by its applicable carrier service such as Bell or AT&T. The firmware hardwired into the SIM determined whether the request was for itself, and, if so, it would activate the phone to an incoming call state. All others, literally thousands every second, were discarded as *not for me.*

"See what you can do about getting Bowers into this office," Nathan continued. "Let him think that we can do what he wants, based on his limited understanding. If he wants us to replicate SIMs so that he can tap into conversations, we will make sure the first and only one is his, but I need to be close enough to clone it."

Thoughtful, James nodded his head in agreement.

Nathan lost some of his nervous reserve and went on excitedly with animated hand motions as his uneasiness dissolved. "I've already installed an application on one of the support phones that will not only create a digital replication of another phone's SIM, but also everything else in its memory. Contacts, messages, email, photos, browsing history, everything: and it will collect the data from built-in memory as well as a micro-SD, if one is installed. While the transfer takes place, and it only takes a few minutes, there can be no incoming call. The program logic of the SIM changes slightly when it acknowledges a call. We don't want that, because the clone will be in a perpetual state of waiting for the call to be answered."

"How can you prevent that?" James asked.

"Sven will be here this afternoon with a small device hidden in a fishing trophy that you can put on your coffee table. It has a very sensitive GPS locator and will disrupt any incoming call in the immediate locale."

"Wouldn't a caller be a little dubious if the number registers as unavailable? They would most certainly think they had dialled wrong and try again. The exact time and place might get back to Adrian in casual conversation, and, would probably raise suspicion."

"No," Nathan answered. "The device will simply broadcast back to the caller as 'Busy'."

"What if his phone is password-protected?"

"Not an issue. The password and phone activation sequence is on the SIM. We are cloning the SIM, not activating the phone, so no password entry will be prompted for."

"And if Adrian's data is encrypted?"

Nathan smiled. "I'm glad you asked. We dump it all on the IBM, and let NSA's snoop software provide the encryption key. I'm sure you can see the irony in that."

James leaned back in his chair, smiled and looked mischievously at Nathan. "I think we're going to have some fun with our good friend Adrian Bowers," he stated sardonically.

"One other thing," Nathan said. "You will have to leave your own phone somewhere outside this office. You can leave it at my workspace if you like. It will be perfectly safe. Besides, the soon-to-be-cloned phone, Adrian's, must be the only one in the immediate vicinity. Oh, and I need Adrian's number."

James scanned his contacts list and provided it.

***

"I don't want any more email conversations," James Clark stated to Adrian Bowers. "Nor am I comfortable with discussing your requirements on the phone. We need to speak face to face. Development has started, but there are a few challenges for which my software development manager has some alternative proposals, so he will be joining us. When is the soonest you can come to SkyTech?"

Adrian Bowers was unaccustomed to such abruptness. He talked, others listened. Under the circumstances, he let it go, and agreed to come to James's office the following morning at ten a.m.

***

"Good morning, Mr. Bowers." Emily Hurst greeted Adrian with a welcoming smile. "Right on time. Mr. Clark is expecting you."

Adrian sized her up. He had imagined that Clark would have an executive assistant with more sex appeal and bigger tits, not Susie Homemaker.

Emily stood from behind her desk and escorted Adrian through to James's office. "Mr. Bowers is here," she announced formally to James.

"Thank you, Emily."

Adrian walked in. "James."

"Adrian."

They didn't shake hands and Adrian promptly made himself comfortable on the Chesterfield without being invited to do so.

The subtle animosity between them was obvious to Emily.

"Can I offer either of you any refreshment?" she asked.

"A Perrier water for me please," James answered.

"Coffee," Adrian replied imperiously. "Black."

"I will bring that through in a moment." Pompous ass, she thought.

"Nathan should be on his way," James said to Emily. "If you see him, tell him to come straight in, and please hold all my calls."

Emily walked out the office to the small facilities area, where fresh coffee and a variety of cold beverages were always available. She poured two cups, knowing that Nathan was sure to want some as well. He seemed to live on coffee. Maybe that was the secret all slim people had.

Nathan McIntosh was already seated opposite Adrian Bowers when Emily returned with the refreshments. She placed them on the small table, inquisitive about the fishing trophy, which she had never noticed before. Emily was obviously not aware of all of James's recreational activities. Discarding the thought, she returned to her desk, closing James' office door behind her.

"So, you've run into problems, have you?" Adrian asked. He was obviously annoyed.

"Not problems, as such, but a few technical challenges that we can easily iron out," Nathan interrupted, before James was able to respond. "I understand from James that you require regular updates on progress. What we are doing is illegal and any communication between us should be direct, not through email or phone conversation."

"You obviously have to agree," James urged Adrian. "I'm prepared to give you a full update once a month. We can meet here or any location that suits you, provided that it's private. Central Park is less than five minutes' walk from here, and, at this time of day, ideal. The early morning joggers are already done for the day and lunch-time pedestrian traffic hasn't started yet."

"Fine with me," Adrian said indifferently.

"Do you know Pilgrim Hill, flanking Fifth Avenue and East 72nd Street?"

"Yes, I've been there."

"There are some park benches surrounding the Hans Christian Andersen statue. We can meet there at ten o'clock on this date for the next three or four months."

"Very well," Adrian said. "Anything else?"

Nathan explained. "We cannot clone smartphones just by knowing the number, but we can get enough information out of the SIM card so that, when overlaid into your own phone's SIM, it will allow you to listen in on any incoming call."

"Go on."

"You obviously haven't given this much thought," Nathan said.

"What do you mean?" Adrian asked argumentatively.

Nathan didn't care if he bluntly followed through with the obvious. "How will you know when one of those phones will have an incoming call? You would need the applicable SIM overlay at just the right moment. And how many phones are you planning to snoop? One by itself would already be impossible to predict."

Adrian was losing some of his arrogance. "What would you suggest?"

"We record the conversations here at SkyTech as and when they happen, simultaneously from as many phones as you require. Then transfer them real-time to a location that you provide. I presume the FDA has a public site for incoming data, but I would recommend that you set up a personal digital drop-box somewhere on the internet."

"I already have one," Adrian replied. "I'll create a public folder with login credentials, and email you the details tomorrow."

"Good, we'll use that. We also want to protect our interests in this little game of yours," Nathan went on. "The recordings will include details of phone numbers and names applicable to both parties for which the conversation took place. The data will be deposited into your folder with sender details logged as *anonymous*. It will be rerouted through a number of global providers, the footprint of which will be totally wiped out after each hop."

"How can you guarantee that?" Adrian asked with scepticism.

"This is what we do. You'll just have to trust us," Nathan replied caustically. "As soon as the digital recording has left our own databanks, it too will be destroyed. It will never be traced back to SkyTech."

James knew very well that Nathan would keep all the communications stored somewhere secure and out of reach.

They needed to know what was really going on. James also had a suspicion that the Food and Drug Administration knew nothing of what Bowers was doing.

"The last thing we'll need from you," Nathan went on, "is the list of phone numbers."

Adrian removed the list from his pretentious FDA-embellished Ralph Lauren briefcase and passed it over to Nathan, who briefly looked over it before handing it to James.

The list was far shorter than James expected - fifty at most.

They would soon know exactly who these numbers belonged to.

Adrian closed his briefcase. Coffee untouched, he hoisted himself up from the Chesterfield with exertion.

Too much time in bars and restaurants and not enough in the gym, thought James.

"We'll talk again in a month at this time," Adrian stated belligerently, as he trudged out of the office.

"Where's the washroom?" Adrian asked Emily impertinently, on his way through reception.

"Just over to the left by the facilities area," she replied, pointing the way.

Adrian swaggered in the direction given and went through the door marked with a small stick-figure signifying "Male".

Inside, he did God's calling, then crossed the room to wash and dry his hands. He noticed a key-card lying next to the sink. Looking around to ensure that there was no one occupying any of the cubicles, he picked it up and concluded that it was an optical security access card. It was marked *Phil Roberts - Sys. Admin.* He quickly slid it into his pocket.

Emily observed Adrian's return from the washroom on his way to the foyer. "Have a pleasant day, Mr. Bowers," she said cheerfully.

He ignored her and went directly to the elevators.

Chapter Eleven

Meeting over, and Bowers out of the way, Nathan pulled the service phone out of his pocket and powered it off. He then reached for the bogus fishing trophy, and flipped the small base-mounted switch to deactivate the signal disrupter.

"I think we should leave the trophy here for a while," Nathan suggested. "Emily noticed it, and I'm sure you don't want to answer any awkward questions if she now sees that it's gone."

"Good point," James agreed.

Nathan replaced the trophy in its original position, oblivious to the fact that, when he had neutralized the disrupter, he had also deactivated the concealed listening device installed by Sven Labrowski.

Nathan returned with James's phone. "Mind if I sit down?"

"Please," James replied. "For the first time in weeks I don't feel like we are the prey anymore, but rather the predators." He leaned back in his chair, visibly relaxing. "Everything okay with our little cloning exercise?"

"Perfect," Nathan said. "I'm dumping the contents to one of our autonomous computers now. If his phone contained any malicious software, I don't want it propagating into our network. It's also easier to scrutinize the data from a computer than doing it directly on the clone."

"How long before we have the eavesdropping application in place?" James asked.

"I should have it done by the end of next week. Goes to show just how ignorant Adrian is. He assumes it will take us months, and we'll let him carry on believing that. It gives us plenty of time to figure out what he's up to."

James raised his eyebrows, tilted his head and smirked. "And what will I tell him when I see him next month?"

Nathan responded with a twisted smile. "Fabricate something about various technical glitches that we've run into. You'll figure it out, just keep him guessing."

"No problem, Nate. And thanks for taking this troublesome burden off my mind," James said earnestly.

"One thing I'm going to have done by the end of today," Nathan said as an afterthought, "is to pair the clone with an app on the IBM. Everything that goes in or out of Bowers's phone will be replicated and recorded in a separate databank."

"Everything?" James asked.

"Phone calls, emails, messages, web searches, downloaded data, the lot," Nathan remarked.

James grinned. "Sounds devious. I like it."

"Just a thought," Nathan said. "Are there any personal emails on your computer? Stuff you'd rather not have anyone in my department delve into? It's probably a bit too late to be asking."

"Other than those relating to business? No," James said, shaking his head. "I manage my private life from my phone or my home computer. Why do you ask?"

"I would like to scan all your emails for the last six months if that's okay. Not the content, just the access dates and times. I want to be sure that it's only emails between you and Adrian that have been probed. If not, the rabbit hole may be deeper than we thought."

"Go ahead and look into whatever it is you might need," James offered.

"Someone is either looking for something or…". Nathan paused in thought for a few seconds.

James frowned as Nathan trailed off. "What?"

"It's almost as if the hack isn't an intrusion into data at all, but rather something else," Nathan said, shaking his head as he stood up.

"I'm going to see how the data dump from the phone is doing. It should be done by now. Also, I want to check if Sven has discovered anything new."

"I don't mind you getting Sven or any others of your team involved all the way, if you think they can keep it under wraps," James said.

"Sven's dependable enough, and if there's anything to find, he's the guy. Phil is also very good at what he does. My only annoyance with him is that he tends to leave his key-card lying around in the oddest places," Nathan replied.

"How does he get in and out?"

"Knowing Phil, he probably created a few extra cards for himself. He did, after all, install our entire security system software."

"Have a word with him," James said. "We can't afford any negligent behaviour, especially now."

"Will do," Nathan said. "See you later."

"Lunch in about an hour?" Emily asked Nathan as he passed her desk.

"See you then," he said reflexively without looking up.

What's up with him? she thought.

Although James was far more positive in his outlook, having the support of Nathan and his team, he still felt very much alone. Motivated by profit or greed, he now realized just how easily Adrian Bowers had manipulated him. Through his own bad judgement, this was a predicament that he and he alone should be burdened with.

Life had been so much more rewarding in the days, seemingly not so long before, when his biggest challenges centered on radical ideas, discoveries and creations. Now the livelihood of his company and its employees was at stake. He couldn't just let this play out. It required very careful strategy, but for now he needed a few more pieces of information from Nathan. James was not going to make any more unwise decisions based on what he thought he knew. If only he had listened to his instincts after his first meeting with Adrian. His gut told him then that something was amiss, but he just wasn't listening. An expensive lesson, and one he had no intention of repeating.

He wondered about the graphic calling card left behind by the intrusion hack. And what was that all about? Adrian Bowers, the FDA, the NSA? He had no hunches to work from. Nathan and Sven had more pressing tasks at the moment, so maybe he should have a closer look into the image and see if he could find anything the others had missed. It was, after all, just a simple JPG image, something he was definitely an authority on.

***

Sitting in the cab on his way to an administrative appointment with a few colleagues at his church, Adrian Bowers considered what Nathan McIntosh had said, and, much to his reluctance, it made sense. Adrian was well aware that a phone couldn't be cloned by the number alone, but threw it to them in that way to gauge a response, or, more accurately, to test their integrity.

Most of the assholes Adrian dealt with told him what they thought he wanted to hear, or what he didn't need to hear. Nathan, as irritating as he was, told him exactly what he needed to hear. Direct and to the point, SkyTech had provided a workable solution. He had no worries about trusting them. He did after all hold all the cards.

That idiot Ryan Hurst had also provided him with what he needed to know about some of SkyTech's security, along with the location and means of access to their primary computer hardware. Information like this could prove to be very useful indeed.

It was purely coincidental that Adrian discovered Hurst's past association with Emily, even if it had taken place many years previously. Having an insider within SkyTech could be beneficial. Much like her ex-husband, Emily Hurst should be easy to manipulate, of that he was confident.

Yes, Adrian Bowers thought, things were falling into place nicely.

***

"You were deep in thought earlier," Emily said to Nathan, who was sitting opposite her at their usual spot in the cafeteria.

"Some issues we've faced with one of JW's business deals."

"You mean with Mr. Bowers?" she prodded.

"Yes," he said. "How is your salad?"

"Same as every day," she responded with a sarcastic grin, wagging her fork at him. "Come on, tell me what's going on."

"It's not something I can talk about now, but I can say that Bowers is trying to put some pressure on SkyTech. The type we are not entirely comfortable with."

"He seems a bit arrogant," Emily observed.

"Arrogant! He's a contemptuous, egotistical prick."

"Don't get so angry. It can't be as bad as all that."

"Sorry," Nathan apologized. "He just annoys me intensely." He gulped down the last of his coffee and looked directly at Emily.

"What?" she said. She adored his eyes.

"Do you like rock music?"

"Depends... Why?"

"Friday night, two weeks from now, I'm going to one of the Summer-Stage concerts. I usually go alone, but it's just not the same without someone else to enjoy it with me. I'm wondering if you'd like to tag along?"

"Sounds like fun, but only if I can pay my own way."

As if he hadn't heard that before! But he was thrilled she hadn't said no. "Great," he said, smiling broadly. He couldn't disguise the relief on his face.

"Where is it?" she asked.

"Rumsey Playfield. We can meet at the info kiosk on Terrace at the 5th Street entrance of the park. Around six in the evening okay with you? And if you're feeling adventurous, there's an excellent street vendor on the corner." Nathan was speaking fast, trying not to stumble over his words. "He sells the best beef-dogs in Manhattan."

"Sure," she said, quickly getting in a response.

"But if you prefer somewhere else to eat..."

"Nathan," she interrupted. "Stop always being so nervous when you ask me out. I don't bite, you know."

"Sorry."

"And stop with all the apologies," she said teasingly. "We're going to have a great time." She had never been to any of the evening rock concerts, but walking along Fifth Avenue during the day, often heard acoustical and orchestral music playing in the distance.

These events, free to watch, continued throughout the summer months into early fall. Many world-renowned and emerging artists have performed in Central Park: the New

York Philharmonic conducted by Leonard Bernstein in the 1990's, Paul Simon, Bon Jovi, and more recently, The Black-Eyed Peas.

She was feeling elated, having been invited by Nathan.

"You seem to have very eventful weekends," she said, knowing that Nate had a ball game to go to this Saturday. "You still going to the game with Daryl?"

"He's been driving me insane talking about it," Nathan said. "I still can't thank you enough for the tickets. That was the best birthday present ever."

"You're very welcome, and I had a really great time," she said thinking back to the party.

Contrary to expectations, Nate's apartment, although masculine, had not been cluttered, in the way she had imagined it would be for a single man. Furniture and décor were tastefully arranged, with colour combinations pleasing and soft on the eyes. Pot plants and cactus below the large balcony window were well-tended, and, much to her surprise, none were artificial.

The only computer equipment she had spotted was in a small office adjacent to the bathroom. The room was functional, with everything in its place, and, along the right wall, a small workbench, with many electronic components scattered about. The condition of the workbench looked more like what she expected to see in the rest of his home. He had probably spilt some coffee that had started attracting a few bugs.

The bathroom was spacious with a Jacuzzi tub - could have fun in that, she thought - separate shower stall, toilet and under-mounted china sink. A quick inquisitive peek into the mirrored bathroom cabinet divulged only the necessities: razor, shaving foam, toothbrush and the like, but not a single bottle of medication, not even cold and 'flu remedies.

Discussions during dinner were varied, and she was surprised at his broad range of interests and hobbies; cooking being one of his obvious specialities. Teasing and light-hearted mockery between Nate and Daryl provided a continuous source for laughter among the small group.

Gone was the serious and disciplined co-worker she knew at SkyTech. With a keen sense of humour, this was a characteristic of Nathan she would never have anticipated. Daryl, playing devil's advocate, was fast, and had an answer or counter-argument for just about everything.

It was well after midnight when the party finally broke up. Everyone helped with cleaning the kitchen and tidying the lounge and dining area. After giving Nathan best wishes and thanking him again for a wonderful evening, Emily prepared to leave with the rest of the group, but not before putting her arms around his waist and hugging him tightly. Perhaps a little too much wine had dispelled some of her inhibitions, but she was okay with that.

Chapter Twelve

"JW, you have to see this," Nathan said, walking excitedly into James's office and closing the door behind him. "Can I put my laptop on your desk?"

Must be important, James thought, diverting attention from his computer monitor to Nathan. He rarely barged in without prior announcement.

Nathan sat in one of the visitor's chairs and put the laptop on James' desk. He looked up in sudden awareness. "Sorry, JW. Er, were you in the middle of something?"

James stood up, walked around his desk and sat next to Nathan. "I was just seeing if I can make head or tail out of that intruder calling card. What's up? You look flustered."

"Okay, first, I've done some research on Bowers' phone calls, emails and contacts. Nothing particularly out of the ordinary. Did you know that he's a deacon at one of the Baptist-Catholic churches in Jersey?"

"He's a priest?" James said, a little startled. He knew very little about a church's chain of command, or *pecking order* as he preferred to call it.

"Not quite. One rank lower. Kind of like a priest's sidekick or glorified altar-boy. In some faiths, deacons also offer moral guidance to members of the congregation."

"Ah." Bit of a contradiction labelling Adrian Bowers as *moral*, James thought.

Nathan continued. "Very few emails to you from his phone. Probably used his computer. Nothing unusual about any of his contacts, except one. A Ryan Hurst working at Magentis."

"Magentis?"

"It's an agricultural research company working out of St. Louis. They also have an office in New York and a few other places. Although *research* leaves a lot to interpretation. They're more into manufacturing genetically modified foods."

"Right, now I remember," James said. "If I recall, they were involved in a scandal a few years back."

"Yes," Nathan agreed, nodding his head. "And the FDA were right in the thick of things, but involvement couldn't be proven. Here's the thing that bugs me though. I did some covert enquiries into Ryan Hurst. He was married to Emily. They divorced some twenty years ago."

"Cause for concern?"

"I don't know yet," Nathan said. "Seems a little coincidental, don't you think? I'll let you know if anything new comes up with that."

"Let me know immediately."

"There's something else that you need to see." Nathan couldn't keep the agitation out of his voice. "Bowers's appointments go back a few years, and every January he goes to the Far East for a few weeks. Thailand specifically. Look at these." He turned the laptop more towards James.

"What the…" James was appalled at what leaped out at him from the laptop's monitor.

"There are hundreds of them," Nathan said, looking very disturbed.

"That piece of shit is a God-damn paedophile," James exclaimed, with a rare burst of emotion.

"And he apparently gets his jollies from one of those houses in Bangkok catering to his sick fetish," Nathan said.

"That mother-fucking son of a bitch!" James couldn't contain his outrage.

Nathan closed the laptop. "Listen, JW. This is something we can use."

"What do you mean?" James asked, calming down a little.

"It's Bangkok, and out of our jurisdiction. There's absolutely nothing we can do about it. Lawyers would be all over us. Their only argument would be that we obtained these photos illegally. And they would be right. You know how the justice system here works. It's all about technicalities in favor of delinquents like Bowers."

"But Nate, some of those girls can't be much older than fourteen," James said, dismayed.

"I know," Nathan said, shaking his head. He flipped the laptop open again. "Look at this." Scrolling further down the array of photos were several selfies. "He seems very proud of himself. Under threat of releasing these anonymously to some interested parties, we have the perfect tool for reverse blackmail."

"You're right," said James suddenly excited. "If it gets to that, we can eliminate any evidence of our tampering with the NSA's spyware, along with what we've put into place for Bowers. Something tells me this is his personal mission, and that the FDA knows nothing about it. But what I want to know is what he's up to. It can't be good."

"Not to lessen the seriousness of his exploits, but look at that," Nathan said, pointing to one of the selfies."

Both smiled knowingly. "No wonder he prefers little girls," James said. "Women would break out laughing at something that small."

Nathan snorted. "It is tiny, isn't it?"

"How's the phone snooping application coming along?" James enquired, getting onto a more serious topic.

"Nicely," Nathan responded, closing the laptop again. "I've added Adrian's phone number to the list but will obviously not be forwarding any of those conversations to him."

"I should hope not," James said solemnly.

"Bowers has actually given us quite a bit of ammunition, but very little, other than his exploits, that we could use against him. He has no unusual software on his phone and very few social media apps. His browsing history doesn't show anything worth noting, and his searches on Google didn't surprise me either. Over the last few months he's been looking for images and videos typical to what one would expect to find on child porno sites, fortunately with very little success, except for one site that he visits regularly."

"Thanks for bringing me up to speed Nate. Let's see what we can do about taking Bowers to the cleaners. But not yet. I still want to know what he's up to. By the way, was the data encrypted?"

"No, and his phone wasn't even password protected," Nathan replied.

"I thought all government departments had some very strict rules on that," James said, shaking his head. "He must be very confident of himself."

"Let's just hope you can keep a straight face next time you look him in the eyes," Nathan said, sharing their private joke about Adrian. "Want me to leave your door open on my way out?"

"Yes, that's fine."

***

Rested and relaxed from a good night's sleep, the first in many months, James Clark walked into his office and put his briefcase on the credenza. He typically arrived about half an hour before anyone else. He was exultant that they would be able to turn the tables on Adrian Bowers. James was out for sadistic and painful revenge on that bastard, and Nate had provided some excellent ammunition.

He ambled over to the corner of his office and turned on the small flat-screen TV to catch up on recent news events. CNN as usual. A New York congresswoman was outlining her plan to convert all public washrooms to trans-gender - if elected to the senate, that was. James listened briefly with mild amusement, as he took a bottle of Perrier water from the fridge bar and walked around his desk to sit down. With everything else that politicians could be focused on, toilets was the best she could come up with as an election promise.

The amount of time and money politicians spent on campaigns was almost criminal. Surely the electorate had a right for some real work to be done, and some real issues to be addressed.

He didn't know why he listened to this drivel: a habit picked up from his father, most likely. James recalled from his youth that stations like CNN used to broadcast real news with reliable facts that were actually investigated. Now it was all manufactured entertainment – sensational, speculative and alleged.

It was mid-morning by the time James finally cracked the electronic calling card left behind by the intrusion hack into his computer. Staring with disbelief at his monitor, he was faced with a situation that didn't make any sense at all.

Using photoshop, he zoomed into the graphic as far as possible. Pixel by pixel revealed nothing. Still just a solid grey image from left to right and top to bottom. He enhanced the brightness, first gradually, then to its maximum intensity. This would expose an embedded watermark if there was one. Still nothing.

Finally, using an editor specifically designed to analyse the binary patterns that defined all digital information, he looked at the internal metadata; that which classified the characteristics of the file itself. Nothing unusual there. A standard true-colour JPG image. No embedded program code, and no *jump* instruction in the header segment.

Computer operating systems read the metadata to determine what application to use when presenting the file to a user. A document would typically be opened by something like Microsoft Word; music files would be opened by a media player; image files with Photoshop and so on.

Creators of viruses, or other malicious code, embed a *jump* instruction into a file's metadata. The computer's processor simply jumped to the location specified and followed the instructions at that point. This could be to corrupt other files, download and run mischievous programs, or pass a contacts list to an interested party, any number of things.

None of that was evident from what James could see. He went to the signature of the formula that decoded and displayed image segments in the correct sequence. As this was a single-colour image, there should only be one segment detailing the colour itself, in this case grey, along with the start and end vectors. That's when he realized that this was not the case.

On computer monitors, individual pixel colours were regulated by intensities of Red, Green and Blue. Referred to as the RGB model, permutations of individual values between zero and two hundred and fifty-five yield over sixteen million colour combinations. Grey was seen when the Red, Green and Blue values were all identical. The lower the values, the darker the grey, zeroing out at black. Inversely, higher values produced lighter shades of grey, moving progressively toward white.

James identified the greyscale RGB values that he expected would define the entire image, but there were anomalies. Most of the image was defined with pixel values that would display a shade of grey perfectly central in the black-to-white spectrum, but there were some where the values were just one unit lower – indistinguishable to the human eye.

But not to a computer.

Importing the image back into Photoshop, he adjusted the contrast. Applying progressively more divergence between greyscale values, most of the image remained the same, but those pixels with a lower RGB value darkened towards black. If they had been a unit or more higher than their surrounding grey background, they would have intensified in brightness towards white.

***

"I'm hoping that you can explain this," James said with deep concern, as he swivelled his monitor to face the other side of his desk.

Chapter Thirteen

"Took you long enough," Emily Hurst said to James with an underhanded smile.

James Clark flinched. This was not the response he expected. James looked at the graphic with Emily's name clearly revealed, then at her, with scepticism. "You know how these images ended up on my computer?"

"Yes," Emily replied. "I put them there."

"Why on earth did you do that, Em? And what's this about?" he snapped between curiosity and momentary anger. "Is this some sort of plot?"

"James, we've known about Mr. Bowers' little game for some time now, and…".

"We?" he interrupted.

"Perhaps I should get the primary conspirator in here. May I?" she asked, reaching over to his desk phone and punching in an internal number. "It's Emily. Can you please come to James' office?" She returned the handset to its cradle.

James seized the handset and dialled Nathan's extension. "Nate, I need you here immediately!"

A few moments later Nathan McIntosh hurried in followed closely by Sven.

"Sven!" James exclaimed, now totally perplexed.

"What's going on?" Nathan asked, glancing quickly to those around him.

"I'm hoping one of these two will tell me," James replied.

Sven Labrowski was fiercely loyal to SkyTech. His *Trinity* internet handle, along with hacking into corporate domains, had started off as nothing more than a hobby. It was only later that he discovered just how financially lucrative his talents were. He couldn't give a damn about helping lawbreakers rip off banks, which were, after all, the biggest criminals of all. They would simply recover their losses by screwing their account holders and investors in other ways, but he would never intentionally harm SkyTech. Something that Sven was passionate about however, was keeping charity organizations honest, or, more commonly, putting them out of business.

Sven knew of Magentis GMP, and had his suspicions. A bit of research within his hacker community joined Magentis to Adrian Bowers. At that point he was sure that whatever Bowers was up to would be detrimental to SkyTech, but he wanted to be absolutely sure.

Sven explained. "When Nathan approached us about two years ago to develop an information analysis application based on the NSA's data, it didn't take me or the other developers long to put the pieces together. Nathan's strategy, of having each of us code separate parts, made perfect sense. It's the fastest way to get things done, and offers some internal security."

Sven looked at Nathan. "Sorry, Nate, but the superfluous functionality you asked us to put in made it kind of obvious that there was something you were trying to hide."

Nathan reddened. His team was obviously more intuitive than he thought.

Sven continued. "With the help of some internet friends, and in particular a hacker's blog, we found some interesting stuff on Bowers. Firstly, he's not as highly placed with the FDA as he likes to make out."

"But the FDA is paying us a substantial amount every month for the service we provide," James pointed out. "Surely it would take a certain level of seniority to authorise such expenses."

"Here's the thing," Sven went on to explain. "Like every government department, a general revenue account is available. Money goes in and out without culpability. We are actually being paid indirectly by Magentis GMP. They deposit into the FDA's slush fund and Bowers takes it out to pay us. SkyTech's accounting department simply records it as a service payment from the FDA."

"Do you think the FDA knows what's going on?" James asked.

"I doubt it," Sven said.

James looked at Nathan. "Much like you suspected."

"Don't take Bowers for an idiot. He's crafty and very sly," Sven said. "Granted, when it comes to technology, there's a lot he thinks he knows, but doesn't. I hacked into the FDA's central mail server..."

"I don't want to know how you did that," James interrupted.

"Anyway," Sven continued, "I didn't find anything of interest on Bowers, so I tapped into the NSA's databanks to see what I could find there."

"Now I definitely don't want to know," James said, shaking his head in disapproval.

"I could just as easily have looked through our own version of the data sent to us for analysis by the NSA," Sven said, "but wasn't sure that they are giving us everything. I found something very interesting, though. What he's doing to SkyTech, he's tried previously with two other tech companies, but they declined his offer. To them, certain things that Bowers said just didn't add up."

Guilt swept over James. Just like his own gut feeling after meeting with Adrian Bowers the first time.

"Don't feel that you did anything wrong, JW," Sven said empathetically, noticing James's shamefaced expression. "Bowers learned some cunning lessons from those previous rejections."

"I appreciate your saying so," James said.

"I also learned a valuable lesson. We know that the National Security Agency records and archives digital communications, phone calls and such, but they don't restrict themselves to North America."

Not surprising, thought James. "I wonder who's contracted out to analyse that data. It's certainly not SkyTech."

"It's kind of scary to think that *Big Brother* has been around longer than we thought," Nathan commented.

"Information that they've accumulated is never deleted," Sven explained. "That's why I found historical emails from

Bowers that had already been wiped out on the FDA servers. "Once I associated Bowers with Magentis, my suspicions went sky high. They are mentioned in a number of conspiracy blogs, and Bowers appears on quite a few."

"I've never taken conspiracy blogs too seriously," James said scornfully.

"Bowers's email discussions with you are almost identical to those he had in his other entrapment attempts. I can show you if you like."

James's surprise was evident. "It's seems that you've been quite busy." Nathan sat there looking from one to the other in complete bewilderment.

"And you knew nothing of this?" James asked Nathan.

Nathan, feeling uncomfortable, shrugged apologetically. "Only that Sven was attempting to associate the emails between you and Bowers with the intrusion hack, but it appears he already knew."

"Don't be too harsh on Nate," Sven said. "There was a good reason why I kept this to myself."

"And why the calling card? What does Emily have to do with this?"

"Your executive assistant is more resourceful than you realize."

Sven turned to Emily with a sideways grin.

"Emily?" James asked, looking at her testily.

"About three months ago, totally out of the blue, my first husband phoned me and invited me to lunch," Emily said. "I hadn't heard from him since shortly after our divorce about twenty years ago."

"Ryan Hurst?" Nathan asked.

"Yes. He told me who he worked for and that he was part of a team of influential people who were doing research towards a healthier planet and the global food crisis."

After all those years, that much of him hadn't changed, Emily thought. Still trying to stress his worth to others. "Ryan told me that SkyTech was providing some research information to the FDA, and they simply wanted assurances that we were still the right company with which to move forward."

"What type of assurances?" James asked.

"I wondered about that," she said. "What he was asking is all a matter of public record, and I told him so. None of his questions really made much sense, though. It felt more like he was prying into something, but I couldn't make out exactly what. He asked me if I was settled in life and happy with my work. A bit of idle gossip about the office environment, that sort of thing. I suppose it was nice to see him again, and he did pay for the lunch." She smiled remembering how obvious Ryan made it that he had a company credit card.

James, deep in thought, frowned.

"After lunch, he said that it was great to see me looking so well, and that it would be nice to stay in touch," she continued. "I agreed, and we parted ways. He's phoned me twice since then, but they were more social calls than anything else."

Nathan felt a twinge of jealousy that he couldn't quite explain. "Next day, here in the office, I bumped into Sven at the coffee machine and asked idly if he'd ever heard of Magentis." Emily recounted some of the events of three months ago.

"Magentis?" Sven Labrowski's face turned to shock.

"What?" Emily said, taken by surprise. "So, you *have* heard of them?"

"This can't be coincidental," Sven muttered, almost to himself. He grabbed her left shoulder forcefully.

"Why do you ask? Sven, what's going on?"

"Hopefully, nothing. We need to talk in private. Come."

She followed Sven through Info Tech's security door and into the sound-proof media center.

"Why do you want to know about Magentis?" he asked sternly.

"I'd never heard of them until yesterday when I had lunch with my ex."

"Matt and Elle's father?" he asked.

"No, the marriage before that."

"Sorry Em, none of my business. Go on."

"He told me that he worked for Magentis, and that SkyTech was doing some contract work for them and the FDA. I presume that's the deal James made with Mr. Bowers a couple of years ago."

"It is," Sven said, "but this whole deal is going to go south."

"How so?" she asked, suddenly concerned.

"Bowers is up to something, that much I know. I'd bet my life on it. When Nate presented the original program specifications to us, there were things that he obviously didn't want us to know about. None of the developers, including myself, were too concerned. Work needs to be done, we just get on and do it without question."

Emily nodded. "So how does this involve Ryan, my ex?"

"Bowers is using him to get to you, in the hope of establishing an inside contact. You can guarantee that Ryan will be in touch with you again. Most likely under the pretense that it's just a social call."

"Sven, you sound paranoid. Are you sure some of those conspiracy blogs you subscribe to aren't twisting your mind."

"I'm serious, Em. Not too long ago I started monitoring emails between Bowers and JW. They were the first hint that something wasn't right."

"In what way?" she asked, with a note of concern in her voice.

"Just things that were said by Bowers, and the way he expressed himself. JW's responses also appeared very vague and uncommunicative. It's not that important, and I can fill you in on the details later if you want."

"Okay, so what now?" she asked.

"I need to put a stop to this entire business venture, but I want JW to be the one pulling the plug."

"How?" she asked, intrigued.

"By raising doubts. And I know how to do it. If JW sees that emails between himself and Bowers are being snooped, it will most certainly make him suspicious, but I cannot do that from inside SkyTech's domain."

"Why not?"

"The programs we develop are automatically monitored by the system, to ensure that no malicious code gets in. Anything slightly out of the ordinary, and Nate gets a notification."

"You and the other programmers are okay with your work being policed?"

"It's standard practice in most IT departments," he said. "It also keeps us developers honest."

"Okay, I see where this is going. You want my help, right?"

Sven came right to the point. "I will provide you with some apps and a few detailed instructions that will get you into JW's emails from your home computer."

"Yeah, right," she said sarcastically. She wasn't feeling at all comfortable about where this was heading. "I don't know, Sven. Shouldn't you be speaking to Nate about this?"

"No. There's something going on that neither he nor JW want any of us to know about."

"Why me?" she questioned with trepidation. "Surely you can do this from your own home computer?"

"Let's just say that there are things on that computer which are not entirely above-board. For legal and moral reasons, I don't want SkyTech involved in any way with that part of my private life."

"Okay, so why me?" she asked again.

"Trust, more than anything else," he affirmed. "Just hear me out. What I have in mind is to create a process that will worm its way through all our security protocols, open up his computer for a few milliseconds and touch his email data. Only those going to, or coming from Bowers and the FDA will be scanned."

"Go on," she prompted, as he briefly halted in thought.

"We need to leave something behind that's obvious. Something that suggests his computer is being probed."

"How about a smiley face pasted all over his monitor," she suggested with a mild attempt at humour.

"That's actually a brilliant idea." He was serious. "Look, what you leave as a calling card can be whatever you want. The intrusion itself will hop through about twenty anonymous internet servers across the globe. They will self-destruct, but it takes a few seconds. Anyone back-tracking will see three or four previous servers at the most. It will be impossible to trace it back to its origin."

"Namely, my home computer," Emily said, still feeling very uncomfortable.

"Right. For the miniscule time interval that JW's computer is exposed, the emails will have their last access time modified and that will coincide with the time stamp on the calling card. It will then reset his computer back to a secure state."

"I don't know Sven. Surely our firewall will detect that," said Emily stating the obvious.

"Oh, yes. All bells and whistles will go off. But that's exactly what we want; for both JW and Nate to be instantly alerted that a security breach has occurred."

They put their plan into action.

Chapter Fourteen

With furled brow, James looked up from his expansive office desk at Emily and Sven apprehensively. "So, you hatched your scheme and kept the rest of us on edge all this time," he said.

"As for keeping you on edge," Emily pointed out, after relaying to James and Nathan her discussion with Sven, "you didn't need any help from us. You've hardly been yourself these past few months, skulking around like you were carrying the world on your shoulders. We knew that there was something far more serious on your mind than your emails being probed. We also had every confidence that either you or Nate would eventually crack the graphic. It was a subtle way to let you know that you're not on your own. We will support and help you in any way we can."

"If the FDA venture proved to be legitimate," Sven explained, "Emily would immediately stop the intrusions, and I would inform Nate that we'd tweaked the firewall to trap the hacks and discard them."

Nathan did not look happy.

"There's another thing," Sven said to James. "I unintentionally overheard the discussion you had recently with Nate in his office. I didn't join the other developers for lunch because I had some stuff to get out the way. I saw no reason to announce my presence from around the corner. Once I heard of Bowers' latest demand, I knew that I was right about him."

"Demand," Nathan growled. "More like extortion."

"You were absolutely right, JW, when you expressed your fear to Nate that the intrusion was within SkyTech itself," Sven confirmed.

Nathan slumped further into his chair.

"In the last few days I've put every effort into digging up dirt on Bowers," Sven said smugly. "You wouldn't believe what I've found. His little trips to Thailand are just a part of the story."

They sat in silence for a moment.

James turned from Sven and looked Emily sombrely in the eyes. "Em, with everything that's come to light, I don't think it's in the best interests of this company to keep you on any longer as my executive assistant."

Emily's eyes dropped. What had she expected? That little prank of hers might have seemed imaginative, even clever at the time, but it was childish. She had no one to blame but herself. She didn't have to go along with Sven, but did, probably looking for some excitement in her life.

Emily would have trouble finding another job. Executive assistants were hardly in demand these days and she had no other professional skills to tap into that could provide a half decent salary.

She would certainly have to find a cheaper apartment outside of Queens. A move like that would be more disruptive to Matt and Elle than it would be for herself.

They had grown up in that apartment and it was the only home they knew. All their social connections were in the neighbourhood, and both had jobs nearby. Would they decide to leave their mother and start with new lives of their own? The loneliness for her would be unbearable.

She'd have to explain it to the kids as best as possible and hope they would understand the situation she had put her family in.

Emily felt tears welling in her eyes.

***

Walking out of Mex's Steakhouse, where he regularly ate lunch, Adrian Bowers popped another Pepto-Bismol caplet into his mouth. He needed to cut down on the heavy lunches, and double shots of Bourbon didn't help matters much either. The problem was that he simply had no appetite for the healthy salad lunches which Sofia, his third wife, packed for him. They always ended up in the trash. He tried to make it clear to her again last night that he was old enough to look after his own wellbeing and didn't need advice from her. As usual, it broke out into a heated argument and he had to backhand the stupid bitch across the face to stop her infuriated nagging. She was obviously asking for it.

What was it with women these days, he thought? As soon as they had a ring on their finger, they owned you. She knew that he had a high-stress job and certainly didn't complain about his income, which gave her reasonable spending power. She should be appreciative of the things he gave her, and, being twenty years younger than him, even more so.

Adrian considered himself an excellent lover, yet Sofia had very little interest in having sex with him. He was getting a little tired of forcing himself on her. It was all her fault that he needed to look elsewhere and if he ever found out that her apathy towards him was because she was having an affair, there'd be hell to pay. Yes, he was justified in his infidelities. She was definitely the one to blame.

The scriptures were clear. In the bonds of marriage, women should love, honour and obey their husbands. Throughout history, men had been the protectors and the providers. Why couldn't women just do as they were told? None of them were capable of rational thought. And not surprising, considering that their brains were between their legs. Whores - all of them.

Walking along the sidewalk to his car, his belt uncomfortably tight again, Adrian pulled out his phone and dialled a number. "Dom, how are you on this fine day?"

"Hello, Adrian. I'm doing very well thank you. Have you seen the latest additions?"

"That's why I'm calling you," Adrian said, bringing to mind the exciting new photos on Dom's website. "Nice new content. They're getting younger every day. I love the little redhead."

"She is quite something special, isn't she?" Dom agreed. "And not even in her teens yet."

"Did you find these pictures, or take them yourself?"

"All my own work," Dom admitted proudly.

"I'm jealous," Adrian laughed. "I'm also as randy as hell."

"Now, now," admonished Dom. "No blasphemous words please."

Adrian smiled. "Are we still on for tomorrow night?"

"Ten thirty as planned," Dom confirmed.

"Great. See you then," Adrian said, ending the call.

Reverend Dominique Francis Garcia, minister to the Baptist-Catholic church in Jersey, hung up his phone.

Plugging away unobtrusively, without any sense of right or wrong, three levels below SkyTech Tower, the IBM Sequoia took a few millisecond time-slices away from regular operations and archived to its databanks the date, time, participating phone numbers and full conversation between Adrian Bowers and Reverend Garcia.

***

"Emily," James said, interrupting her thoughts. "You misunderstood when I implied that I don't require to keep you on as my assistant. I think you'd be more suited working in Nate's department."

"What?" Emily said, looking up.

"I said that you'd be better suited working in Nate's department," James repeated. "You obviously have some hidden skills none of us, except perhaps Sven, knew about. And Nate is always complaining that he doesn't have enough creative talent."

Her face lit up in sudden relief. "I thought you were firing me."

"Good grief, no," James exclaimed. "Let's get through this problem with Bowers and work towards your transition as soon as possible afterwards. It's going to be difficult for me to find a replacement as efficient and dedicated as you."

Emily beamed with delight.

"Oh, and there's one last thing," Sven said, sheepishly. "I have a recording of the discussion which you, Nate and Bowers had in your office. It's not much use, though. Bowers is very shrewd and nothing he said points directly back to him. In fact, that entire discussion would incriminate us more than it would him if it ever got out."

"Jesus, Sven. What else didn't I know about?" Nathan barked with displeasure. "I take it you installed a listening device into that fishing trophy."

James laughed out in genuine pleasure. "Sven, I don't know if I should reprimand you or hug you."

Sven grimaced and dropped his eyes.

James looked at each in turn. "I don't know what to say, other than being glad you're on my team and on my side. And in case you've been wondering, Em: no, I did not win any fishing trophies."

"Look James," Emily said, "Sven and I risked our jobs exposing our scheme to you, but if it prevented SkyTech from being put into serious jeopardy, it was worth it. We like this company just as much as you do."

Sven nodded in agreement. Nathan said nothing.

"Sometimes the obvious glares out at us, and we don't see it immediately," Sven said, turning to Nathan and then to James. "Has either of you noticed his email address? The domain name ends in .NET. All government departments, including the NSA, FDA, FBI and CIA are all on the .GOV domain, much like all commercial sites are almost always on .COM and educational sites are on .EDU."

Nathan's sudden interest jolted him back into the conversation. "Good catch, Sven. I didn't notice that."

"Me neither," James admitted.

"That's why I found very little communication from Bowers on the FDA's email server," Sven explained to James. "All exchanges between the two of you go through his personal account on public domain. Emails he thinks are sensitive get dumped into his *deleted* folder, which he cleans out religiously, but all are still securely tucked away in the NSA's databanks."

"We'll play Adrian's game until we find out more," Nathan suggested. "Sven, I presume you now know about the program I'm developing to tap into phone conversations."

"Most, but not all the details. Emily knows nothing of this."

"No reason why not," James said. "Like it or not, Em, you're now in the thick of things."

Nathan turned to Emily. "Keep up the casual conversations with Ryan. I'm sure he will be reaching out to you again soon. It goes without saying that you need to be careful what you say to him."

"Of course," she said.

"Let us know what sort of questions he's asking about

SkyTech," James added, "and answer him as honestly as you can. He doesn't realize he's being played by Bowers. Will you be okay with all of this? He *was* your husband, after all."

Nathan looked expectantly at Emily.

"He didn't seem to be coming on to me," she said. "I would have had mixed feelings if he did, and probably just gone along to see where it went." She thought about it for a moment. Ryan Hurst had never truly committed himself to anything. After so many years, he still seemed unsure of the direction in which he wanted his life to go, and always to be trying to prove something along the way.

Maybe she was wrong. Maybe he *had* changed, and had started taking life a bit more seriously. It was well over twenty years ago. Surely he must have matured in that time. Was she prepared to rekindle an old relationship? She wasn't getting any younger. Niggling reflections of the years of loneliness started surfacing again in her mind.

With a resolute expression, she looked at James. "Any emotional attachment I had died years ago," she said abruptly, getting her thoughts firmly back to reality. "Maybe I'm being unfair, but quite frankly, if he's being played, he probably deserves it."

Nathan quietly breathed a sigh of relief.

James looked at his Rolex. "It's already an hour past lunch. Sorry that I kept you all here this long," he apologized. "Let's break. Tomorrow we can discuss everything we have on Bowers. Let's get Em up to speed. Sven, you can also let the rest of us know what else you've uncovered on Bowers.

On their way out of James's office, Emily teased Nathan. "Looks like I'll be working under you, Nate." Nathan blushed.

Chapter Fifteen

"You were right," Emily said to Nathan. "That was the best street dog ever."

"Told you," Nathan replied, as they walked along Terrace and down towards the east entrance of Summer-Stage. The evening was warm, with just a few wispy clouds. Sunset was still two hours away. Trees, abundant with leaves, offered shade to the well-tended walkways. Elm, birch, cedar, maple and pine were among the many varieties that provided vibrant colour to the grounds.

"Looks like quite a line-up of people ahead," Emily observed.

"No worries. We go directly through the members' entrance over there," Nathan said pointing to the left of the crowd.

"You're a member?" she asked.

"Sure. I come here often enough. I'm surprised you've never been to one of these concerts."

"I've often heard distant music coming from here when I'm window shopping along Fifth," she said, "but I've never actually come into this part of the park before."

"Come," he said, taking her by the hand and leading her around the Witch Statue towards the members' admission gate a little further ahead. "If you're worried about walking through the park on your own, you are probably in one of the safest areas. Not that there are any real concerns elsewhere, but did you know that in the late nineteenth century, this part of the park had what was called a Ladies' Refreshment Saloon? It was a very respectable Victorian establishment, where women could dine in public without a male escort."

"Oh." She didn't know that. The fact was, she knew very little history at all about Central Park.

"It's been through a lot of changes," Nathan went on. "By the 1920s it changed to a casino, a co-ed restaurant, and then an Art Deco gentlemen's night club. Jimmy Walker, the Mayor of New York at that time, dined here almost every night with his mistress."

"How long has Summer-Stage been around?"

"It was built in 1990," Nathan explained. "The casino itself was torn down in the 1930s, and the Rumsey Playfield or *Playground,* as it was usually referred to then, was constructed."

"Who was Rumsey?" she asked.

"Mary Harriman Rumsey. She founded the *League for the Promotion of Settlement Movements.* Even in those days, politics ruled when it came to naming places and monuments. Her father, Edward Harriman, was a very wealthy railroad magnate, and her younger brother William, a New York State Governor and US Diplomat. In 1933, Roosevelt appointed Mary to chair the Consumer Advisory Board. She died the following year."

Emily recalled that the Settlement Movements played a large part in making the administration a little easier for the volumes of new immigrants coming from Europe, but she had no idea that the founder was a woman. "Quite an achievement for her time," she said.

"Mary was a remarkable woman," Nathan agreed.

"Oh my God! Is that the Rolling Stones playing?" Emily exclaimed, hurrying them up the wide stone steps leading to the gate. "I can't quite see the stage from here."

Nathan laughed. "This concert certainly wouldn't be for free if that were the case. No, they're a tribute band called Hot Rocks."

"They sound just like the Stones," she said excitedly.

"Come," he said, guiding her through the entrance where he displayed his membership card. "See if we can get as close as possible to the stage."

"Are they from New York?"

"Toronto, actually. They play here quite often. Wait till you see them up close. Their lead singer, Bob Wotherspoon, looks exactly like Mick Jagger."

"You're kidding," she said, looking at Nathan with astonishment.

"You wouldn't believe how many world-famous musicians performing to American and international audiences originated in Canada. Our own music industry has become stagnant. Country music is dying, bluegrass has lost all its momentum, except perhaps in Nashville, and the best we have to offer now is rap, something the rest of the world couldn't give a rat's ass about."

They traversed their way through the dense crowd closer to the base of the stage. From her vantage point, Emily looked up at the lead singer blasting out a perfect rendition of "Jumping Jack Flash".

"He does look like Jagger," Emily shouted over the clamour with a wide grin, bouncing up and down in time to the beat.

"What?" Nathan said, leaning his ear closer to Emily.

"I said," she shouted louder, "he looks exactly like Mick Jagger. And moves like him too."

They were still holding hands.

For the next three hours Nathan, and more so Emily, were captivated by the booming rock music and spellbinding performance of Hot Rocks. They were totally immersed in the energy of the crowd, and were encouraged to sing along with any and all of the songs.

This was yet another side of Nathan that Emily had never seen before. He was more like a teenager than the serious-minded software guru she had become so familiar with at SkyTech.

They shared an Uber to get home, Emily's apartment being just a few miles further from Nathan's condo in Elmhurst.

"My ears are still ringing from the loud music," she said as she got comfortable in the back seat. "I had so much fun. Hot Rocks are fantastic; and I thought you were joking when you said their lead singer looks like Jagger. He's just like him."

"Glad you enjoyed yourself," Nathan said, turning to face her. "That's the third concert I've been to. They perform here twice a year."

"Always at Rumsey?"

"Yeah... well, the free concerts anyhow. They perform at other New York venues and tour across the States and Canada, but those you have to pay for," he answered. "The shows they give here are more for self-promotion and publicity. A lot of famous musicians have started off at Summer-Stage."

"You seem to know a lot of Central Park's history. Is that another of your specialities, besides being a master chef?"

Nathan laughed. "Thanks, but my cooking skills really aren't that great."

"Yes, they are! Didn't you notice at your party that we were all so engrossed in the food, nobody was talking? Even Daryl had very little to say," she said, smiling.

"Cooking is just something I really enjoy. But to your point about history. New York's past has some fantastic stories to tell, and I love reading about it."

"I've lived in the city my whole life," Emily said, looking out the open cab window, "but know almost nothing of its history." She turned to face him. "So, what else about you, besides your interest in cooking, New York's past and rock music, don't I know about?"

"A few things I guess. I certainly have enough personal time on my hands."

"No romantic attachments?" she pried, not really wanting to know the answer.

He looked at her in silence for a few moments and Emily wondered if his reticence was cautionary or calculated.

"Not for a while," he said. "I've been single my whole life, Em, with very few serious or long-term relationships. Over the years I kind of got buried in my interests and hobbies."

"Like reading cookery books or historical journals?"

"Journals, no. But I do read a lot of fiction based on historical fact. As for cookbooks, can't really remember when I last looked at one of those. I just experiment with all sorts of foods and spices, and remember those recipes that worked. And a few that were complete disasters," he chuckled. "Never try curried sardines!"

"I'll be sure to avoid that," she said. "Anyway, I don't really care for sardines, no matter how they are flavored or disguised."

"I don't eat them anymore either," he admitted.

"I noticed a small workbench in your office with tools and electronics," she said. "Sorry, didn't mean to snoop. I looked in on my way to the bathroom. Are you building your own computer parts?"

"Micro-bots actually. You probably saw some bugs on the table and a fly walking around in circles."

Emily covered her mouth with her right hand and grabbed his forearm with the other. "Oh, Nate!" she exclaimed in an embarrassed tone. "I saw that but thought you'd spilt something which was attracting insects."

He grinned. "They're very realistic, don't you think?"

"Very! But why are you building robotic bugs?"

"It's far more interesting than radio-controlled toys and less of a challenge than creating nano-machines," he said. "Maybe that will be my next hobby."

What's with the fly?" she asked.

"I'm testing a self-charging battery. The fly has been following the same circular pattern for a few weeks now. It will recharge from any light source, or the infinitesimal magnetic field given off by a nearby power supply. I want to see how long it continues before breaking down or losing power. So far, it's behaving beyond my expectations."

"That's fascinating," she said with wonder.

"From my laptop, I can switch it over to full remote-control and get it to fly where I want. It's got excellent range. It's the third-generation of that particular model. The first one demolished itself against a wall, and the second model flew out of range. I never found it again," he explained. "This version has full audio and video capabilities. I can see where it's going and what it hears. Its range is about two miles; much further than my first attempts."

"I'm impressed," she said, looking at Nathan with admiration.

"One thing that I haven't quite perfected is its behaviour when it lands." he went on. "Sorry, Em, is this boring you? Once I get started on my *bugs*, I tend to ramble on."

"God, no!" she said with sincerity. "This is exciting stuff."

"Well, what I was saying," he continued, "is that insects don't land and become dead still. They immediately start moving around in what seems to us like senseless erratic behaviour, but it's actually a survival mechanism."

"I didn't know that," she said.

"I got the unpredictable movements figured out, but the fly keeps walking into walls or off the table. I'll figure something out."

"I know you will," she said with assurance.

"The beetles are another problem entirely," he continued with enthusiasm. "With their body-mass to wing-size ratio, actual beetles shouldn't be able to fly. It baffled science for years, until high speed photography was developed. Their wings don't move up and down or front to back like many other flying insects, but angle and shape themselves to scoop up the surrounding air. It grants them flight, but does nothing for maneuverability. That's why they keep on flying into things. It's only their exo-skeleton that protects them from permanent damage."

He seems to know a lot of stuff, she thought.

"Nature has created a very effective mechanism for beetles, but their wing mechanics are incredibly complex," Nathan said, almost to himself.

"We're at the first stop," the driver interrupted.

"That's me," Nathan said. "How much do I owe you?"

"Twelve fifty."

"Here's fifteen. Keep the change."

"Thanks, buddy," the driver answered, taking the money.

Emily leaned over and kissed Nathan lightly on the cheek. "I had a really wonderful time, Nate. Thanks for the invite. We should do it again."

"Me too, Em," Nathan replied. "Have a great weekend, and say hello to Elle and Matt."

"Will do," she responded. "See you Monday."

A few minutes later, the cab arrived outside her apartment block. She paid the driver the remaining fare and gave him a small tip. She walked up the short flight of stairs, through the building entrance and called for the elevator. It annoyed her that there was no accessible staircase, the only one available being the fire escape; the door could only be opened from the inside.

It was just after ten thirty p.m., and Emily was exhausted from singing, bouncing up and down to the music and her overall excitement. She was ready to flop on her bed and unwind for a bit. She dropped her small bag on the dining room table, and walked through to her bedroom, where she kicked off her sandals, sat down on the bed and massaged her feet which were killing her.

After a few moments, she got up, closed the bedroom door and struggled out of her jeans. She threw them into the corner laundry basket along with her loose top. She'd take care of the small ketchup stain in the morning.

"Hope that stain wasn't too obvious," she said to herself. Bra and panties, suitably discarded, Emily slumped backwards on to the bed. It was good to be lying down.

With the sounds of *Paint It Black* echoing in her mind, she reflected on the different sides of Nate's personality. Having worked with him for so many years, how could she have failed to know what a remarkable and interesting man he was? She wondered what her reaction would have been if he'd invited her up to his apartment after the concert. Her mind responded with an instant *yes*, even before she put further thought into her own question. And if he had asked her to stay the night? Again, *yes*. Putting some serious thought into that however, the answer would have had to be an apologetic *no*. She deliberated on whether or not he would have been offended.

Emily had no intentions of phoning her kids and telling them she'd be out for the night. This was not something she'd be ready to justify or negotiate. They would be totally grossed out at the thought of their mom having sex. She certainly had been at their age, thinking that about her own parents.

She let her thoughts wander freely for a few minutes. From her long association with him, it was clear that Nathan didn't want Emily as a friend with benefits. Just a friend. And she was content with that.

Or was she?

After some mild deliberation, Emily had finally let Nate pay for her hot-dog and soda before they walked through the park to the concert. Although not quite the same as if he had invited her to an expensive restaurant, she trusted that, either way, Nate wouldn't have expected anything in return.

She wondered what it would be like making love to a skinny guy like Nate. She had a fleeting thought of him lying on top of her, with her legs clenched tightly around him, feet hooked together. Emily felt her face going red. She needed to stop these whimsical thoughts. They were office colleagues, and, more recently, social friends; nothing more.

Emily fluffed up two pillows against her headboard. Leaning into them, she opened her bedside drawer and pulled out this month's edition of Vogue, exposing her dildo hidden underneath. She really needed to find a better place for her toy. Emily didn't suspect that Matt or Elle were rummaging around her personal belongings, but still.

What the hell, she thought suddenly. The kids wouldn't be back for hours. She discarded the open magazine on the floor and reached for her dildo.

***

Realistically, they would never be more than co-workers and friends. No hint or suggestion was ever given to the contrary, but there was nothing wrong with a bit of imaginative make-believe. Thoughts of friendship disappeared into oblivion and were quickly replaced by visions of their naked bodies locked together in urgent and lustful desire. Orgasm was rapid and powerful at the thought of Emily lying underneath him with her firm shapely legs wrapped tightly around him. Just a few miles away in his Elmhurst condo, Nathan drifted off to sleep with a contented and satisfied smile on his face.

God, she had great legs.

Chapter Sixteen

Nathan walked towards Emily's anteroom, excited at the thought of passing her desk for the third time that day. Sven Labrowski was close behind. Emily stood up from her chair, followed them into James's office, and closed the door behind her. She sat down on the Chesterfield in her usual spot, opposite where James was already seated on the left. Nathan and Sven made themselves comfortable in the easy chairs flanking the center table. Emily had already provided coffee, Perrier water and cookies a few minutes earlier.

James Clark looked up from his phone and smiled briefly at each of them. "Right on time as usual," he said. "Thanks for being punctual."

One does not arrive late to meetings with the CEO and sole owner of SkyTech, Emily thought with mild amusement.

James switched his phone to vibrate mode. The others, on cue, did likewise. Emily put her phone down on the side table. This was their third scheduled meeting since Adrian Bowers's appointment with James and Nathan a few weeks ago.

"Let's make this as fast as possible," James said. "I have a luncheon appointment with AT&T in an hour, so let's start. Sven?"

"What I have so far is all of Bowers's trips to Thailand and the places he's frequented. Bangkok appears to make very lucrative profits from people like him. One place he favors is Hung Sin Escorts. It specialises in very young girls." Sven looked further down his notes. "He spends an average of two weeks there and all expenses are paid from his FDA credit card account."

"In other words, the government's slush fund," Nathan commented.

"Our tax dollars at work," James said, with a scornful expression on his face.

Sven continued. "Occasional calls to Ryan Hurst, but nothing of note there. Bowers is doing nothing more than making Hurst feel involved and important. Most intriguing, though, are the daily calls between himself and Garcia, mostly discussing church business and other items of mutual interest, which I now have most of the facts on."

"Who is Garcia?" Emily asked.

"Dominique Garcia, minister to the Baptist-Catholic church in Jersey," Sven answered. "Nate is mostly up to speed with what I've uncovered there, but I didn't want to report back to you, JW, or, of course, you, Em, without absolute proof and all the facts. Garcia and Bowers are part-time lovers."

James looked up in surprise. "Has Bowers got any scruples at all?"

"You haven't heard the rest," Sven went on. "They both share an interest in little girls and boys. Garcia regularly sends images to Bowers on his latest findings. Now, here's the real core of something tangible that we can use against Bowers when we're ready. He spends a lot of time perusing one particular website that specialises in child porn."

"Yes, you mentioned that at our last meeting," Emily recalled. "How can we use that against him?"

"That specific site is owned and administered by Dominique Garcia," Sven answered. "By association, Bowers is a collaborator." Now everyone's eyes were drawn to Sven.

"And you're certain about this?" James asked.

"Yes," Sven replied. "That's why I haven't mentioned it until now. One thing that I will also have conclusive proof of very soon is that Garcia takes most of the photos on that site himself, which suggests that he's luring children from his own congregation."

"Oh my God," Emily said, shocked, raising her right hand to her chest. Her blood was starting to boil.

"I doubt God will be of any help," James said cynically. "That's why it's probably so easy for Garcia. In his position, he's trusted by his congregation and more so by the children."

"I'd hate to know what fictitious crap he feeds those kids to entice them into his sacristy and in front of the camera," Nathan said.

"Ah yes," James growled. "In the name of religion and the righteousness of Christian doctrine, I'm sure." He was mortified at what he was hearing.

"Also," Sven said, "he's on to his third wife, who is much younger than he is. I doubt she will stick around much longer. Like his other two exes, he beats her up regularly."

"Scumbag," Nathan muttered to himself.

"Are you having him followed?" James asked.

"Not necessary," Sven said. "We've been recording his location. Well, the location of his phone, through its GPS. Since we cloned it, we know exactly where he's been, and where he is now. Like the rest of us, he always has his phone with him. Our clone doesn't really serve much purpose any more except to record and store all his incoming and outgoing data, web searches and phone calls. Most of what's useful now comes from his phone directly. Something I should have done from the start, but only activated last week, was his microphone: we've been recording everything that his phone hears twenty-four hours a day."

"Isn't there some visual indication on his phone that the microphone is active?" James asked.

"I don't want to overwhelm anyone with the technicalities, but you need to understand that cloning a phone works both ways. Our clone will mirror all his phone calls, as you know, but if we change something on the clone, it also changes the behaviour of Bowers's phone," Sven explained.

Nathan nodded in agreement.

"This is something I've been very careful with," Sven said. "Firstly, I've modified his Location app, so that, if he turns it off, it will wait about ten seconds and turn on again. That way it doesn't arouse any suspicions. He'll just think one of his other applications, like Maps, or his Uber app, reactivated it. We always know where he is. The phone's front notification light will turn on when the microphone is listening, and I have no direct override for that behaviour. Like all smartphones however, you can control the colour of the light for different apps and notifications. I've simply set the colour to black for his mic, so the light is technically on but nothing shows."

James was impressed. "Nice move."

"I can't take any credit for that," Sven clarified. "It was actually Nate's idea."

"Well done," James said, redirecting the compliment to Nathan.

"Listening in on him a few nights ago was how we found out that he abuses his wife," Nathan said. "It's all securely recorded on the IBM. I found it very disturbing to listen to."

"Don't all these tweaks to his phone drain the battery?" Emily asked.

"Not to any great extent," Sven said. "Certainly not enough to arouse suspicion. Also, we are using his own technology against him. He has voice recognition installed, and I've refined it to exclude everything except human speech. All background sounds, even the discordance of large crowds talking in unison, are ignored."

"Thanks, Sven," James said. "We need to move on. If you can, let us know how Garcia is getting the photos for his website, and as soon as possible please."

Sven nodded and got stuck into the cookies.

"Nate," James said, turning away from Sven. "How is the phone monitoring coming along for the numbers Bowers gave us?"

"We've started testing and it will be complete by the end of the week."

"That's excellent progress," James said. "I have my update with Bowers next week and will simply tell him that we are progressing well, and that he should see results in about two months."

"That's a conversation I'd like to listen in on," Emily chuckled.

"Unfortunately we can't," Nathan said.

"Oh. Won't his mic be on?" she asked.

"Something that I didn't think of at first, but glad you reminded me of it now," Nathan said. "After we cloned Bowers' phone, we had an exact replica of everything; not only the SIM, but all data stored in its memory and SD card. Even now, the clone will mimic almost all activity, but I discovered something interesting. Some apps are entirely local to the phone. They use their own memory space, and are completely isolated from Wi-Fi or any other external access. After we dumped the clone's contents on the computer, we found a bunch of text-notes as well as numerous voice-notes."

"Are they important?" James asked.

"The text? No. But the voice-notes, although of no particular value to us in this case, clearly prove that Bowers covertly records his business meetings. He was doing so when he was here in your office."

"That doesn't surprise me," Sven said.

"Yeah, right, Sven," Emily teased. "Like you weren't doing the same?"

"The point I'm trying to make," Nathan continued, "and to answer Em, is that when he turns on his voice-notes app, it will override the microphone's current activity. I have no doubts that he will be recording your conversation with him, JW."

"I could always turn on my own voice-notes app," James said, a little hesitantly.

"Why not get one of your bugs to listen in," Emily suggested in all seriousness.

"Are you still working on those micro-bots?" James asked.

"With a great deal of success," Nathan replied. "I took your advice and experimented with the dynamic frequency modulation that you suggested. The *fly* now has a range of about two miles. We can easily record sound and video from up here. Unless the agreed location has changed, you and Bowers will be less than half a mile away."

"No change," James confirmed. "It's still scheduled to take place by Andersen's statue. Won't Bowers be a bit suspicious if his recording light doesn't come on?"

"Smartphone manufacturers are clever," Nathan said. "Developers don't have to code notification functionality into their apps. Instead, they call on the phone's built-in service; that does this for them. All the app needs to do is provide the preferred colour and optional blink rate. The phone does the rest. Most app developers don't bother with providing special parameters, and just rely on the phone's default behaviour – a slow blinking red light." Nathan looked to each of them. "Try it on your own phones. Whether you are recording voice or video, you will likely get the same slow blinking red."

Emily picked up her phone from the side table. A few moments later, after Sven washed down the last of the cookies with his coffee, she confirmed exactly what Nathan had just said.

"I've modified the mic's behaviour on Adrian's phone, via the clone, to request a continuous *black* light only when his phone is listening and transmitting to us," Nathan said, as Emily returned her phone to the table. "There are no changes to the way his apps behave. Bowers won't notice anything out of the ordinary."

"Might be worth a shot, using your *fly*," James said thoughtfully.

"Another idea I've just had," Nathan said. "The fly can disrupt the app's ability to record. All I need is the exact frequency that the microphone operates at, and that I can get from the clone. When he plays it back, all he'll get is static. He will most certainly turn the recorder on beforehand, and we will know the instant he does, because his phone will stop transmitting to us."

"Won't that raise any suspicions with Bowers?" Sven asked, looking at James. "Suddenly his faithful app starts giving trouble, but only when meeting with you?"

"You have a valid point Sven," James said. "But in this I would concur with Nate's suggestion. It's time Bowers started getting a bit nervous. I suspect he doesn't particularly like things he can't explain, or situations he has no control over. Let's see what we can do to erode some of his confidence."

The others all nodded in agreement.

"We're agreed then," James said. "We use the fly. How is the audio quality?"

"Excellent," Nathan said, with a proud look on his face. "Also the video quality, but that's not much use to us in this case. The power supply will continue uninterrupted for about two hours, without the need to recharge."

"I didn't know miniaturisation was so advanced," Emily commented.

"My little hobby toys are nothing, compared to how far government labs have progressed," Nathan said. "Fully functional micro- and auto-bots are already down to a microscopic level."

Emily jolted in astonishment.

"Emily has verified the numbers Bowers gave us," Nathan went on. "Five are doctors specialising in health and nutrition, and the others are all pharmacists. When we're ready to start sending those conversations to Bowers's internet drop-box, we will use Sven's intrusion hack process, but such that it works backwards."

"I've removed those programs from my home computer," Emily said, "and Sven has installed them on one of our autonomous servers here at SkyTech."

James frowned.

"Nate has confirmed that there would be no security risks," Sven hurriedly justified.

"I have no choice but to trust your judgements on that," James said, looking in turn at Nathan and Sven. He still felt a little uncomfortable every time mention was made of the intrusion into his computer.

"Sven, you would be better at explaining the details to James," Emily said.

"As soon as a phone conversation has concluded, the IBM will send the entire data package to the autonomous server from where it will be transmitted," Sven explained, "It will be routed through twenty global providers, looping back on to itself. In other words, the autonomous server is both sender and receiver. After each hop on to the next global provider, the data on the previous one will be permanently wiped out. All except on our own, of course. Here it will be securely archived and we can do some analysis on it."

"Any thoughts on what you might expect to find?" James asked.

"None," Sven replied, "but we at least want to have a listen before it gets out there. If we have any indication that it's sensitive, or could cause major problems for these or other individuals, we might want to stall before giving it to Bowers. I don't want this sitting on some easily accessible internet provider. And we really don't know yet what Bowers is up to."

"Assuming we do send it," Nathan interjected, "Sven will then take out all firewall blockades and redirect to Bowers' drop-box. For now, though, we need these measures in place because the destination is within SkyTech. It's also imperative that this information never filters through the National Security Agency's snooping process."

"Well, you've obviously thought this through," James said. "Em, anything else you want to add?"

"I had two calls from Ryan," she said. "Not sure what they were all about though. He didn't ask me anything specific about SkyTech. It was more like he was trying to impress on me how important his job at Magentis is. That part of his nature, at least, hasn't changed since I was married to him, and I think that's an advantage to us."

"How so?" James asked.

"It makes him easier to read," Emily responded. "He might think he's devious enough to lull people into a false sense of security and get sensitive information out of them, but he's not."

James nodded. "More like an open book."

"Oh, he's completely transparent. I get the distinct feeling he's trying to come on to me again."

Nathan, apprehensively wondering if she had more to say on the topic, raised his head and looked at her.

Emily changed the subject. "I had an idea on how we might be able to help those poor children in Bangkok."

"Give us your thoughts when we reconvene next week, Em," James said, nodding to her. "I'm sure you have something creative in mind. Sorry to call this session short, but I need to get to AT&T. Good work, everyone."

Chapter Seventeen

With Nathan seated in the center, Emily and Sven made themselves comfortable on the Chesterfield in the privacy of James office. Nathan's laptop was open on the coffee table, a gamer's joystick plugged into one USB port and a transmitter-receiver in another.

"The video quality of your robotic fly is amazing," Emily said, leaning slightly forward so that her feet could touch the floor. "Nice to get a bird's eye view of the park. Why isn't there any sound?" she asked, turning towards Nathan on her right.

"The bot ignores all ambient noise except human speech. Look, here comes Bowers now."

Under Nathan's remote control, the micro-bot descended towards Adrian Bowers and hovered unnoticed scarcely two feet behind him as he passed the few shallow steps leading up to Andersen's statue. They watched Adrian casually slide his left hand into his trouser pocket. His phone's listening mode ceased instantaneously.

Unobserved on the thirty-first floor of SkyTech Tower, Nathan, Emily and Sven knew that Adrian's voice-notes app had been activated.

At the western edge of Conservatory Water, the cast bronze sculpture of master storyteller Hans Christian

Andersen, roughly twice the size of an adult, is one of the most popular climbing structures in Central Park. Seated on a marble bench, leaning on his right arm, Andersen holds an open book, displaying a few lines of "The Ugly Duckling" while he looks at the free-standing stray duck at his feet. Andersen's ever-present top hat rests on the bench behind him on the right. The statue commemorates the one hundred and fiftieth anniversary of Andersen's birth, maintenance being funded largely by the Danish-American Women's Association.

Created by Georg J. Lober, and cast at the Modern Art Foundry in Queens, it was donated to the park in 1956. The two most popular spots for children to climb on are the book and the hat, much to the enjoyment of their camera wielding parents. The association's story telling program delights youngsters throughout the summer months.

James Clark, sitting comfortably on one of the shady benches surrounding the statue, regretted not picking a hot sunny spot, if for no reason other than to annoy Bowers.

Sweating, and fatigued from his short walk, Adrian sat down opposite to James.

Nathan rested the micro-bot out of sight from Adrian on the topmost brace of the bench's wooden backrest. The wide-angle video showed only his broad back, shoulders and neck, wet with perspiration. Crystal clear audio immediately started transmitting to Nathan's laptop, where it was recorded and simultaneously broadcast on the computer's speakers. Nathan initiated the micro-bot's signal, to disrupt

Adrian's phone. The discussion Adrian thought he was recording would yield nothing more than static.

"Are you ready to receive some test data into your internet drop-box?" James asked, purposely not giving Adrian a chance to catch his breath.

"Yes," Adrian wheezed after a few moments. "Looks like you're progressing faster than expected."

"It will be another few months," James lied. "Nate is busy with the application that collects the phone conversations, but that's still a few weeks to completion. The development work to securely route those calls across multiple anonymous global providers is still ahead of us."

There was actually no work required for the global data routing, all development having already been done by Sven on the intrusion hack into James's email.

Adrian was still a little breathless as James continued.

"What we can do now, and you've just confirmed that you're ready, is to test your drop-box's ability to receive data using the address and login credentials you provided. At first, it will be a simple ten-second random audio clip transmitted directly from our local server. When we have your confirmation that it arrived successfully, we will send another longer one, then multiple audio clips in succession. The final test will be two thousand five minute clips, all being transmitted simultaneously."

"Seems a little excessive," Adrian said argumentatively.

"We want to ensure that even the most extreme scenarios can be successfully accommodated by your service provider, who, incidentally, we've confirmed as being TeraCom Inc. operating out of eastern Asia."

Adrian's facial expression didn't change, but the *fly* recorded an instantaneous, but very subtle nervous twitch in his shoulders.

Both Nathan and Sven noticed it, but not Emily. She was far more excited about the micro-bot's impressive technology, than about what she could see or hear, and, even more so, about Nathan's ability to have created such a miniature marvel.

Sven turned to Nathan. "He's getting nervous."

Nathan smiled. "Shame we won't be able to gauge his reaction when he plays back his recording and hears nothing but noise."

"What exactly do you plan on doing with these phone conversations?" James prodded. "It's obviously not research, but I am curious."

"That's of no concern to you," Adrian answered with scorn. "You're getting paid very well for what we at the Food and Drug Administration require, and that's all you need to know."

"Very well," James said. "We'll carry on playing by your rules."

"You don't have a choice," Adrian stated.

You have no idea just how many choices we do have, James thought. Hopefully the smugness he was feeling didn't show on his face.

"Mid-afternoon today, we will run the first audio clip test. We will add instruction to the clip, such that your service provider notifies you by email that something has been deposited in your drop-box. There's no reason why this shouldn't work, but please confirm with me before we proceed with more complex trials."

"Look, his shoulders twitched again," Sven said, pointing at the laptop. "I didn't know you were putting notification instructions into the sound clips."

"I'm not," Nathan said. "TeraCom's firewall would almost certainly reject the entire data package because any imbedded code would be seen as a potential virus."

"That's what I figured," Sven said. "So why... Oh, I get it," he smiled. "JW is feeding Bowers's mind with a few uncertainties."

Nathan laughed. "The provider is going to send notification to Bowers regardless, but his nervous twitch suggests he didn't see that as obvious. I'm surprised at how otherwise composed he's remained."

"Years of practice, I imagine," Sven commented.

"James is handling this really well," Emily observed.

"Listen, Adrian," James said. "We really don't have to be so cold towards each other. I apologize for the way I've been acting. I will treat this undertaking of yours as a simple business proposition, and ask no further questions."

Adrian waited for James to continue.

"As much as I don't particularly like what we're doing," James said with a repentant smile, "I'm sure this isn't as underhanded as some of SkyTech's past endeavours, a few being somewhat questionable from a legal point of view. I agree, Adrian, you are paying us handsomely for our service, and we will take this project seriously and keep it at a professional level."

Adrian still seemed to be catching his breath and just nodded. James continued. "I would prefer that we keep our meetings out in the open. This location is well situated for both of us, but if you have another preference, let me know."

Adrian looked seriously at James for a few moments. "You're right, Clark. Let's put our personal differences aside and focus on the FDA's requirements. I too should apologize to you. We do after all have the same motivation."

"Motivation?" James questioned.

"Profit," Adrian responded with laughter.

"Ah, yes."

"So what kind of questionable activity could a successful enterprise like SkyTech possibly have been involved in?" Adrian prompted.

"A company our size doesn't get to where it's at without crossing a few boundaries," James admitted. "A few years ago, we sold some encryption software to the federal telecommunications division and charged them fifteen million."

"What's wrong with that?" Adrian asked. "Everyone overcharges the government."

"The thing is, we sold it as proprietary software." James looked around him cautiously, leaned more towards Adrian, and lowered his voice. "We had developed an identical solution for German Tel-Com two years before. There was no additional work involved. All we did was change the logo."

Adrian smirked.

James's voice was almost a whisper. "A bit of creative accounting by our financial department, and the government gladly paid up. I'm sure that you can keep that bit of information just between the two of us."

"Don't worry," Adrian said softly, and with practiced sincerity. "It will go no further."

Sven looked at Nathan. "Did you know anything about this?"

Nathan grinned. "It's complete fabrication. JW is playing the underdog. He's taken Bowers into his confidence, and now Bowers believes that he has something else to hold over JW."

"He's going to be pissed when he finds that his voice app didn't record any of that," Emily said. "James plays this game well."

"In his position, boardroom games can make or break a business," Nathan said. "You have to be good at it. Let's just hope JW was able to keep a straight face when he looked at Bowers."

"Why shouldn't he?" she asked.

"Let's just say that JW and I share a very sensitive private joke about Bowers."

Oh," said Emily. "And what's that?"

Nathan recalled the selfie on Bowers' phone. "Let's just say that the size of his 'equipment' wouldn't impress too many women."

Emily wondered how they could possibly know that, but said nothing.

Following a few minutes of stilted small talk about the warm weather, James and Adrian agreed to meet here at Andersen's Statue the same time next month. They stood up and shook hands, James's grip enclosing firmly around Bowers' podgy, damp hand.

Unnoticed by either of them, an insect took flight from the park bench and made its way towards SkyTech Tower.

Chapter Eighteen

Over the years, James Clark and Warren Ellison, each firmly established in their own commercial endeavours, had kept in touch regularly during their respective business trips between the East and West coasts. Warren was due in New York later that day, and James was looking forward to seeing his life-long friend again. He was also keen to know how Warren's latest brainchild was coming along.

Smiling, James turned his chair towards the corner windows of his office and looked out to Central Park in the distance. With the recent seasonal change and cooler temperatures, trees had started displaying their radiant fall colours.

The discussion with Adrian Bowers, two weeks previously, had been the last, with further updates from James no longer necessary. All their meetings had been faithfully recorded by Nate's micro-bot, but Bowers's voice recording was no longer disrupted. James was careful not to say anything that could be detrimental or misinterpreted in any way. It was agreed that, if they did need to discuss anything sensitive, they would exchange a phone call or email and settle on a time and place.

Recordings of calls to and from the phone numbers provided by Bowers had over the past several weeks been successfully deposited real-time into his internet drop-box. Nathan and Emily had done extensive research into the conversations, and agreed that there was nothing that could be used in a harmful way.

Social calls were discarded as irrelevant, and many were, to a certain degree, embarrassing to listen to. It was apparent that non-life-threatening social diseases were as rampant as ever, and Viagra was a hot topic among middle-aged men.

Nathan and Emily's attention was primarily on medical and nutritional advice provided by the applicable doctors or pharmacists. Emily had commented, during their weekly meetings, that the information was really very good. Preferred fruits and vegetables, depending on the condition of your health; which food groups shouldn't be mixed; recommendations on substitutes for meat products; all sound advice.

Counsel was given on the detrimental effects of consuming highly refined foods such as wheat and sugar. Avoiding restaurants was stressed, not because of the actual food, but rather because of the sauces and artificial spices that were added to enhance their flavour. Fried foods totally lacked nourishment, and diet products containing aspartame were regarded as toxic.

To all intents and purposes, it was excellent advice, steering people towards natural products and a healthy lifestyle. To Emily's mind, it didn't make any sense. Why would Bowers want this? The only conclusion James could come to was that the health-care system was running out of money and was putting pressure on the Food and Drug Administration to do something about it. Yet the FDA didn't seem to know anything about what Bowers was doing.

It was mid-afternoon when Emily looked above her monitor, face breaking into a broad smile. "Date night?" she asked Warren Ellison as he walked with a bounce in his step through reception towards her desk.

"Em. It's good to see you again," he replied with a wink.

Emily stood up. "Looks like you've come straight from JFK. Here, let me take your carry-all. I'll put it out of the way."

"Thanks," he said, passing it over.

"Go straight through," she said. "I will bring refreshments shortly."

James' relationship with Warren was no secret at SkyTech. James had no problems with that, being more concerned with running a successful company and treating his employees fairly than what opinions they might have about his private life.

A few minutes later, Emily returned with Perrier water, tumblers with ice, a small plate of mixed sugar-free cookies and some paper napkins. Moving James's briefcase slightly to one side, she placed the refreshments on his credenza.

Emily briefly glanced at Warren, who, sitting comfortably in a visitor's chair at James's desk, looked very slick, dressed in navy-blue jeans, black loafers, casual white shirt and black sports jacket.

"Should I arrange dinner reservations?" she asked.

"That would be great." James looked at Warren. "Donatello's okay with you?"

"Sounds good," Warren replied.

"I'll make reservations for seven p.m. then," Emily said, walking out the office and closing the door behind her.

"How was your flight?" James asked, reaching over and passing a tumbler and bottle of Perrier to his friend.

"Uneventful," Warren said. "I dozed on and off most of the way. There was a bit of a hold-up landing. We circled for about half an hour before finally getting clearance from the tower. At least the cab ride along Grand Central was quick."

"Well, I'm glad you got here without too much delay." James looked at Warren affectionately. "It's good to see you again."

"And you," Warren said, smiling.

"How's Med-Bot progressing?"

"A few revelations," Warren said. "My response base has doubled to almost thirty million in the last couple of months."

"That's excellent," James said, reaching for a bottle of water himself. "This would almost make it the largest medical artificial intelligence service on the internet."

"Almost," Warren agreed. "There are still two ahead of me, but I'm getting there faster than expected. Strange thing, though; most of the advice comes from a select group of medical professionals, and it's mostly on nutrition and health."

James, stopping halfway through unscrewing the cap of his Perrier, became perfectly still and glared at Warren.

Warren looked at him in surprise. "What? It looks like you've just seen a ghost."

"Does your database store the names of people providing medical advice?" James asked.

"Yes, they must be registered with Med-Bot, but responses to questions do not include those names, just the most likely remedy or treatment based on probability. Also, the A.I. engine is programmed never to guarantee a cure."

"Warren. This is important," James stressed. "Can you get me a list of those names?"

"Sure, but not from here," he replied. "It's securely buried in the metadata."

"Do you recall the discussion I had with you a few weeks ago about the work I'm doing for the FDA?"

"Yes," Warren said. "You suggested that it's causing you some grief."

"I didn't give you all the details," James said. "I have a very bad feeling that my concerns are somehow tied in to the sudden growth you've seen in Med-Bot's responses, but I need some proof."

"Okay," Warren said, a little confused.

"Let me get my team in here and we'll put you in the picture." James dialled Emily's extension. "Em, can you, Nate and Sven come into my office, please?"

"Let me go and get them. We'll be right in," she replied.

All were now assembled in James's office. He suggested they get comfortable around the coffee table.

"What's up?" Nathan asked when they were all seated.

"I don't know for sure yet," James said, "but I have a suspicion that Med-Bot is somehow connected to Adrian Bowers's little game."

"What's Med-Bot?" Emily asked.

"An artificial intelligence, or A.I. engine," Warren answered. "It's used primarily to collect medical information, and provide intelligent and well-researched responses to ailments."

"Like a wiki for doctors?" That explains why they all walk around with tablets these days, Emily thought, sceptically.

"Sort of," Warren said. "But unlike wikis, to which almost anyone can contribute, Med-Bot collects questions, but will only allow answers provided by medical professionals. They have to be certified and registered."

"A.I. is something I know nothing about," Emily said. She looked at Nathan and Sven. "I suppose you know all about this stuff?"

"Some," Nathan said.

Sven nodded non-committally.

"You've probably received more online answers from A.I. engines than you're aware of," Warren said. "I'm sure you've even heard of some of the more popular ones, like Apple's Siri, Microsoft's Cortana, or the various Echo devices out there, such as Alexa and Google Home."

"Yes," Emily answered in surprise. "I do know those."

"IBM's Watson is one of the largest," Warren explained.

"There are countless others, much smaller. I'm sure you've been to many online retail sites that have a link asking, "How can I help?" Click on that, and you're instantly communicating with an A.I. engine, not a person."

"You're kidding," she said.

"Not at all," Warren said. "I'm hoping to make Med-Bot the largest medical A.I. engine on the planet."

"How do they work?" she asked.

Warren considered briefly before answering Emily's question. "They learn by what people are asking and what responses they get. And it's not just based on keywords. It's the complete context of the question or answer. In some ways, it's no more than a numbers game, where the most common response to a question is considered the correct answer. Most A.I.'s will get you into a question and answer session before providing the resolution you're looking for. That's how they learn."

"Oh," she said, not quite sure she fully understood.

"Let's say, for example, that people are looking for quick pain relief," Warren went on. "In some cases, it's a headache; in others, it's anything from shingles to backache to haemorrhoids. Doesn't matter, but the chances of an A.I. bot finding a common answer based just on specific words would be very difficult. It has to consider the context of what's being asked. Most bots go through multiple layers of previously collected dialog to find some commonality. Ten similar questions asked in totally different ways can often result in the bot's searching through hundreds of thousands of possible responses to determine what to answer, or what to ask next. They respond in a matter of milliseconds. Often they formulate new answers that may be relevant to a specific question. Those too are stored for possible future retrieval."

"They can answer that fast?" Emily asked.

"Today's processor and network speeds allow it," Warren said.

"Also, they are not just conversing with only one individual, but thousands simultaneously, each trying to find a remedy for their particular disorder. In the case of headaches and hemorrhoids, the A.I. would likely associate "pain" as the collective condition, then search for the most common remedy suggested by a doctor."

"Something like 'take two Tylenol every six hours and call your doctor in the morning'," she said, with a wry smile.

"Something like that," Warren said, grinning. "In the case of Med-Bot, I do try and make it a little more scientific."

"I hope so," she said.

"Tylenol would certainly work for a mild headache, but is definitely not a solution for haemorrhoids, even if pain is the common denominator."

"Hence the science that would be required," Emily commented.

"Artificial intelligence exists on almost all social media sites," Warren went on enthusiastically. "If you're writing an email to someone, and you haven't blocked popup ads, you will see adverts from companies claiming to specialise in products for which you've provided certain keywords. Marketing is a multi-billion-dollar industry. They are going to get their message to you one way or another. A.I. ensures that these messages make sense. If I'm writing an email, and I use a word such as "nails" without any context whatsoever, I will likely get advertising from Home Hardware. You, on the other hand, will get ads from Maybelline Cosmetics."

Emily looked at Warren with a dubious expression.

"It's simple, Em," Warren said, perceiving her doubt. "A.I. queries relevant personal details provided when we signed up into our respective online accounts, and has determined that I'm male, and probably talking about something like roof nails. Yours, on the other hand, knows that you're female and are probably referring to fingernails."

Chapter Nineteen

Listening to Warren Ellison's passionate discussion of artificial intelligence, Emily found it a little disturbing just how much personal information about her existed on the internet; much of it having got there without her knowledge or consent. What Warren said made a lot of sense.

"Only fools believe claims that their privacy is protected," Nathan commented.

"If your phone's *location* feature is active, you will get pop-up ads from businesses in your immediate location, or most certainly in close proximity," Warren said. "As I mentioned, marketing *will* get their messages to you. Let me ask you this. How many really cool apps do you have on your phone?"

"Quite a few," she said.

"How many did you pay for?"

"None," she admitted.

"So how do the developers of those apps make any money if they're not charging you?"

"Never really thought about it," Emily said.

"Advertising," Warren said. "Almost all apps require internet connectivity in order for you to use them. I presume that you've played some games?"

"A few," she said.

"So now you want to go to the next level, but just before you tap the appropriate button, your new high-score slides in on the left of the screen. Space is made by shifting everything slightly to the right. A.I. has already calculated the average time it takes you to tap to the next level, but instead, you hit a new button occupying that space and end up at a commercial site."

"That's happened to me so often!" Emily exclaimed. "I always thought I was having finger trouble."

"And that's the idea," Warren said. "It's a science, and A.I. ensures that there's a very good chance you tap something that you didn't mean to. Through online gaming, marketing has the ability to reach millions of people every second of every day. It never sleeps."

"My weather app has a tiny advertising banner located just above the *Close* button. It's unbelievable how often I've accidentally tapped that," Emily said. "You've also explained why so many of my apps were free. Developers must make a fortune."

"The developers of Warcraft made more money in the first month than that made by all the Super Mario and PacMan game consoles sold in the eighties," Warren said. "Today's online game developers have to be very creative, and almost all rely on simple A.I. Most games work on trial and error. Fail at a certain level and you get the chance to respawn. You are learning by your mistakes, and the A.I. is learning how you play. Most will adjust the dynamics of the game according to your level of anxiety or boredom."

"Why would a game do that?" she asked.

"To keep you engaged," he said. "The longer you play, the longer you're exposed to marketing."

"It sort of leads into whether you are playing the game or the game is playing you," Nathan observed.

James cleared his throat. "We've digressed a little," he said, addressing Emily, Sven and Nathan. "I'd like to get back on track. A few weeks back I spoke to Warren about our arrangement with Adrian Bowers, but without any detail as to what's really going on." He turned to Warren. "I'll fill you in on those details as we go."

"And you think Warren's A.I. engine is somehow connected?" Nathan asked.

"I don't know for sure yet," James said, "but over a very short space of time, the last few months, if I'm correct, Med-Bot's dialog base has doubled in size."

"In fact, exponentially just in the last several weeks," Warren added.

James continued. "Responses have been coming from a very small group of individuals, and the majority of advice centers around health and nutrition."

"Coincidental?" Nathan asked.

"I don't know. It's just a very strong feeling I have. Nate, do you have any idea how many calls we've sent to Bowers so far? A rough guess will do."

"I would say about twelve thousand," Nathan said.

"No," James said, shaking his head thoughtfully. "That's far too small a number to explain Med-Bot's growth in such a brief time span."

"What do you mean by calls?" Warren asked.

James briefly explained Bowers' initial business proposal to snoop and record conversations to and from selected phone numbers, and how SkyTech was subsequently steered towards being blackmailed. He voiced his opinion that the Food and Drug Administration probably weren't involved, but left out any reference to the dirt they had on Bowers.

Warren listened intently with a concerned expression on his face. "You said that the number of conversations sent to Bowers weren't enough to have such an impact on Med-Bot's rapid database growth, especially in such a short time-span. I would disagree."

Warren had their full attention.

"Med-Bot records, indexes and catalogs an entire dialog," Warren explained. "Not just a single answer associated with a single question. Let's say, for example, that one of the phone conversations you sent to Bowers is very general. It's accurate in context, but not specific to only one query. If a thousand questions about stomach complaints or constipation are asked and the answer 'eat more fruit and vegetables' is given, that single answer can be applied to all those questions. It's simple enough for the doctor or pharmacist to provide such a remedy to Med-Bot. Typical A.I.s automatically interrogate all responses to questions, and make determination where else that solution could be applied."

"That makes sense," James said.

"Sort of like those small tubes of super-glue," Emily stated, off-hand. "It can conceivably be applied to more and more products."

"Exactly," Warren acknowledged, facing Emily and then turning back to the rest of the group.

"Cataloging, re-indexing and topic association goes on continuously in the background," Warren made clear. "A.I. databases are in a perpetual state of reconstruction. A single response can end up being the probable solution to thousands, even millions of scenarios. Many previous answers to questions are replaced, based on the probability that a more recent one is correct, or more accurate."

"So the more general the answer is, the more it can be associated. That would explain rapid growth in the size of the database," Nathan said.

"One problem all A.I. developers have is determining fact from fiction," Warren expressed, gesturing with his hand for emphasis. "We want to provide working solutions to situations, and the more data we have to work with, the better the application becomes. Here's the issue. Let's say that someone makes a statement on social media that's incorrect. Another person, likely looking for attention, agrees with that statement. Next thing, everyone climbs on the bandwagon in agreement."

"So in A.I. terms," Nathan said, "the probability of that statement's being correct is because it outweighs contradiction."

"Exactly, Nate," Warren said nodding. "Extrapolating from unbelievably large volumes of data should provide accuracy based on the probability principle. But don't forget, it's artificial, not intelligent, and it cannot reason. Nor is it aware of its own existence. The larger the data it has from which to reach a conclusion, the closer it should get to a correct response. In today's world of self-promotion, however, A.I. often has to search its data banks specifically for contradiction before making a rational choice between right and wrong."

Emily wasn't quite sure she understood that last bit. She would have to ask Nate at some point to explain it better.

"Med-Bot," Warren said, "is for use by the medical profession. By definition, it cannot provide incorrect or ambiguous answers. Human lives are on the line. Its database is continuously being refined."

"That must take up a lot of computing power," Emily said.

"Today's technology can handle it," Warren said. "Imagine a spelling mistake was discovered in something as large as the printed version of the Encyclopaedia Britannica: the same word misspelt, over and over. We take it for granted that an encyclopaedia is one hundred percent accurate. It has to be. It would take a human decades of reading through every page of every volume to find and correct the word in question. With an electronic version of Britannica, Med-Bot would be able to do the same job in just a few seconds. Med-Bot's answers, like any encyclopaedia, are expected to be correct, so it's constantly updating and re-referencing every time new information is introduced."

James, raising his eyebrows, looked at Warren.

"Sorry, James," Warren apologized. "I'm getting a little side-tracked again."

"Warren can provide the names of those doctors and pharmacists who he thinks have contributed the most to

Med-Bot's growth in recent weeks," James said to the rest of the group. "The problem is that he won't be able to do it from here."

Warren looked at Nathan. "I was saying to James earlier that we keep the names of all medical contributors to Med-Bot, but those names are not provided with any answers or possible remedies. Can you imagine the lawsuits we would face?"

"I have a suggestion," James said. "Warren, with your permission, would you mind if Sven got into Med-Bot's database?"

"I have no problem with that at all," Warren said, surprised. "It's on public domain."

"Not the application," James clarified, "but the actual database itself. Sven should be able to extract those names. It goes without question that the information remains confidential."

"That not possible," Warren said. "To guard against any intrusions and leaks, those names are protected by multi-layer encryption procedures, code which I didn't write myself. I can get to the raw data, but only through my personal administrator account. Unfortunately, it's been set up such that I can only use it from my office computer. If anyone stole my laptop, they could possibly hack into the database that way."

"That would certainly be catastrophic," James said. "Many of our own admin accounts at SkyTech are set up the same way. They can only be used within this building."

"Either way," Warren said, "it would require the skills of an expert hacker to crack through the encryption and get at the data. Someone like Trinity for example."

Sven juddered slightly and sunk a little into his seat.

"Who's *Trinity*?" Emily asked, looking from face to face.

"Surely you've seen that name on social media," Warren replied. "Trinity certainly gets mentioned enough on conspiracy blogs."

Emily shook her head.

"Blogs aren't exactly my thing either," James said, with a smile. "Warren, you of all people should know that."

"Okay, maybe not blogs," Warren said defensively, "but you must have remembered when Trinity exposed that *Feed the World* charity."

"I do remember," Nathan said, recalling a news article he read last year. "Millions of dollars were involved, and none of the money actually went to the hungry. Trinity transferred it out of the charity's numerous off-shore bank accounts into the private accounts of destitute families."

"Yes," Emily said, recollecting. "I read about that. Then, six months later, when the charity was operating under a different name, Trinity did the same thing. After their third attempt, some wealthy investors, who were associated with the scam, ended up behind bars. I doubt they tried again."

"They didn't," Sven muttered almost to himself, attempting to slide even further into his seat - a little difficult for someone so tall.

"Pity. It would have been nice to get hold of those names before you go back to California next week," James said to Warren.

Nathan looked at Sven. "Aren't you connected to some of those hacker groups?" he asked. "Maybe you can get to Trinity and ask for some ideas."

"Thing is," Warren interrupted dejectedly. "From what I've heard, nobody knows who Trinity is, nor has even met the person. Trinity is reputedly the best there is. Certainly, the most elusive."

"So, we scrap the idea," Nathan said, already considering alternatives.

Warren ignored Nathan's comment. "Any thoughts on how we could reach out to Trinity?" he asked, turning to face Sven.

"Not necessary," Sven said almost cagily.

"How so?" Warren asked.

"You're sitting next to him," Sven replied. "And I'd appreciate it if that knowledge didn't leave this room."

Chapter Twenty

By early evening, Sven Labrowski, using all the hacking skills available to him, had access to the names of all those who had contributed to Med-Bot in the last few weeks. He was impressed by the level of sophistication used in the encryption code and assured Warren Ellison that Med-Bot's database was about as secure as it could get.

Within two days, the media center became the hub of operations for the team to group together in their attempt to figure out what Adrian Bowers and the FDA's plan was. Located within Info Tech's security zone, the room offered privacy, was sound-proof, and out of the way of regular day-to-day interruptions.

Nathan set up a central server and four workstations interconnected through a private intranet, allowing for data sharing and analysis. There were no wireless, ethernet or fibre-optic connections into this network. It was completely isolated from the outside world.

James Clark temporarily restricted access to everyone except Nathan, Emily, Sven and himself. Any of the team coming into this room were under strict instruction to leave their smartphones outside. For that purpose, Emily placed a small basket on top of the filing cabinet by the door leading into the media room.

James had taken the rest of the week off to spend time with Warren, but reminded the team to let him know immediately if anything important came to light.

"Hacked into any interesting places recently?" Emily asked Sven, still with a sense of admiration at what he had revealed about himself.

Sven, sitting opposite her in the media center, looked up with his usual twisted smirk. "Nothing beyond what we're doing here."

"Isn't what you're doing considered criminal activity? I don't mean with what's going on here at SkyTech, as I'm sure this is all highly illegal, but some of the other hacks you do in your spare time."

"Oh, for sure," he said. "The trick is not to get caught. Like so many things, though, there's always a grey area. With a few simple search refinements, you will find Trinity listed on various internet blogs as an *ethical* hacker."

"What can possibly be ethical about hacking?" she asked with amusement.

"There are thousands out there who have made it their full-time career," he explained, leaning back and running fingers through his unruly hair. "It's a totally legal profession, and our services are highly sought after."

"For what?"

"Almost all large enterprises are paranoid about their data. They hire ethical hackers to break into their databases and expose vulnerabilities," he said, leaning back in his chair. "Contracts drawn up by corporations hiring our expertise are usually interspersed with all sorts of non-disclosure clauses. Violating those would most certainly land the hacker in prison."

"So why hasn't SkyTech hired one?" Emily asked. "The data we process for the government is about as sensitive as it gets."

Sven tilted his head. "Really?"

"Oops, sorry," she laughed. "Senior moment... I forgot that we already have *you* on the payroll."

He smiled and continued his research into Adrian's personal life.

"Ha!" Sven slammed his hand on the table after a few minutes, startling Emily.

She looked up in surprise. "What?"

"Other than Bowers' regular checking and savings accounts, I haven't been able to find any unusual activity. No large deposits, nothing." Sven shook his head. "That bastard."

"Well, don't leave me hanging," she said.

"His wife, Sofia Bowers," Sven said after a pause.

"What about her?"

"She has an account with Deutsche Bundesbank in Hamburg, Germany."

"So deposits are being made there?" Emily asked.

"Yes. But here's the thing. It's an inheritance account, and she cannot access it until she's thirty-five."

"How old is she now?" Emily asked.

"Twenty-four. Sofia is almost twenty years younger than Adrian. Knowing him, he will have divorced her before she can touch that money. No doubt the account has been set up such that Adrian has complete control. If my suspicions are correct, Sofia doesn't even know about it."

"Wouldn't surprise me," she concurred.

"Sofia's his third wife," Sven said.

"Yes, you mentioned that the other day. How much is in the account?"

"Just over thirty million Euros," he answered. Emily let out a slow whistle.

***

Monday morning.

James Clark walked into the media center, now referred to as the *War Room*. The others were already seated at their workstations. It had been agreed that this would be the best place to convene for their regular weekly updates. It was also understood by the team that James would manage all aspects of this investigation. Not because he was the boss, but because he asked the right questions and came to the right conclusions.

"Morning, JW," Sven and Nathan said in chorus.

Emily looked up. "Good morning, James. You don't look very happy. Bad weekend?"

"Morning, all," James said, lifting his frown. "Weekend was great, but I have some concerns about how we're collecting all this data."

"You've got nothing to worry about, JW," Sven assured. "It's all done from my home computer. I bring the latest info on that flash-drive you see plugged in over there."

"And with the war room isolated from the internet," Nathan said, "we're safe from external access. And that also includes everyone within this building."

"You can deny all awareness of what I do in my spare time at home," Sven said earnestly. "Provided that your knowledge of Trinity is never revealed, SkyTech remains out of harm's way."

"Well, let's hope it doesn't come to that," James said, placing a bottle of Perrier on the desk and pulling up a chair. "Sven, let's start with you. What's new on Bowers?"

Sven disclosed to JW what he had discovered about the inheritance account in Hamburg under the name of Bowers's third wife Sofia, and that she likely knew nothing about it.

"Thirty million Euros," James said in astonishment. "That's a lot of money."

"Regular deposits started shortly after the account was opened three years ago," Sven said, "the largest amounts being within the last few months. That's about all I've found on him, but I'm still searching."

James took a sip of water and cleared his throat. "Thanks, Sven. What have you got, Nate?"

"Aside from three pharmacists and one doctor, all the names from Bowers's list of phone numbers coincided with those providing answers to Med-Bot in recent weeks," Nathan replied. "Those four, who contributed regularly in the past, haven't provided anything to the A.I. database during the time period I looked into."

James listened intently.

"Sven looked into their personal bank accounts," Nathan continued. "Each contribution to Med-Bot is followed a day later by a generous compensation paid out from the FDA's slush fund. Based on the transaction dates and times, those deposits coincided precisely with expenditures incurred by Magentis GMP."

"Magentis?" James looked at Nathan with a startled expression. Interesting, he thought, and put it aside for later consideration.

"That's who we traced the transactions back to," Nathan said.

"And my assumption," James said, "is that no deposits were made into the accounts of those four not contributing to Med-Bot."

"Correct," Nathan said. "Bowers is monitoring the phone conversations to ensure that those on his private payroll are promoting Magentis foodstuffs. Emily did some analysis, and there's no doubt that there's some dissention amongst the ranks."

James, deep in thought, raised his head after a few moments of silence.

"Adrian put such pressure on me about snooping into those conversations that I started wondering why," James said. "Think about it. There's absolutely nothing of real value there, besides being a typical, if somewhat unethical, marketing ploy. Blackmailing SkyTech was a desperate move to get me to comply."

"I don't get where you're going with this?" Nathan questioned.

"Look at it this way," James said. "Adrian's initial request to filter out medical discussions from the NSA's data and feed it to the FDA for the purpose of nutritional research could have sparked some questions here at SkyTech. The FDA is in tight collusion with big pharma, not private enterprise. That in itself could have raised some questions. Next, he forces our attention on phone calls to and from a select group of doctors and pharmacists."

"And that's exactly what we've been wasting our time on," Nathan said.

James looked directly at Nathan. "You and your team have spent a great deal of effort ensuring that these phone conversations cannot be traced back to us," he said. "You demonstrated to Bowers that the data packets hop around the globe from one anonymous server to the next, leaving no trace of their source."

"Right," Nathan agreed.

"And you also assured him that we would delete them from our own systems to protect ourselves from any liability," James said. "I really don't think Bowers is that ignorant. He knows that we're keeping the data and digging into it."

"Oh my God," Emily said in sudden comprehension. "It's complete misdirection."

James smiled and slapped his hand lightly on the table, almost spilling his Perrier. "Exactly, Em. We've been so focused on the phone conversations and avoiding blackmail that we haven't had any time to consider what's really going on."

"I think you're right," Nathan said. "He's kept us very busy chasing shadows. Bowers is playing a very deceitful game. But why?"

"Well, two can play at that game," James said. "Em, I want you to dig up everything you can on Magentis. I hate to ask this, but use your ex-husband Ryan Hurst if you must. Considering the millions of dollars going from Magentis into private bank accounts, this 'rabbit hole' is a lot deeper than we think."

"I do have something I can feed back to the group now," she said. "Magentis holds the monopoly on seeds for fruit and vegetable produce. It's exactly those foodstuffs being recommended by the medical professionals on Adrian's payroll."

"Okay," James said. "And we've already determined that four from his list are not promoting crops harvested from seeds distributed by Magentis, and those four aren't getting paid either."

Emily continued. "Progressively more competitive seed farms are going out of business. Farmers are buying from Magentis because it's cheaper and they offer faster delivery. Smaller operations that aren't going bankrupt are bought out by Magentis and closed down within days."

"And what they're doing is quite legal," Sven said, smiling. "It's called capitalism."

"Thing is," Nathan said. "Here in the good ol' US of A, we lean more towards *neo-capitalism*."

Emily looked at him with curiosity. "Meaning?"

Sven butted in. "Meaning our capitalist system ensures that only the wealthy are entitled to make money." Emily grimaced at that.

Sven went on. "Although the FDA isn't exactly endorsing the remedies suggested by Med-Bot, they cannot raise any objection that natural products pose a health risk."

"Pharmaceutical companies certainly aren't going to sit back while Magentis puts them out of business," Nathan said, stating the obvious.

"Alright, let's continue feeding Bowers his phone conversations like nothing has changed," James said. "But we'll see what we can find out about Magentis."

They all expressed agreement.

"Is there anything else?" James asked.

"Other than Bowers still physically abusing his wife Sofia, and regular contact with his Catholic priest friend Dominique Garcia, there is just one anomaly," Sven said. "I haven't been paying too much attention to where he goes. We're still tracking his GPS locations, by the way. Thing is, he takes bi-weekly trips to the Magentis seed farms near Iowa. In fact, he has an appointment there this Wednesday. A few minutes after he arrives at the admin block, his phone goes completely off the radar. No GPS location, no transmissions, nothing."

"Maybe he switches his phone off," Emily suggested.

"Doesn't matter," Sven said. "Unless he physically removes the battery, his phone will still be listening, but it's not transmitting. I don't think that's it."

"Your thoughts?" James asked.

"The *silent* period is about half an hour," Sven said. "He goes to a meeting room that disrupts a smartphone's signal, or..."

The others looked at Sven expectantly.

Chapter Twenty-One

The atmosphere in the War Room was tense. Sven Labrowski leaned back in his chair and looked sombrely at James, Emily, then Nathan. "Bowers doesn't go to a meeting room that disrupts phone signals," he concluded after a short pause, "but rather, to some place that's located deep underground."

"That can only mean one thing," Nathan added. "Whoever he sees, or whatever they talk about, obviously has to be in complete secrecy."

"Of that, there's no doubt," Sven agreed. "He flies from New York to St. Louis in Missouri, drives for about four hours to the Magentis seed farms, talks to someone for half an hour, and then returns to New York. Nobody spends an entire day travelling for a thirty-minute meeting."

"Unless what they say cannot be discussed over the phone or exchanged on the internet," Nathan pointed out.

"Where the NSA could pick it up," Emily finished off. The room fell silent.

"Do we know much about the seed farms?" James asked, after a short pause.

"Not beyond what's available on public domain," Nathan answered. "The place is huge, covering quite a few square miles. Its operation is well documented."

"See if you can help Em get some more info," James said to Nathan. "But don't spend too much time on it. We have more pressing issues now, with the NSA's yearly audit coming up. Time permitting, I will do some digging myself. We need to find out what's going on."

"No problem," Nathan said, nodding.

"I can probably get into the operation's security cameras," Sven suggested.

"Might be worth a shot," James said.

"Alright," Sven acknowledged. "I'll see what I can do."

"Any more information on how that loathsome priest Dominique Garcia lures the children of his congregation in front of his camera?" James asked as an afterthought.

"Nothing," Sven said. "But there don't seem to be any new additions to his website - much to Bowers's disappointment."

"A small consolation, I suppose," Emily said almost to herself.

"Let me not waste any more of your time," James said, reaching for his Perrier and getting up. "Keep up the great work, everyone. I unfortunately still have a business to run. Oh, and Em, I have a temp starting today just to help out with a few mundane tasks."

"Let me know if she needs any help," Emily offered, assuming that the temp was indeed a *she*.

"Thanks, I will," James said, leaving the war room. "I'll see you all later."

***

"Something I meant to ask you, Nate," Emily said, looking up from her lunchtime salad. "I kind of get what Warren was saying about artificial intelligence coming up with the right solution based on probability, but got a little lost when he explained that the correct answer sometimes rests with a conflicting point of view. If I got it right, A.I. finds contradiction, then considers all references to that, which, in turn, puts the contradiction in a higher probability of being correct."

"Think of it this way," Nathan said, chewing on his burger. "It's accepted that oil is a fossil fuel. And why? Because everyone says so." He took a swig of his coffee. "Not sure exactly when, but I think it was first suggested by a Russian scientist around the end of the nineteenth century. His reasoning was sound - he postulated that crude oil formed from decayed plants and animals exposed to heat and pressure in the earth's crust over hundreds of millions of years."

"And that's wrong?" Emily questioned.

"No, it's probably accurate," he said. "Problem is that it was misinterpreted. People started saying that the oil comes from decomposed dinosaurs."

"That's what I've always believed," she said.

"And because of that belief, you know that oil will eventually run out," he said.

"Sure," she said. "There could only have been so many dinosaurs."

"Speak to anyone about life millions of years ago, and the first thing that comes to mind are brontosauruses, pterodactyls and T. Rexes," he went on. "No one thinks in terms of birds, fish, insects and plant life, or the countless microbes and bacteria."

"You're right," Emily said, considering her own thoughts on the subject.

"In the grand scheme of things, and the age of the Earth, the presence of dinosaurs was fairly recent. They evolved like all other life-forms, endured for a period of time and became extinct. There was life before, and there is life after. Crude oil is nothing more complex than a hydrocarbon," he explained. "All life on this planet is carbon-based. If my own body was compressed for long enough, I'd eventually be nothing more than slushy black goo that can be refined into gas."

"That's a disgusting thought," she said, rapping him lightly on the knuckles with her fork.

"We call it gasoline," he said, getting a little off topic. "The rest of the world refers to it as petroleum."

"Your point," she said.

"Petra Oleum. Latin for Rock Oil," he clarified. "When it was first discovered as a fuel by the Phoenicians, it oozed out of rocks. Many of those rocks were formed long before dinosaurs came into existence."

"Okay," she said, "I see where you're coming from."

"Of course, dinosaurs did have a part to play, but only a very small one," he said. "Carbon life existed long before, and has existed long after, that era. If artificial intelligence engines reasoned like humans, we might as well get all our facts from social media. We'd rather agree with popular opinion than make ourselves unpopular by disagreeing."

Emily nodded, mulling over what Nathan was saying. "I'm sure social media is where news channels get all their crap."

"A large portion of it," Nathan concurred. "There's no such thing anymore as investigative journalism. News anchors are more concerned with appearance than with what they're reading off the monitor behind the camera. They don't care if there's any truth in what they say, only that it's sensational and that they look good on TV. It's all about the ratings. People automatically assume that what they hear is fact, because it's broadcast on a news channel. Nobody thinks to contradict that."

Emily loved these lunchtime debates with Nate, and he seemed to keep up quite well, with her thoughts drifting all over the place. His diverse knowledge was really impressive, and she was appreciative that he didn't dumb things down for her. Besides the ones she knew about, Nate probably had a few other activities or hobbies, affording him little time for social engagements.

She'd be over the moon if he ever asked her out on a real date, but the chances of that were slim. She was sure that like most men, he preferred women with more sex appeal, and certainly those a little taller than herself. Sensual thoughts of her and Nate occupied much of her time lately, particularly when she was at home alone with nothing else to keep her mind busy.

"What?" Nathan asked.

Emily quickly dropped her eyes, not realizing that she had been looking at him so intently.

"So," she said, getting back to fossil fuels. "Crude oil doesn't necessarily come just from dinosaurs."

"No, but it also suggests that it's regenerating continuously, because plants and animals are always decomposing," Nathan pointed out. "There's now strong scientific evidence supporting that. Oil companies will, of course, argue. Their profits are based largely on false perception."

"In other words," Emily said, "if people believe that oil is in limited supply, they are more likely to accept that prices will go up."

"And oil companies use that to their advantage," he added.

"But there's another thing. If they need an instant boost in profits, they create a news leak that there might be a shortage. Prices don't necessarily increase immediately, but people do start panic buying. In some respects, it becomes a self-fulfilling prophesy. Suddenly there really is a shortage, and guess what?"

"Higher prices," she said. "Scary, the way we're always held to ransom by big business."

Emily had another thought. "If scientific evidence is correct, isn't there a good chance that we're consuming oil faster than it can regenerate?"

"A very good chance," he said, swallowing the last of his burger, now cold. "And ask any A.I. application today if oil is limited in supply, it will most certainly answer *yes*, because there's not enough supporting data to suggest otherwise. If it were proven that oil regenerates faster than demand, artificial intelligence could only answer on what it knows today. If it must consider future availability, then population growth, based on historical trends, would need to be considered. Artificial intelligence engines are unbelievably complex, and hunger for more and more data. It can make your head spin."

"Mine's already spinning, thanks," Emily said, smiling. "Warren said that A.I. engines continuously rebuild their data cross-references as more information becomes available. Isn't there a point where there's so much data and so many references that it can never come to a conclusion, or if it does, that it just takes too long?"

"It could easily end up going down a bottomless pit," he said. "But no, they're programmed to stop searching after a reasonable limit of probability is reached. They also need to avoid a situation where two topics cross-reference each other resulting in an endless back and forth search loop."

"Isn't that what programmers refer to as a 'Cartesian Join'?"

Nathan was astonished that she knew that. Her understanding of some of the things he spoke about were often a complete eye-opener - the stuff his brother Daryl referred to as "jargon".

Nathan's attraction towards Emily had grown over the last few months. Her bubbly and relaxed demeanour outside the office was in such sharp contrast to her professional, no-

nonsense work attitude. He wondered how women managed to do that.

Erotic thoughts about her were becoming progressively more regular, and he contemplated whether there could ever be a chance for a more intimate relationship. Probably not, he thought dismissively. Anyhow, he could never bring himself to broach the subject. He'd hate to put any barriers between their mutual friendship. In Nate's mind, intellectual women like Em projected strong sex appeal; and she was so cute.

"The idea of A.I. goes back about sixty years," he said, getting back to reality. "It's only recently, the last fifteen years or so, that computer and network speeds have made A.I. practical. Sifting through a million inter-related topics would take today's processors less than a second."

"Well, they say knowledge is power," she said.

"And money," Nathan added. "Countless trillions of dollars are made annually just on collecting and using information. Even more so on manipulating it. We all know that politicians rewrite history to suit their own agendas. Power and money - that's what it's all about." He shook his head.

"And speaking of power and money," she said, "we should get back to work."

***

"I was just bouncing something off Sven," James said to Nathan and Emily as they came through the door into the war room. "I'm convinced that what Bowers is doing is more closely related to the data we're collecting for the Food and Drug Administration than it is to collecting phone conversations. The more I think about it, the more certain I am."

Emily walked around the table and sat down. As usual, Nathan remained standing for a few minutes. He claimed that it helped digest lunch.

"There's absolutely nothing in those calls that has any value other than giving Adrian a tool to check that Magentis-harvested foodstuffs are being promoted by people on his private payroll," James said. "There are any number of ways he could be doing that. He certainly doesn't need the services of SkyTech."

"I think we're all of like mind with that," Sven said, looking to the others, who were nodding slowly in thoughtful agreement.

"Bowers made a huge issue of getting me to do this, and threatening blackmail reinforced the importance of what he wanted," James said. "In my mind, he was pushing just a little too hard. If there's one lesson I've learned over the last several months, it's to trust my instincts."

"So what do you have in mind?" Nathan asked.

"By nature of your job as a developer, you've been conditioned to think in a certain way," James said.

"Yeah," Nathan said, smiling. "We're all a little psychotic and filled with self-importance."

"No, hear me out," James said, with a stern look on his face.

"Sorry, JW," Nathan said, with an apologetic grin. "You were saying..."

"Faced with a problem," James went on, "you look at what you have and what you can do, not what you don't have and what you can't do. We need to change our mindsets."

"Go on," Nathan prompted.

"When we look at the data that we're collecting for the FDA, we can come to certain conclusions from what's in front of us," James continued. "What we need is to analyse that data using what we don't see. Kind of like reading between the lines, or finding the true meaning of a politician's speech."

"Sort of like looking at a blackboard," Emily said, "and instead of saying it's black, we can say that it's not white."

"Perfect analogy, Em," James said, looking at her in surprise. She had interpreted precisely what he was trying to convey.

"Which would unlock many possibilities," Sven added.

James let them think on this a few minutes.

"Something became apparent this morning about the information we're filtering out of the NSA's data for the Food and Drug Administration," James said. "In this, Bowers was honest. It *was* requested by the FDA. I had Monica, our temp, check the financial statements. Our payment comes directly from the FDA's R&D account, not some general revenue slush fund."

"So the question remains," Nathan pondered, "why is Bowers trying to lead us away from digging deeper?"

"And that's what we're going to find out," James said. "Another thing. I don't want all of us going in different directions, so if I can recommend that you, Em, find out a bit more on Magentis' seed farm if you can. Nate, help Em if she needs it, but I want you to start sifting through the data we're gathering for the FDA. And Sven, continue your research on Bowers. Tapping into the farm's security cameras might reveal something. Think you can get it done before Wednesday?"

Sven just smiled with a single nod of his head.

"I take it, then, that we put no further effort into those phone conversations from Bowers's list," Nathan said.

"It's a waste of time," James said. "I'll leave you to it, then." He walked out of the War Room.

Chapter Twenty-Two

Situated about thirty miles south of Iowa State, Magentis GMP's seed farms in Missouri cover three hundred thousand acres of rich, fertile land. Several climate-controlled greenhouses, each spanning almost an acre and spread throughout the vast domain, are used to grow seed for research towards manufacturing higher yielding crops. Each has an adjoining maintenance yard, along with structures that house massive mechanization vehicles and assorted farming implements. Water for irrigation is provided by pump-houses drawing from Hazel Creek Lake and the Chariton River.

With convenient access to road and rail transport, over seven hundred tower-silos occupy the south-eastern region of the estate. Magentis is by far the largest commercial enterprise of its kind on the planet, yet there isn't a single sign or logo anywhere that declares who they are or what they do.

Being a highly automated operation, Magentis needs very few field workers. The majority of their staff, living mostly in Kirksville a few miles to the south, work in the main administration building.

Adrian Bowers stopped his car in front of the closed security gates and handed his credentials to an armed guard for verification. Satisfied that the visitor was who he claimed to be, and that he had an appointment, the guard jotted Adrian's name, along with the current date and time, on a log-sheet attached to his clipboard. He walked into the guardhouse and returned a moment later with a temporary identification card. Adrian grabbed the card and attached it to his jacket pocket.

The security guard, content that everything was in order, spoke briefly into a hand-held intercom, then activated the electronic gates. The surrounding eight-foot-high razor-wire fence extended from the guardhouse in both directions as far as the eye could see. As soon as the gates opened wide enough, Adrian drove through and proceeded along the neatly tended tree-lined asphalt road to the five-storey administrative block a short distance ahead.

As with his previous appointments, Adrian took an early morning flight from LaGuardia to Lambert International, hired a rental and drove to the Magentis seed farms. Taking Interstate-70, and then driving north along Highway-63, Adrian could usually make the trip in less than four hours – breaking a few speed limits along the way.

Adrian parked by the entrance of the admin block, in a visitor's bay clearly marked for the physically handicapped, and killed the engine. He opened the car door, reached over for his briefcase and stepped out into the warm afternoon sun. After stretching and adjusting his trousers, he walked into the building and announced himself at the main reception desk.

The stone-faced clerk looked at Adrian's identification tag, noted the number, said something, and then pointed towards a row of comfortable visitors' chairs. Adrian declined the offer, preferring rather to stand for a while. Clutching his briefcase in front with both hands, Adrian looked around absent-mindedly.

The clerk spoke to someone on an inter-office phone.

Two minutes later, Adrian turned and looked beyond the reception area towards a set of heavy wood-panelled doors adjacent to a single elevator. A tall, elderly man, well dressed in a black suit and patent leather shoes, came through the door on the right. His name was Davis Eldridge. He approached Adrian with a broad smile; they shook hands and exchanged a few polite words. Both walked towards the elevator. The old man swiped his security card across a scanner; the elevator door opened and they stepped in. The elevator door closed promptly.

Adrian's phone listened unobtrusively, and, along with its GPS, transmitted faithfully to SkyTech. Anything Bowers or his acquaintance had to say could be played back later from the recording.

***

"So far, nothing of importance," Sven said.

He had successfully linked to the seed farm's main security center, from where all cameras were controlled. Magentis' security setup was common to most surveillance systems; one computer monitor showed a matrix of small video feeds, and a second monitor displayed a zoomed version of the camera currently selected from that matrix.

Sven's setup at SkyTech mirrored that arrangement, except that he redirected the zoomed image from his secondary computer screen to the media center's large 80-inch flat-screen TV on the far wall. He also dimmed the room's lights.

For the purpose of tracking Bowers, he isolated his own computer, as well as Emily's, from the War Room's intranet, and temporarily exposed both to the internet.

For now, Emily, Nathan and Sven were interested in surveillance of the gatehouse and the admin block, and, in particular, in Adrian Bowers's movements. The rest of Magentis' operation, also closely monitored by cameras, could wait until another time.

Superimposed over a close-up map of the surrounding area, Bowers's GPS location presented itself as a small blip on Emily's screen.

Nathan and Emily watched attentively as Sven switched between cameras, zooming in from one feed to the next. The piggy-back link at SkyTech ran independently, and caused no interference or unexpected visual behaviour on Magentis' security center monitors.

They watched Bowers drive through the main gate, get out of his car and stretch for a moment. He then scratched his balls, trying to make it look as if he was adjusting his pants.

"I don't know why men always have to do that," Emily commented with a sly grin, looking from one to the other.

Sven and Nathan, quietly clearing their throats in unison, declined an answer.

"Magentis have a very sophisticated surveillance system," Nathan said, quickly changing the subject.

"How can you say that, Nate," Emily said, looking at him. "The cameras don't even capture in colour."

"Look how clear and fluid the video is," he said, pointing at the TV screen. "It's ultra hi-def. You can zoom in to the tiniest portion and still get excellent definition. Security cameras that record in colour are actually the cheaper inferior types, but most people think they're buying a better product. They don't capture as fast and when you zoom in, especially real close, the colours just start blending into each other. Detail completely disappears."

"Oh." She hadn't thought of that. It was a problem Emily often had when manipulating images in Photoshop. Small slices of colour images could only be zoomed in on and focussed to a point before they became a complete granular mess.

They were looking through the eye of the camera mounted inside the admin block and pointing towards reception. The clerk was talking into an intercom.

Bowers was facing in their direction, idly looking around.

"Can you read the number on his identification card?" Nathan asked.

"No. It's much too small," Emily replied.

"Sven," Nathan said. "Freeze the screen and zoom in as close as you can."

"My God!" Emily exclaimed. The ID number, now clearly visible, splashed halfway across the screen. Underneath, she noticed something that looked like text, but too small and out of focus to make out accurately.

"Sven, apply focus to that line below," Nathan said.

"*Printed in the Philippines*," she read, shaking her head in astonishment.

"Shit!" Nathan exclaimed anxiously. "When you zoom in, don't they also see that at Magentis?"

"No," Sven replied. "I'm not connected directly to any of their cameras. All I've done is piggy-backed onto the video feed of their surveillance network."

"Oh," Nathan said, visibly relaxing again. "I got quite a fright there."

Sven switched to the elevator's interior camera just as the door closed. Bowers and the old man, neither saying anything, shuffled towards the back and turned, partially facing each other.

"They're going down, not up," Emily observed.

Nathan and Sven looked at her.

"How can you tell, Em?" Nathan asked. "The elevator's floor selection panel isn't visible."

"You mean I know something that neither of you two geniuses knows," she said with a sly grin. "I presume this is all being recorded."

"Yeah," Sven said, still looking at her quizzically.

"Okay, you can play it back afterwards," she said, "but when an elevator descends, people react subconsciously, sort of preparing themselves to grab onto something. It's barely noticeable. You don't get that reaction when an elevator goes up."

Nathan laughed. "Now I'll be looking at everyone around me the next time I step into an elevator."

Bowers and the old man stepped forward a bit, waited for a second or so, and then walked out of video range.

Sven switched cameras. The two could be seen walking away from the elevator toward a closed door at the end of a short, well-lit corridor. A small red light illuminated above the door.

Nathan chuckled to himself. "From behind, they look like Laurel and Hardy."

"I never know which one is which," Emily said.

"Hardy is the fat one," Sven replied indifferently, looking closer at the video feed.

Bowers handed over his phone, which the old man, now mockingly branded by the team as 'Stan Laurel', placed in a secure container. Emily looked over to her screen. The phone was now officially off the grid. Its GPS location blip had disappeared.

"Shit!" Nathan remarked.

"At least that question has been answered," Sven pointed out.

Laurel swiped his card, the light turned green and the door opened automatically into an expansive office. Laurel gestured to Bowers to go ahead.

Sven switched feeds. Adrian Bowers, with his back towards the camera, seated himself comfortably in a chair in front of a small utility desk. Stan Laurel walked around the desk, pulled up another chair and sat down. From the higher elevation and angle of the camera, Laurel's head and shoulders were clearly visible; the rest obscured by Bowers's large frame.

With the dim ambient light of the media center and the scene unfolding on the huge TV screen, it felt to Emily as if she was also in the room with Bower and Laurel, rather than being an impartial observer over a thousand miles away in New York.

Behind Laurel, a glass partition, extending almost the entire width of the office, revealed what appeared to be an enormous sunken laboratory. On the right, just in view of the camera, a set of double doors provided access to a small flight of stairs leading down to the lab.

Neither Emily nor Nathan noticed Sven stumble back slightly in astonishment at seeing the operation behind the partition.

"That place is massive!" Emily exclaimed.

Nathan was awestruck.

"And spotlessly clean," Sven quickly added. "All stainless steel and ceramics. This is a biologically sterile environment."

"And fully automated," Nathan said. "I only see about ten technicians. All they seem to be doing is walking around in their protective bio-gear with clipboards, making observations."

With a wide central walkway, the left and right sides of the brightly-lit underground complex mirrored each other. Inclined chutes, five on each side, delivered seed directly on to adjoining conveyor belts, which slowly transported the goods from one processing unit to the next. The ten-foot-tall rectangular units, twelve on each side, could be seen extending into the distance.

"From what I can make out," Nathan said, "final packaging and shipping is at the very end." He pointed at the monitor. "That room with the partially open roll-up cage-door looks like one of those huge transport elevators."

Just then, James walked through the door. "This is impressive," he commented, looking at the large TV screen.

"We're looking into a small office adjoined to what appears to be a lab and production facility beneath Magentis' admin building," Emily said, glancing briefly in James' direction.

All watched the operation with fascination. At regular intervals, the conveyors stopped for a few seconds, and bright red lights, like those mounted on emergency vehicles, started flashing. A few technicians looked at digital readouts and scribbled something on their clipboard sheets.

"What are Bowers and that old man talking about?" James asked. There was no mistaking Adrian's broad back and shoulders.

"Wish we knew," Sven answered. "The video feed has no sound and Bowers' phone is off the grid. It's locked in a cabinet outside the area we're looking at now."

"Why would a seed manufacturing and distribution operation need to be so sterile?" Emily asked to no one in particular. "And why underground?"

James looked at her. "Underground?"

"Yes," she replied. "Sven did a great job getting into Magentis' surveillance network. We've been following Adrian's movements from all those cameras you see on his screen."

James briefly scanned the matrix of video feeds displayed on Sven's computer monitor.

"They got into an elevator and descended to the level we're looking at now," she said. "My guess is that they're down about three floors, but it could be more."

"Can you zoom into one of those contraptions being fed by the conveyors?" James asked Sven.

"I can, but for now would rather see what's going on with Bowers and Laurel," he replied. "We're recording exactly what my computer monitor and the TV are currently displaying. Zooming in could cause us to miss something from the overall view."

"Laurel?" James tilted his head.

"We dubbed them Laurel and Hardy," Emily said with a grin.

"You'll see why when we play back the entire recording."

"To answer your question, Em," Nate said. "If this is the operation that creates genetically modified produce, hence their name, 'Magentis GMP', it would have to be fairly sanitary and germ-free."

James looked closer. "This isn't an alteration or mutation operation for genetic engineering."

He had Emily and Nathan's attention.

"You sure?" Nathan asked. "It's definitely not manufacturing."

"Actually it is," James contradicted. He pointed to one of the processing units. "Have a closer look."

They watched as the conveyor slowed and stopped in its cycle.

A sliding door sealed the small conveyor entry portal.

Red lights started flashing. Technicians took notes.

A few seconds later, the portals opened, the lights turned off and the conveyors continued through the next cycle.

"It's not that easy to make out from the camera's viewpoint," James said, "but the warning symbols on the sides of each of those large contraptions look very familiar."

Nathan pushed his glasses closer towards his eyes. Six equilateral triangles joined to form a circle and alternating in colour between light and dark. From a colour camera and monitor, the triangles would have been captured and displayed in black and yellow.

"The international symbol for radioactivity," Nathan said. "Now I understand why their protective clothing looks so unusual. They're not bio-suits at all."

Chapter Twenty-Three

Staring intently at the war room's large TV screen, James, Emily and Sven looked closer at one of the signs Nathan was pointing to.

"No," Sven said knowingly. "They're not bio-suits. They're hazmat suits used in operations susceptible to radiation."

"Genetic modification," James explained, "happens shortly after seed germination. It's largely a chemical process that works on groups of closely coupled molecules. With the right process, you can get fruit to grow larger than nature intended. You can get tomatoes to grow into cubic instead of spherical shapes. All sorts of alterations are now possible."

"And that's not what this is?" Emily asked.

"All those units you see will be heavily lined with lead," James said. "The seeds are being exposed to small bursts of gamma. With just the right exposure and energy levels, you can change the gene structure of DNA and RNA, but at an almost atomic level. Each station along the production line provides slightly higher levels of radiation, but in shorter bursts."

Emily and Nathan listened intently. Sven, who knew all of this already, was more interested in Stan Laurel and Adrian Bowers.

Laurel appeared to be doing most of the talking. Bowers, from behind, could occasionally be seen shifting in his chair or nodding his head in agreement.

"This entire production line probably cost Magentis ten to fifteen billion," James said.

No surprise there, thought Nathan.

"That which you see being packaged at the end of the line," James said, "will produce fruits or vegetables that, when harvested to maturity, will be one hundred percent sterile."

"I don't really know what that means," Emily said, "but it doesn't sound good. Why would they do that? Wouldn't the resulting fruit or vegetable be radioactive and hazardous to eat?"

"Not at all," said James. "Gamma radiation is just a super-high frequency within the electromagnetic spectrum. Like X-rays and microwaves, gamma does not leave any radioactive particles behind. In fact, you probably eat more sterile foods than you're aware of."

"Such as?" she asked.

"Seedless grapes, seedless watermelons, zucchini, corn," James said. "The list of harvested foods that are sterile is endless."

"So why do it?" she asked.

"Take an apple seed," James explained. "Under the right conditions, it will germinate and grow into an apple tree. In order to have offspring, the tree produces enticing fruit. An animal comes along, eats the delicious apples, but doesn't digest the enclosed seeds. They pass undamaged through the animal's intestinal tract and are subsequently dumped unceremoniously on the ground. They now have the opportunity to germinate. The animal has even provided some 'fertilizer' to help the cycle of life succeed."

"I like the way you put it," she said.

"Apple seeds from Magentis will grow into the same tree with the same fruit," James said. "But with one subtle difference."

"The apples are seedless," Nathan interrupted.

"Exactly," James said. "So now, farmers sell their fruit harvested from Magentis' seeds, but keeping some of the apples aside for next year's crop is fruitless - no pun intended. Their farm is no longer self-sustaining. If they want to grow more apples, they have to buy a new batch of seeds."

"Oh my God! And the way Magentis is monopolizing the market," Emily said, "farmers will have no choice but to buy from them."

"Or, what's also likely," James said, "is that those farms that can afford to do so will change their operation to dairy. But it's a very expensive undertaking."

"Sorry to interrupt this gloomy conversation," Sven said, "but it looks as if Bowers is about to leave."

Switching cameras, they followed Adrian Bowers and Stan Laurel back to the admin reception area. Bowers's GPS had reactivated, the blip showing again on Emily's screen. She turned up the volume of his phone's microphone transmission.

"I'll see you in two weeks, Adrian," Laurel said.

They shook hands.

"By then I'll have more accurate timelines on when the FDA will be starting research," Bowers responded.

"Have a safe return trip to New York." Laurel turned back in the direction from which they had come.

The parking area camera showed Bowers climbing into his car. Through his phone, they heard him curse the interior heat and what sounded like a severe case of flatulence. Engine started, air conditioner turned to maximum, Bowers drove off towards the gate.

"Sven, you can stop recording now," Nathan suggested. "We'll keep the footage here on the central server where we can all access it. I don't want any copies leaving this room."

"I want to switch back to their underground operation and record a bit more," Sven said. "According to the feeds displaying in the matrix, the only camera in that area is the one where Bowers and Laurel had their little meeting."

"This has been a very successful exercise, Sven," James said.

"Even though we don't know what Bowers and the old man were talking about, at least we know a key part of Magentis' operations. I agree, keep that video feed going for a bit. Good work."

"There's something I quickly need to look into," Nathan said, with a more thoughtful expression than usual on his face. He followed James out the war room.

"5... 4... 3... 2... 1..."

Emily looked at Sven. "Why are you counting backwards?"

Nathan barged back into the room and looked around. "Did anyone see where I left my glasses? Oh, never mind. Here they are." He picked them up and rushed back through the door.

Emily laughed. "Same old Nate." She looked at Sven questioningly. "Any idea what's suddenly niggling at him?"

Resetting the War Room lights to their normal brightness, Sven shrugged, unconcerned. "Nope. No idea at all."

***

No one had seen or heard from Nathan the rest of that day, and the following morning he came into the office later than usual.

"Where have you been, Nate?" Emily asked, as he walked through the glass doors towards her desk. She was helping Monica, the temporary executive assistant, with some invoices that needed James's attention.

"Is JW busy?" Nathan asked, looking hurriedly around the door into James' office.

"He's in the War Room, looking at the recording we took yesterday," she said, wondering why Nate appeared so agitated.

"Come with me," he said abruptly. "Is Sven also there?"

"He wasn't when I left about twenty minutes ago," she answered. "I think he's back at his desk."

"We'll get him on the way," he said, turning and walking in the direction of Info Tech.

Emily gave a few instructions to Monica and hurried after him.

James was watching the recording which they had been looking at the day before, on one of the computer monitors, not on the media center's large TV.

Nathan, Emily and Sven walked into the War Room.

James hit the keyboard's spacebar, pausing the video, and looked up. "Been wondering where you were, Nate."

"I've been up most of the night," Nathan said. "Just took a few hours early this morning to go home, nap for a bit and change clothes."

"You look a little unsettled," James said. "Everything okay?"

"I had an idea." Nathan pulled a portable hard-drive and USB connector from his pocket. "Just give me a few moments to set things up." He faced Sven. "Before I plug this in, have you disengaged yours and Emily's computer from the internet?"

"Did it yesterday shortly after I stopped recording from Magentis' surveillance system," he answered.

"Good," Nathan said. "So the war room is completely isolated again from the outside world?"

Sven nodded. "Yes."

Emily turned to James. "While Nate's busy, can I ask something about what you said yesterday?"

"Sure," James said.

"If Magentis holds the monopoly on foodstuff seeds, you said that many of the other seed-producing farmers, well, those that can afford it, will convert to dairy. What happens to the others? Will they simply go out of business?"

"Most likely," James said.

"Thing is," Emily continued, "it's obvious that once Magentis does have the monopoly, prices will escalate to a point where regular food-producing farms that rely on seed can no longer afford to operate."

"And this is puzzling to me," James replied in deep thought. "If there's no one left to buy their merchandise, they would consequentially put themselves out of business."

"Government mentality," Sven added sarcastically. "Biting the hand that feeds you."

"Except unlike private enterprise," Emily said, "governments don't go out of business."

After a few minutes of plugging away at his keyboard, Nathan looked up. "I hope this wasn't a waste of time."

"What is it that you're doing Nate?" James asked.

"As you know, I contributed quite a bit of technological expertise to the NSA's eavesdropping software, which we run on their behalf," Nathan said. "The entire process is very complex, but it's all compartmentalized. Depending on what's being analysed, the data is passed through a specific module, singular in its analytical ability. Most of the algorithms and formulas I provided are based on language, dialect and sentence context, both written and verbal. I had nothing to do with video and imaging, yet that particular module seems to be the largest of them all. Surveillance video is almost always self-contained within businesses that have their own security setups. None of it goes out on the internet, and none of it has audio."

"For security purposes, there'd be no benefit recording audio," James said. "Although, if a business relies on an external company to monitor their premises, then that would certainly be transmitted across the web."

"Much like traffic cams," Emily said.

"Yes," Nathan agreed. "The NSA has tons of this sort of footage, and much of it is replicated on our own databanks."

"That seems a bit weird," James said. "Unless they're recordings of sting operations, or clandestine videos of a North Korean lab refining uranium, why keep them?"

Nathan had considered that. "Why indeed? But they're not. I did some random sampling on the data and almost all are recordings from the type of feeds expected from malls, subways, convenience stores and airports. The surveillance equipment used is also inferior. Video quality is atrocious."

"To a degree, airport security monitoring makes the most sense," Sven cut in. "Although I doubt that passenger behaviour is scrutinized by software. It might be useful after the fact, but as far as I know, they train their security personnel for that."

"Yeah, two hours of hard-core theoretical classroom instruction, and then they pay them bottom dollar," Nathan responded sarcastically.

"Extremists are trained for years to shroud suspicious body language," James added. "The aggressive or anxious behaviour you see with regular passengers is largely because of their fear getting into an airplane."

"For airports, audio would probably be useful," Sven said. "Pity that surveillance equipment delivers nothing more than *silent movies*."

"And airport check-in is hardly a pleasant experience these days," Emily added.

Sven nodded in agreement. He had had his fair share lately of getting pissed around by inefficient and uninterested airport employees. No matter what the question, or who you asked, it was never their job.

"I think it's a case of the NSA just consuming everything that crosses the internet, whether it's of any use or not," she concluded.

"I would agree with that," Nathan said, still hammering away at the keyboard, "but my point is the sheer size of that video analysis module. What's there to analyse? Traffic cams are actually an excellent example, Em. Evaluate traffic movement, and then adjust signals accordingly."

"That makes sense," she said, "although gridlock is hardly a question of national security."

"Coordinating traffic lights requires, at most, a few thousand lines of code," Nathan said. "The algorithms are very simple. Colleges teach them in the first year to computer science students."

"So, you think there's more to this?" James asked.

"Yes. And we're about to find out," Nathan said. "Last night, I partially reverse-engineered the video analysis module. Not the whole thing, of course. There are millions of lines of code. All I wanted was the code address of the entry point where the analysis logic starts."

"That must have taken some time," James said.

"Most of the night," Nathan said. "The quick part was creating a simple stand-alone program that opens a video file and passes control over to the appropriate initialization function within the module. The video will be shown real-time in an embedded media player window while the content is being examined in the background. I compiled the three parts together into a single fully functional application. That's what I've just transferred to this workstation from my portable drive."

While they waited for Nathan to finish, Sven made a comment. "You raise a good point, Em, about the NSA consuming everything on the internet. The CIA is even worse."

"In what way?" she asked.

"Until recently, they were only focused on the highest levels of classified information, both local and abroad," he explained. "Everything they had on print was mostly unreadable being blacked out or redacted in other ways. The documents proved useless, because everything deemed confidential was no longer available for analysis. All they managed to achieve was hiding their own secrets from themselves. Their paranoia almost put them out of business."

"Pity it didn't," she said. "So what happened?"

"They followed the same strategy as the NSA," he continued.

"They started looking at anything not considered secret. It didn't take long for our adversaries to realize that the best place to hide something was out in the open – newspapers, magazines, social media, that sort of thing."

Emily considered that.

"The Central Intelligence Agency probably has more sophisticated data-mining techniques in place than the NSA," he said. "As much as I'm not in favor of *big brother* watching over me, I honestly think that the CIA has squashed many potential threats to the US. Stuff we will never hear about."

"Well, it sounds more like a contest between government departments as to who has the most intel," Emily remarked in idle thought.

"All right," Nathan said, starting his program. "Let's see if my suspicions are correct. JW, can you please close the video feed to your screen. My program will require exclusive access to the file."

James did so.

Enter file location or URL, the program prompted.

Nathan faced Sven. "You sure the War Room is isolated from the outside world?"

As proof, Sven reached over and grabbed the end of the ethernet cable, now unplugged from the wall socket leading to their internet server.

Nathan, nodding in acknowledgement, entered the directory path and filename of the video captured the day before from Magentis' surveillance cameras.

Chapter Twenty-Four

Crowded around Nathan's computer monitor, James, Sven and Emily stood motionless in eager anticipation as Nathan clicked the 'Play' button.

All four watched, as they had done the day before, Bowers's arrival at Magentis' main gate.

"I'm going to fast forward to when Bowers and Stan Laurel enter the basement office," Nathan said, running his finger on the keyboard touch-pad. After a few seconds, he switched back to standard playback mode.

Laurel swipes his card.
The light turns green.
The door opens automatically.
Laurel gestures Bowers ahead.
Bowers sits down comfortably, his back facing the camera. Laurel walks around the table. He sits.

James, Emily and Sven watched the scene unfold with mild interest, not knowing where Nate was going with this. The video didn't seem to have quite the same clarity and definition as the original recording.

Nathan, picking nervously at his index finger with his thumb nail, looked at the scene with anxious uncertainly.

Laurel opens his mouth to speak. "I trust that things are going according to plan?"

"Perfectly," Adrian responds, seating himself more comfortably.

"Christ!" James recoiled, looking quickly between Nathan and the screen.

"How in the hell..." Sven trailed off with an amazed expression on his face and running fingers through his hair.

"My God," said Emily absolutely stunned. "That explains the millions of lines of analytical code."

Nathan let out a deep breath that he had unconsciously been holding. His shoulders visibly relaxed.

The embedded module was lip-reading.

Simulating a gender-neutral voice, it was clear and articulate, with near perfect intonation.

Nathan paused the playback and looked at them. "We can carry on listening in a moment, but I need to stress this to all of you. What you've just seen, or to put it more accurately, *heard*, is a result of my breaking the NSA's contractual agreement with SkyTech."

James was the first to recover his composure. "Right," he said. "Legally, we're not permitted to dig into their code. The penalties are harsh. The NSA would be very unsympathetic if they found out we had reverse-engineered some of it."

"To put it bluntly," Nathan said, "they'll lock us away for life and throw away the key."

"This does not leave the War Room," James said as sternly as he could. "Nate, is this program of yours anywhere else?"

"No. Just on this computer and my portable drive," he said.

"The copy I made of the NSA's original module, along with my own development files, are already wiped out."

"Where were you coding?" James asked.

"The same autonomous computer to where we're archiving Bowers's personal phone activity."

"Is there anything else of importance on that portable drive of yours?" James inquired.

"Nothing. Why?"

"I want you to physically destroy it," James said. "Don't worry; I'll buy you a new one."

Nathan understood the importance of this. Portable equipment had a bad habit of accidentally ending up somewhere else.

"I've always prided myself on being up there with the best of them," Sven said grimly, "but what I've just seen is a little disturbing. I had no idea their spyware was already so advanced."

"None of us can claim any level of privacy anymore," Emily said, with a worried look. "What else do they have that we don't know about?"

"Hang on," James said, pointing out the obvious. "How are we able to hear what appears to be Bowers? His back is to the camera."

Nathan's smile broadened. "Have a closer look at the screen," he said, still elated that his suspicions the previous day about the NSA's video analysis module had proved correct.

They all leaned forward.

"What am I missing?" James asked, squinting.

"Oh, I see it," Emily said, with excitement. "There in the background on the left. Adrian's reflection in the glass partition."

Sven leaned closer. "It's almost impossible to see."

"Ignore the poor quality of the video," Nathan declared. "The module is scanning the original hi-def recording and putting all available processing power into analysis. It steals some additional CPU cycles and memory from the video output encoding functionality."

"So instead of wasting valuable computing resources on image quality, "Emily reasoned, "it dumps the video output to the computer's graphic card, and lets that take care of it."

"Exactly," Nathan said. "The graphic card isn't getting any program instruction on preferred image quality, so it simply spits out the lowest resolution by default. That's why I didn't bother redirecting the video from my computer monitor to the media center's TV."

James grasped Nathan's shoulder and looked at him in admiration. "Nate, I've got to hand it to you. What you've done here is remarkable."

Sven and Emily voiced similar compliments.

"All right," James said, enthusiastically rubbing his hands together, "Let's listen to what *Laurel and Hardy* had to say." He'd been itching to refer to them that way, and now seemed the appropriate time, when everyone was a little less on edge.

Chapter Twenty-Five

"The chief administrator will be with you shortly," the executive secretary said, with courteous professionalism. "Please, have a seat. Would you like some refreshment brought through while you wait?"

"No, that won't be necessary, thanks," Ryan Hurst replied politely.

She smiled and went about her duties.

Ryan Hurst, senior logistics consultant for Magentis GMP, sat down in one of the low visitors' chairs. It was hard and uncomfortable, a technique many top executives used as a subtle reminder as to who was in charge around here.

Ryan, sitting upright with his hands clasped, looked around the plush reception area. His palms were a little damp from nervous anticipation. He had never been to the New York office executive suite before and it was obvious that they made themselves very comfortable. Aerial photos of the Magentis Seed Farms were opulently displayed on the walls behind and to the left of the secretary's ample office space.

Shipping of seed to the Svalbard seed vault was managed from the Missouri offices with the logistics being administered here in Manhattan. In the light of that, Ryan's trips to New York had become more regular in the last six months. He usually stayed overnight and flew back to St. Louis the next morning.

Ryan heard a discreet buzzing sound from somewhere behind the secretary's desk.

"Mr. Hurst," she said, standing up. "Please come this way."

Ryan followed her down a short carpeted hallway which ended at a baroque mahogany door.

She opened it. "Please go right in."

Ryan quickly wiped his hands on his suit trousers, hoping to dry the sweat.

The administrator, squat in stature, balding and smelling of cigar smoke, stood up from his high-backed leather chair. "Ryan," he said, with a smile. He leaned forward and stretched his hand over the wide oak desk.

"Administrator," Ryan acknowledged, shaking his hand and reminding himself to apply a firm confident grip.

"Please sit down."

Ryan did so. The chair was just as uncomfortable as those at reception.

The administrator sat down and opened a folder in front of him. He slowly perused the papers inside.

Ryan was starting to feel uncomfortable. Why he had been summoned here? His hands were clammy again.

"I've been looking at your employee record," the chief administrator said, looking up. "You've been with the company close on twenty years."

"Yes sir. Eighteen in fact."

"Yes, right. In that time, you've been a loyal employee with a commendable track record."

"Thank you, sir. I try to take my work here very seriously." Ryan swallowed, hoping he wasn't stumbling over his words.

"Our company has always seen great value in people like you, Ryan," the administrator said. "Faithful, trustworthy and getting the job done."

"Magentis has treated me very fairly over the years," Ryan affirmed, eager to say the right thing.

"Adrian Bowers from the FDA has spoken very highly of you."

"That's good to know, sir."

"Adrian was at our seed farm yesterday and he made a very valid observation with regard to the production line," the administrator said. "It runs very smoothly, but lacks oversight. We believe that productivity could be improved."

Ryan nodded, wondering where this was going.

The administrator continued. "Speaking with the VP of the facility, he agrees with Adrian's opinion and therefore, we would like to make you head of that department."

Ryan knew that he was going places with Magentis, but didn't expect this. He felt a little off-balance. "Er, that's quite an honour, sir."

The administrator took one of the sheets from the file and handed it to Ryan. "This form outlines your new contract. Your official position will be *Director of Operations*, and if you accept, it will require permanent relocation from your St. Louis office to the seed farm. A company-owned house in Kirksville has already been made available to you, free of charge, and as usual, all moving expenses will be taken care of."

Ryan looked down the form, trying to keep up with what the administrator was saying.

"You're also entitled to what we call an inconvenience allowance," the administrator said, with mild humour. "Kirksville is a nice enough place, but hardly the hub of entertainment for single people like yourself. The largest population group are the students at Truman State University, but, being highly academic, they aren't much into night-life."

Ryan's smile broadened as he looked further down the form. A nice increase in salary.

Yearly bonus based on performance. Company car. Platinum credit card.

Ryan looked up at the administrator who was now leaning back comfortably in his chair, hands folded across his stomach, and smiling.

"This is an extremely generous offer," Ryan said with enthusiasm. His palms were no longer sweating.

"If it all looks in order, sign at the bottom, add today's date in the adjacent box, and have my assistant take it over to payroll. She will give you the keys to your new car and tell you which parking bay it's in."

"Yes sir," Ryan said, smiling.

"Your existing credit card is coupled to a limited expense account. Please return that to my assistant and she will provide you with a new one which is linked to our corporate account. It has no limit and I trust that you will use it responsibly."

Ryan patted his suit pockets in search of a pen. He really needed to remember these things.

The administrator handed him one.

"Thank you, sir," Ryan said with embarrassment. "I must have misplaced mine."

The administrator took a second document from the folder. It looked to be about twenty pages. Opening it to the last sheet, he passed it over to Ryan.

"This is our standard Non-Disclosure Agreement," the administrator explained. "It will require your signature at the bottom."

Ryan was familiar with NDAs and signed on the line above his printed name. There was no box to fill in a date.

He handed the papers back to the administrator, who returned them to the folder.

Ryan neglected to read the document before signing it.

***

Emily really admired the men around her, or maybe "envied" was the right word. They all seemed to be so smart. In some respects, she felt almost inferior by comparison, but none of them, James, Nate or Sven, ever treated her as subordinate to themselves. They simply regarded her as an equal and a key member of the team. She wondered if any of them belonged to Mensa, that elite group of geniuses. She'd have to ask Nate one of these days. How did he even figure out that the NSA's analytical software had such capability?

Anxiously crowded around the computer, Nathan, Emily, James and Sven waited eagerly to see what Adrian Bowers and Stan Laurel had to say.

Nathan hit the *Play* button.

Laurel: *"We forecast that the majority of farmers will be out of business within the next five years."*

Bowers: *"Sounds a little optimistic."*

Laurel: *"We believe that we can do it."*

Bowers: *Are you going to expand into other produce types, or is the focus just on foodstuffs?*

Laurel: *Just fruit and vegetables for now, but there's quite a bit of profit to be made in other areas. Cotton, for example, but that's a future endeavour.*

Bowers: *Can the operation here handle it?*

Laurel: *In limited quantities, yes, but if we do diversify, a new production line would need to be constructed in the south, in Georgia or Alabama, most likely.*

Bowers: *For the immediate future, though, the idea is still to control most of the continent's food supply.*

Laurel: *All except dairy. Government subsidies are getting less. Only a small handful of today's farmers can afford to change their operation from traditional food to milk and cheese. Cattle are also becoming a less viable venture. People are eating less meat.*

Bowers: *And you see no profit in dairy?*

Laurel: *Not much, but there's no real point. Most dairy products sold today have absolutely no nutritional value anymore.*

Bowers: *With pasteurization, homogenization and other refinements, I can understand that.*

Laurel: *The long-term health risks will take care of themselves.*

Bowers: *Good.*

Laurel: *Within the next few years, those farmers who can't change to dairy will be going out of business.*

Bowers: *Most of them either selling their land or simply abandoning the farm.*

Laurel: *Without subsidies, the value of those farms will be a tiny percentage of what they are now. We can pick and choose at a price that we dictate.*

Bowers: *And farmers will have no choice. Either accept what we offer, or walk away with nothing.*

Laurel: *Precisely.*

Bowers: *How much seed are farmers buying from Magentis, in comparison to other suppliers?"*

Laurel: *About seventy percent. We've made it convenient and affordable for them. By this time next year, we'll be close to eighty percent.*

Bowers: *From what I understand, Magentis isn't buying out the smaller independent operations anymore.*

Laurel: *Not necessary. We've killed almost all competition, and those that remain will be bankrupt soon enough.*

Bowers: *That must be saving Magentis millions.*

A short pause. Bowers adjusts his seating position.

Laurel: *SkyTech still providing what you asked for?*

Bowers: *Very much so. They're convinced those bogus numbers I gave are the key to my end-game. Clark tried to convince me that they don't keep the phone conversations, but I have no doubt they've been archived for analysis.*

Laurel: *As long as they don't dig into the original data the FDA is collecting from National Security.*

Bowers: *Clark doesn't worry me so much; it's his senior tech guy, Nate McIntosh. He's sharp. Anyway, they wouldn't know what to look for, so I see absolutely no risk there.*

Laurel: *Good.*

Bowers: *Have you spoken with the administrator yet?*

Laurel: *Yes. He'll be calling Ryan Hurst into his office sometime today or tomorrow.*

Bowers: *Do you think he'll go for it?*

Laurel: *No question. Hurst is an idiot. The administrator will make him an offer he can't refuse.*

Bowers: *So Hurst gets a high profile post with absolutely no real authority or decision making, and if things go south, he'll be accountable for everything.*

Laurel: *Exactly. Our operation here is totally automated. It doesn't need oversight. Our productivity level is as high as it can get.*

Bowers: *And you don't think Hurst will realize that?*

Laurel: *As I said, he's an idiot.*

Another short pause. Laurel is thinking about something.

Laurel: *Has the FDA started any preliminary research yet?*

Bowers: *No. Their plan is to start in about two years. It will give us enough time.*

Laurel: *And Med-Bot?*

Bowers: *Biggest surprise of all. Its database has almost doubled in size.*

Laurel: *That's encouraging.*

Bowers: *It's simply emphasising what people already know about healthy eating.*

Laurel: *And you're quite confident that SkyTech's interest is still in those phone conversations?*

Bowers: *Yes.*

Laurel: *That was good thinking. It will most certainly grant you a nice lump sum, on top of what we already agreed on.*

Bowers: *Thank you.*

Laurel: *Well, it sounds as if everything is on track then.*

Bowers: *It is. When our long-term goals are fulfilled, only the very wealthy will be able to afford to eat.*

Laurel: *Thanks for the update, Adrian. As agreed, we have transferred the initial two million into your Cayman account. We'll see each other again in a fortnight.*

Bowers and Laurel stand up, shake hands and walk towards the camera out of sight.

Chapter Twenty-Six

"I have to give you credit," James said, turning away from the computer monitor and looking at Sven. "I didn't think for one moment that hacking into Magentis' surveillance system would turn out to be so successful."

"Would have been a complete waste of time without Nate's assumption on the video analysis module," Sven said modestly.

"This answers a lot of questions," James remarked.

"Yes," Emily said, now even more disturbed than ever. "Magentis wants to control the country's food supply."

"There's more to it. It's more important than ever Nate, that you do some in-depth analysis on the FDA's data.," James said.

"Not necessary," said Sven.

They all turned to him.

"Weren't you listening?" Sven asked.

"Well yes," Nate said.

"Wind this back about five minutes," Sven said.

Laurel: *In limited quantities, yes, but if we do diversify...*

"Too far. Forward just a bit," Sven said.

Bowers: *With pasteurization, homogenization an...*

"There. Stop," Sven instructed. "Listen to what's next."

Nathan hit *Play*.

Laurel: *The long-term health risks will take care of themselves.*

Bowers: *Good.*

"You can stop," Sven said.

"Good catch, Sven," James said.

"What did I miss?" Emily asked.

"I'm obviously also missing something," Nathan said.

James explained. "The FDA has been completely honest with us. They really are interested in knowing what people are talking about when it comes to healthy eating."

"But the FDA is hardly in the business of keeping people healthy," she said.

"They're not telling us the whole story," James went on.

"Magentis provides all the food; the FDA along with Med-Bot indirectly endorses those foods, but they're all harvested from sterile seed."

"Yes, that part I get," she said. "Food farms are no longer self-sustaining; they're forced to buy seed from the only supplier, namely Magentis."

"The farms go out of business due to escalating prices, and the next thing, Magentis owns all the farms," Nathan rationalized.

"Magentis now holds an entire population at ransom. If we want to eat, we have to buy from them."

"Let me finish," James said. "And I'm sure that you, Sven, have come to the same conclusion. We know that genetically modified foods have long-term side effects, many only manifesting themselves years into the future. I believe that sterile foods could have the same result, and that the FDA is undoubtedly aware of this. These risks may not be evident for many years to come. Bowers said that they will start research in two years, but research on what?"

"Cures or cover-ups for the illnesses those foods will cause," Sven added.

"Good God," Emily raised her hand to her mouth.

"Fuck!" Nathan exclaimed. "Sorry, Em..."

"And pharmaceutical companies will provide all the addictive medications needed to relieve those life-long ailments," James finished. "We were all wrong in assuming that the Food and Drug Administration knows nothing about what Bowers is up to. They know exactly what's going on, but I believe that this whole scheme was set in motion by Magentis. The FDA is simply doing what they've always done; keeping big pharma in business."

"There's already talk about Magentis merging with one of the large drug consortiums in Europe," Sven voiced.

"Where do we go from here?" Emily asked, after clearing her thoughts a little.

"We certainly can't go head-to-head against the FDA," James said, "but we have a good chance with Magentis."

"What do you have in mind?" Nathan asked, noticing a subtle grin on JW's face.

James looked at Sven and Emily. "We do what you two did to me with that intrusion hack, which I'm still a little annoyed about, by the way."

Both dropped their eyes slightly.

"We start by making Bowers's life a living hell," James said with resolve.

Chapter Twenty-Seven

Sitting opposite each other in the lunch room, Emily looked up at Nathan. "Who the hell thinks up this shit? I've hardly had a good night's sleep after listening to that conversation last week between Bowers and Laurel."

"Whoever it was, and I doubt it was Bowers, obviously had a very long-term plan in mind," he said. "You don't think it was Bowers?"

"No. Don't get me wrong, he's sharp and very devious, but this scheme is far too ambitious to have come from any one person. Companies have always tried to hold the monopoly on things. Look at all the data centers available today: IBM, Microsoft, Amazon, Google, countless others, each contending to control the world's information. Be interesting to see who wins out in the end, but my point is that there's value in information, and profit is guaranteed almost immediately. It takes a lot of sharp minds to make something like that work. What Magentis and the FDA are doing is also motivated by profit, but it's a completely innovative concept."

"How so?" she asked.

"It's extremely long-term," Nathan said.

"Yes, hold the current and future generations to ransom," she concurred. "We can survive without information, but not without food or shelter."

"Right," he said, "but somehow I don't think your kids would survive a day without the internet."

She had to smile at that, and it lightened her mood a little.

"But here's what I think," he said. "If they succeed, the next generation will be totally dependent on new types of food and drugs.

The human body will adapt naturally. Switch all those foods back to the way nature intended, and guess what?"

"The body treats it as poison, and new drugs have to be developed," she said.

"And Magentis doesn't have the expense any more of genetically altering seed. So now they generate even more revenue, but the other way."

"Scary thought," she said, and then added with thick sarcasm, "They'll have to rename themselves from *Magentis GMP* to *Magentis Au-Natural*."

Nathan laughed at that. "In some respects, I'm almost glad I didn't bring any children into this world," he said thoughtfully.

"Surely you have some regrets," she said.

"I do, but we live in a world that's almost become foreign to me. Children today aren't taught to think, they're taught to follow rules, and as far as I'm concerned, schools are nothing more than day-care centers. College students can't express themselves freely anymore; creative ideas are frowned on and independent thought is discouraged. I find it all just a little disheartening."

"It's all part of social engineering," Emily said. "Mankind's perpetual quest to control everybody and everything. Doesn't matter what you say or do, someone will have a problem with it. I remember when Elle was small. Her favorite thing for Halloween was to dress up as Pocahontas. Try doing that now! You can't. Some culturally-sensitive asshole will have issues with it."

"All part of political correctness," Nathan said.

"Ah, now that's a special brand of stupid," she agreed. "I don't even know who starts all this bullshit. Politicians trying to gain favour, I suppose."

"Somehow I doubt it," he argued. "Unless it's nearing re-election time, they tend to keep themselves busy inventing new ways to reach into our pockets."

"True," she conceded. "What pisses me off is all the tax breaks given to the wealthy. A poor subway musician is taxed, a waitress getting a free lunch-time sandwich, employees getting coffee paid for by their companies; they're all taxable in the interests of regulating the industry - but not millionaires with off-shore tax-havens."

"Yeah, it is kind of sad," he said, shaking his head.

"Anyway, I have no regrets at all about bringing Matt and Elle into the world," she said. "I would be really lonely without them."

How did you manage with them? They seem to be very well grounded."

"With kids, you take it one day at a time," she said.

"I couldn't do it," he said.

They sat in silence for a few moments.

"Are you done with your coffee?" she asked. "It must be quite cold by now."

He swigged down the last mouthful.

Emily stood up. "James asked us to come directly to his office when we were finished with lunch."

"Let's go, then," Nathan said.

***

"Come on in," James motioned. "And please close the door."

Sven was already seated comfortably on the Chesterfield near the cookies. Emily and Nathan joined him.

"I'm about to phone Adrian Bowers," James said from behind his desk, "so please keep it down. Sven was telling me about a very rare disease that Bowers has."

"PCD," Sven said. "It affects about one in five million men. Nathan looked at Sven.

"Primary Ciliary Dyskinesia," Sven explained. It's an autosomal recessive genetic condition where the microscopic cilia cells in the respiratory system don't function.

"In English please," Emily said.

"Rare lung disorder," Sven said. "That's why he always appears to be out of breath."

"I've heard of that," Nathan commented. "Drugs to keep it under control cost a small fortune."

"Quiet, please," James said, dialing a number.

Emily, Sven and Nathan could only hear one side of the conversation.

"Adrian. James Clark here. How are you? ...Excellent. Did I catch you on the run? You sound a little winded... Oh, I see. Well that's good. I just wanted you to know about a very minor problem we had earlier today... No, nothing too serious... Yes, it's fine to talk on the phone. There was a trace on one of the data packets we sent... No, some college kid. Nate picked it up almost immediately... Yes, Nathan McIntosh, whom you've met... Yes, that's him. You may find one or two files an hour or so behind 'real-time'...Nate stopped the application and did some quick security tweaks to our internal firewall... Yes, he's restarted the process and assured me that it's now secure... No, that's it, but I thought you should know. Listen, Adrian, I'm a little concerned about your health. I wouldn't want a business partner getting sick on me... Yes, I take mine very seriously with diet and exercise. Maybe you should cut down on some of the heavy lunches... No, I'm quite serious... Not related to your diet?... PCD! You're kidding? ...I know all about it. That's a very rare disease. My brother has it... I know how much it costs. Have you tried the generic variety? It works just as well, but at a tenth of the price... Just ask for it next time you fill the prescription... You're welcome... Great. We'll talk again soon." James hung up.

Chapter Twenty-Eight

"Brother?" Emily asked James as he returned the handset to the cradle. "You don't have a brother. And what was that about his prescription?"

"I did some research this morning on the drug used to control PCD," James said. "What I said about a generic version is also true, but it has a major side effect with some unfortunate consequences if taken with alcohol."

"Fatal?" Emily asked.

"No, just unfortunate," James said with a conniving look on his face.

"Surely there must be a warning on the bottle," Sven said.

"When did you last read one of those labels?" James asked.

"I get your point," Sven said. "Come to think of it, every single drug on the market warns against using alcohol."

"But if he requests the generic variety, won't the pharmacist caution him?" Emily asked.

"Unlikely," James said. "Like doctors, their job is to sell you something. Even if he was advised, Bowers wouldn't take such a warning earnestly. He has a serious drinking problem."

"So, what happens now?" Sven asked.

"Bowers's life is about to get very difficult," James said. "I want Magentis to disassociate themselves from him. I figure that if we can break the link between Magentis and the FDA, it's a start."

"Like throwing a spanner in the works. Slow down their ruse and perhaps even put a permanent stop to it," Nathan finished off.

"Yes," James replied. "But I also have a personal debt to pay back, and in this I have every intention of being mean, petty and vindictive."

"Are you that angry with Bowers?" Emily asked.

"Let's just say that I have a very real problem with paedophiles," James said, with an angry look.

Nathan turned to Emily. "Em, you said a while back that we might be able to do something to help those kids entangled in that escort service in Bangkok; the one Bowers goes to once a year. What did you have in mind?"

"I don't see how we can help," Sven interjected. "Thailand is a little out of our jurisdiction."

"Actually Sven, it will involve your particular area of expertise," she said with a grin.

"Okay, let's hear it," James said.

Emily continued. "If we can hack into Magentis' accounts, we can make a generous donation to the Children's Rights Foundation of Thailand, but with the condition that the money is used to close down Hung Sin Escorts in Bangkok, perhaps a few others as well."

"As sad as it may seem, organized prostitution is the only life those children know. Putting them back on the street would be worse for them," James said.

"One of the conditions, then, should be that the foundation finds caring homes," she suggested, "or at the very least, a reputable orphanage."

"Won't they just keep the money for themselves?" Nathan asked.

"No. I did a lot of research on them," she said. "They appear to be completely above board. The foundation is run largely by volunteers and relies heavily on donations. They've spent years fighting with the Thai government, but with no success. Thailand simply turns a blind eye to the legality and ethics of these child prostitution services."

"They would. It brings in foreign revenue," James said.

"So, let's give them some," she said.

"That's only going to hit Magentis," Sven said. "We're after Bowers."

"Hear me out," she said, "and I'm sure you can do this, Sven. We create a transaction trail that Magentis can easily trace back to Adrian's credit account linked to the FDA's slush fund."

"After which, Bowers will be hearing from Magentis. And there'd be no way he could explain it," Nathan said.

Sven laughed. "It would be interesting to see how he talks his way out of that one. So, what were you thinking of in terms of a *generous donation*?"

"Fifty million should do the trick," she answered seriously.

Nathan looked at her in surprise.

"I agree with Em," James said. "It certainly won't go unnoticed by the FDA, even if it is their general revenue account. Bowers won't know what happened and wouldn't be able to explain it - either to Magentis or the FDA. His credibility would be shot on pure denial."

"I can get started right away," Sven said.

"No, hold off," James cautioned. "Nate, I need a plan in place so that we can instantly remove all evidence of Bowers' phone scam. We're in very serious trouble if the NSA or FDA find out we've tampered with their code-stream."

"I can have that in place by the end of the week," Nathan said. "What about payments received? Wouldn't they be able to trace that?"

"Internal to the FDA, yes," James said, "but we have a valid contract with them to collect health and nutrition communications from National Security's eavesdropping data. We get paid by the FDA for services provided. As to which of their accounts those payments come from, it's none of our concern. The FDA wouldn't want to dig too deeply without exposing themselves or the NSA." He paused in thought for a moment. "No, in this I'm confident that SkyTech is secure."

"And if they do start digging, Bowers would have some more explaining to do," Emily said.

"Precisely," James agreed. "Nate, once you have your action plan in place, let us know. It may need some careful co-ordination."

"In the meantime, there's something that I'd like to do," Sven said.

"And that is?" James asked.

"Provide some charity to a worthy cause," he answered.

Chapter Twenty-Nine

Thankfully, Adrian was already gone for the day, Sofia Bowers thought, looking at her bruised cheek in the mirror. She would have to conceal it with make-up again. He had back-handed her harder than usual last night, and it was all because she wanted to finish watching a documentary on TV and he expected her in the bedroom.

The bastard could hardly get it up when he was sober. How could he possibly get any satisfaction being in the drunken state he was in when he came home? And what was that awful rash he had all over his body? It was disgusting.

Sofia didn't know how much more of her husband's abuse she could take, but had no idea where else to turn. She had no family nearby and very few close friends who would be prepared to take her in for a while.

Walking through the hallway, the phone rang. "Hello," she answered.

"Am I speaking to Sofia Balasco?" a polite man asked.

"No... Well yes, but that's my maiden name," she replied. "Sorry, what's this about?"

"We would like to arrange a time for you to come in and speak with our investment advisors," the man replied.

"I think you may have the wrong number," she said.

"You're not married to Adrian Michael Bowers?" he asked quickly, sensing that she was about to hang up.

"Yes," she said, after a brief pause. "What's this about? Who are you?"

"I'm sorry, Mrs. Balasco," the voice on the other end of the line said. "It was very rude of me not to introduce myself. I'm William Sutton, Vice President of Chase Manhattan Investments."

"I think that you should be speaking with my husband, Mr. Sutton," Sofia said, wondering why he was using her maiden name. "He deals with all our financial matters."

"The documents I have clearly state that we speak with you directly," Sutton explained. "It concerns the deposit made into your private bank account yesterday."

Now she was totally confused. "I do have a small savings account, but that's under my married name, Sofia Bowers."

"With Chase Manhattan?" he asked.

"Yes."

William Sutton read an address back to her.

"Yes, that's my current home address," she confirmed.

"Won't you please hold for just a few moments," Sutton said.

Sofia heard the subtle clatter of a keyboard in the background.

Sutton came back on the line. "Thanks for holding, Mrs. Balasco. I've just run a query, but there's no record of there ever having been an account under the name of Sofia Bowers listed at your address."

Sofia was stumped, and didn't know what to say.

"Mrs. Balasco," Sutton asked courteously. "Perhaps, if you could come into the bank, it can be quickly resolved." He asked a few more personal questions based on what he had on record. All of Sofia's answers corresponded perfectly.

"Do I need to bring my husband?" Sofia asked.

"No," Sutton answered. "In fact, the directive I have in front of me is that your husband has no access to this account under any circumstances whatsoever. There is also a clause that prevents you signing any of these funds over to him."

Strange, Sofia thought. What *was* this about?

"We will however, require you to bring suitable identification," Sutton stated. "A birth certificate or old passport would be ideal."

"Yes, of course," she said. "How much money is in the account?"

"Well," Sutton said, "there is of course a very small percentage the bank claims for administrative purposes as well as a trivial fee required for all foreign transactions, which in this case is from the Deutsche Bundesbank in Hamburg. The largest portion unfortunately, as is typical with any inheritance, is that claimed by the IRS and it has already been deducted. The total amount bequeathed to you after all deductions is just over twenty-three million dollars.

***

Emily had just walked in the front door, kicked off her shoes and sat down at the dining room table when her phone rang. "Hello, this is Emily."

"Hi Emily, it's Ryan."

"Oh, hi, Ryan. How are you?"

"Great," he said. "I'm phoning to invite you to dinner. There's something I'd like to share with you."

He sounded very excited. "Tonight?" she asked.

"Yes. It's the only night I have available. I've been permanently transferred to Magentis Seed Farms and won't be back in New York for quite a while."

She had no other plans, and, since it was Friday night, Matt and Elle wouldn't be home until after midnight. Emily also didn't feel like cooking just for herself. "Well, whatever it is, I'll be glad to celebrate with you. Where should we meet?"

"I can pick you up at seven, if that's okay?"

"Perfect. See you then." Emily ended the call. That would give her about an hour to have a leisurely bath and put on something nice. Ryan hadn't been in touch for a few weeks and Emily was curious about what he wanted to share. She also needed to see what else she could get out of him about Magentis, yet she figured that, at this point James, Nate, Sven and herself probably knew more than Ryan did about what Magentis and Adrian Bowers were up to.

The bathwater was warm and relaxing. Being as short as she was, Emily could lie back and stretch out completely. The bathroom vanity lights created a small and subtle sparkling effect across the rippling surface a few inches above her submerged face. Perfect silence. She had a fleeting thought of what it would be like lying in Nate's large Jacuzzi tub. Probably be able to swim in that, amongst other things.

She had a few particular outfits that she really liked, but with rare opportunity to wear any of them. For tonight, she decided on the burgundy dress, cut just below the knee, with matching earrings, necklace and kitten heeled shoes. Emily looked at herself in the full-length bedroom mirror with approval. Her hair was still slightly damp, but that would dry out soon enough. She was expecting Ryan in a few minutes, so, with nothing else to do but wait, she went to the dining room and checked her emails. Other than a few marketing promos, which she deleted, there was nothing else of any interest.

A few moments later, her audible phone notification sounded. She read the message. Ryan Hurst, her ex-husband, had arrived precisely on time. Maybe he really had matured over the years, she thought. Punctuality was never one of Ryan's formidable characteristics.

To guard against the cooler evenings, Emily grabbed a light leather jacket off the coat-rack and slipped it on. She picked up her small clutch bag, checked that she had the door keys and made her way out the apartment and down the stairs to the street.

"Nice car," Emily said, stepping into Ryan's BMW 5-Series Coupe. "I just love the smell of a new car."

Ryan beamed. "Thanks, Emily, glad you like it. It's just panel glue, you know."

"What?"

"Panel glue," he said. "It's what gives all new cars that particular smell."

"Well, the leather upholstery also helps," she added, strapping herself in. "So, where are we going?"

"I know a great little Italian restaurant in Queens Village. It's only about ten minutes from here if we take Grand Central."

Ryan really has grown up, she thought. Twenty years ago, he would have driven a high-performance sports car such as this like a complete lunatic. The BMW gave a remarkably smooth and quiet ride, making the short drive along the highway a very pleasant experience. At no time did Emily feel unsafe or the need to kick her feet against a non-existent brake pedal on the passenger floorboard. The soft sounds of classical music came from the car radio. His taste in music had obviously also improved.

What did surprise her, something she noticed when they met again a few months ago, was that he had matured into a remarkably good-looking man; maybe not so much in his looks, but rather in his demeanour, the confident way in which he presented himself.

"You look very nice," he said, interrupting her thoughts. "Thanks, Ryan. It's not often I get to put on an elegant dress," she said. Compliments had also not been one of Ryan's strong points when she first knew him. "I'm glad to see you in a suit. I've never been to any of the restaurants in Queens Village, and wasn't sure if I was over- or under-dressed."

"Well, you're dressed just right," he affirmed.

After a few minutes of pleasantries, they arrived, lucky enough to find a parking spot just two doors down from the restaurant. Ryan helped her with the car door. Yet another surprise, she thought. He had fostered some good old-fashioned manners.

Chapter Thirty

Canelli's Ristorante was a typically authentic Italian eatery – wood and brick accents, cheerful lighting, an over-kill on the Venetian décor, servers rushing around balancing more plates than seemed possible, and generally loud and boisterous. Smartly dressed patrons thronged together around candle-lit tables exchanged views and opinions all at once. Emily felt instantly relaxed and at home.

They were swiftly escorted to an intimate table for two, near the street-facing side of the restaurant. Both removed their jackets, draped them over their backrests and sat down. Emily had just pulled her chair closer to the table when another server placed glasses of iced water in front of them and lit the candle.

Within a minute, another server approached. "Good evening," he said, nodding with a smile to Emily, then Ryan, as he placed menus in front of them. "My name is Luigi and I will be your host for tonight. Can I start you off with something from the bar?"

"A glass of white house wine, thanks," Emily responded.

"IPA for me," said Ryan. "Lagunitas, if you have it."

"We do," Luigi replied, and hurried off.

Why was it always *Luigi* or *Tony*, Emily thought. If it were a Greek restaurant it would probably be *Nick* or *Costas*.

"What are you smiling about?" Ryan asked.

"Luigi," she said. "He's a New Yorker through and through. He's as much Italian as I am. He has absolutely no trace of an accent."

"Probably not his real name," Ryan suggested, "but it does add to the whole dining experience."

"So, tell me your news," she said. "I take it that it's good, and that this is a little bit of a celebration."

"It is," he said. "You know, I've been with Magentis for years, always between the St. Louis and New York offices, but in all that time, have never been up to their executive suite here in the city."

"Ah, the ivory tower," she joked.

"And they make themselves very comfortable," he divulged, with a jeering smile. "It's also the first time I've spoken with Geoffrey Townsend."

"Who's that?"

"The CEO," he answered, "but he prefers 'Chief Administrator'. Nice man."

"And he offered you a transfer to some farm?"

"The company's seed farms in Missouri. The place is massive. It's where they grow all their seed produce for distribution to farmers."

Luigi returned with their drinks. "Do you need a few more minutes to decide on what to eat?"

"Goodness. I haven't even opened my menu yet," Emily said.

"Give us a few more minutes, please," Ryan said.

"Of course." Luigi nodded politely and marched swiftly towards another table he was hosting.

"Well," Emily said, raising her wine glass. "Here's to farming."

"I won't actually have anything to do with that at all," he said, pouring his India Pale Ale into a chilled glass mug.

Emily took a sip of wine. It was semi-sweet and surprisingly smooth for a house wine.

"I'll be working in the production plant as Director of Operations," he said, almost modestly.

"That's a nice step up from logistics," she said. He sounded more matter-of-fact than boastful. Was this the same Ryan Hurst from a few weeks ago? She could only figure that he had finally reached the level of his ambitions and had nothing more to prove.

"You're not fussy about food, are you?" he asked, changing the subject.

"No. Why?"

"Can I order for you?" he offered.

"Sure," she said with mild amusement.

They started with Antipasto Mediterraneo, portioned for two, consisting of premium cheeses, cured meats, marinated vegetables, Kalamata olives and garlic bread.

"Excellent choice for starters, Ryan. Mind if I use my fingers?"

"Glad you asked," he said. "Makes it easier for me as well." Both got stuck in.

"When are you moving?" she asked.

"Next week, Tuesday."

Emily sampled a slice of rolled prosciutto. "Mmm, this is delicious. Do you have to live on a farm?"

Ryan piled a few assorted meats and cheeses onto a slice of garlic bread. "Although there are farmsteads along the northern parts of the estate where the labor force lives, I'll be moving to Kirksville."

"Kirksville?"

"Small college town a few miles south of the estate. It's where most of the administrators and technicians live," he said, between mouthfuls.

Emily took some more cheese and a few olives. She'd been far more conscious recently of what she was eating. The olives were still capped, but had no seed. Sterile, she concluded.

"Is it a good career change?" she asked.

"Yes. The salary is a little better than what I'm earning now, but the perks make up for it. I guess getting people to move from the city needs some motivational offering. My new contract gives enough incentive for me to make the move."

Emily finished the last of the vegetables "What exactly does a Director of Operations do?"

"Oversees the process, and, where possible, improves productivity," he said. "It's a new post Magentis created, and they figured I'd be a good candidate for the job. Don't really know why, but I'm glad they offered it to me."

"So there's a seed processing plant on the estate?" Emily hoped that she sounded convincing in her question.

"Yes," he replied, "but I've never seen it except from aerial photographs. There's a huge multi-story complex alongside hundreds of silos, so I presume that's where it all happens."

One of the servers, different than the one before, refilled their water glasses, even though there was no real need.

"They also have labs on the estate. Much of the research into higher yielding crops is done there," he explained. "From what I understand, the processing plant genetically engineers seeds to the specifications proposed by the labs. I still have a lot to learn about the entire operation."

Luigi walked over to their table and removed the empty plates. "Can I bring the main courses now, or would you like to wait a little?"

"Now would be good," Ryan said, looking at Emily for confirmation.

She nodded.

"Anything else from the bar?" Luigi prompted.

"I'll have another wine," Emily said.

Ryan took a last swig and handed over the empty mug "And a refill for me, thanks."

The main course arrived a few minutes later, along with the wine and beer. Ryan had made an excellent choice for both, ordering the linguine with tiger shrimp, calamari, scallops and mussels blended into a spicy garlic marinara sauce. The salad was a mix of organic greens tossed in a homemade red wine vinaigrette.

Enjoying their meal, Ryan continued. "I'm really excited about what Magentis is doing. They could very well be the pioneers to ending the global food crisis. They're doing research right now on seeds that can yield crops in the harshest of conditions, even in the most barren regions on the planet."

Ryan had absolutely no idea at all, Emily thought. If left to succeed, Magentis will be the cause of even more famine. The only survivors will be the wealthy. Big surprise.

Regardless of what the future might hold, she wasn't going to do or say anything to quell Ryan's enthusiasm. As much as she doubted their true intentions, Magentis may have provided a valid career opportunity for him, and she wasn't about to take that away.

She listened politely as Ryan's thoughts unfolded on seed mutation and his own involvement overseeing the operation. It was apparent that he knew nothing of the underground production plant, or that it was a highly secure radioactive environment. She assumed that this would be Ryan's area to manage, but said nothing.

He spoke of his most recent trip to the global seed vault in Svalbard and his fascination at what the Norwegians had accomplished there. This was new to Emily. She didn't know that such places even existed. She was genuinely captivated by Ryan's description of the vault and his account of Henrik's family dinner with their unusual food and lively topics of conversation.

Putting all concerns aside, Emily decided to enjoy the evening for what it was – a humble celebration of Ryan's future. She enjoyed the food and wine, and much to her surprise, Ryan's company. He was so different. It was like going on a date for the first time with an interesting and well-spoken man.

Too full for dessert, Emily and Ryan ended their dinner with espresso. Emily enjoyed the natural bitter taste. Ryan preferred his with sugar. When the bill arrived, Emily offered to pay her share, but Ryan refused, taking care of it discreetly with his new company credit card. The smile on Luigi's face suggested to Emily that Ryan had granted a reasonable tip. She often wondered how they shared it out at the end of the evening, with so many different servers all doing their part for a single table.

The drive home was quick, even though the volume of traffic was much the same as earlier in the evening. Emily was relaxed, but a little light-headed. Probably shouldn't have had that third glass of wine, she thought to herself.

"Do you want to come up for a nightcap?" Emily asked.

"Sure," he said, pleased that she had offered.

"Drive around to the back," she said. "There are some visitor's parking bays that are usually empty."

Inside the apartment, Emily beckoned Ryan to make himself comfortable. "What can I get you? I have beer, red or white wine, and I think I may still have some Bourbon."

"Might as well stick with beer," he said, walking into her lounge area and sitting down on the sofa.

Emily returned with a beer and a small glass of wine for herself. "Okay out of the bottle, or do you want a glass?"

"Just fine the way it is, thanks," he said, reaching for the beer.

Emily sat down next to him. Perhaps a little too close. She took her shoes off, pulled her legs up on to the couch and tucked her feet under. "It was a lovely dinner, Ryan. Thanks for inviting me."

"I had a wonderful time, too. It would have been a little depressing celebrating a promotion on my own."

"I'm sure the new job will work out just fine." She felt a little hypocritical and hoped that it didn't sound too artificial, but what else could she say? He hadn't once mentioned SkyTech or tried to pry anything out of her. There was no pretence about tonight. He was moving to a new position, and genuinely wanted to share the news with someone.

He looked into her eyes. "You know, you've hardly changed at all in the last twenty years."

She welcomed the compliment. "Well, I'm glad to say that you *have* changed."

"Oh?" he questioned.

Emily smiled at him sincerely. "You're not the dork that I was married to anymore."

"Yeah, I guess I was kind of a jerk," he agreed.

They sat in thoughtful silence for a while, Ryan engrossed with his beer, Emily sipping her wine. He had been a perfect gentleman all evening. Wistful thoughts were surfacing from the back of her mind. She so longed for the company and close contact of a man. Was this really what she yearned for, or was it the wine talking?

"Do you have any regrets?" she asked.

"A few," he said, reflectively. He understood what she was asking. "I was always in too much of a hurry with everything and too ready to blame someone else for my own shortcomings."

She looked at him without comment.

"Not that I can justify my actions now," he said, "but there's definite truth to being young and stupid. Hindsight is always twenty-twenty."

She nodded. "We think we have it all figured out, and then reality hits us when it's too late to do anything about it."

Did Emily see the reality in Ryan's situation now? Did his new post at the seed farm seem authentic, or was it simply a ploy by Magentis or Adrian Bowers? Should she tell Ryan what her team knew and let him decide for himself?

Too many unanswered questions were racing through her mind. What *could* she say to Ryan? Come clean, which she knew deep down was morally right. But then what about all they had done recently at SkyTech? Was she willing to sacrifice that in favor of ethics?

Maybe she was just overthinking the whole dilemma and should simply let it play out on its own.

Were there any doubts as to what she wanted here and now?

For most of her adult life, Emily always felt that she needed someone else's approval on everything. And why did she think it was always necessary to justify her actions? She never understood why. Certainly, nobody ever asked for her approval; they just went ahead and did what they wanted, regardless of whether or not it was agreeable to her. The need to try and please everyone, along with her fear of being judged poorly or sending out the wrong message remained in perpetual conflict with what she wanted.

There were few times in her life where she simply jumped into a situation feet first without forethought or concern of what the outcome might be. They turned out all right.

What about tonight? Should she just throw caution to the wind? She knew what she wanted, so why hold back?

Ryan put down his beer bottle. He grasped her wrist in a light embrace, his hand jittery. His other hand tenderly cupped her breast.

Emily shuffled a little nearer. His touch was strange, yet distantly familiar.

Their lips drew closer.

Chapter Thirty-One

"Sofia?" Where the hell was she now, Adrian Bowers thought, walking into the living room. The lights were on, but the TV was off. Maybe she was already asleep. Strange, it was only a little after ten p.m. Well, she'd just have to wake up again and perform the duties expected of a wife.

He'd come home in a very good mood, having spent the last few hours with Dominique Garcia in his sacristy. The new additions to Dom's website were unbelievable. He had found some extraordinarily raunchy images of three girls, probably no older than ten or eleven, engrossed in very explicit actions, not only with each other, but with a variety of innovative toys. They looked to be Southern Asian, which in itself was a significant discovery.

The images themselves, and thoughts of what he could be doing with those girls would normally have given Adrian an instant erection, yet in the last few days he was having some difficulty. With urgent desires brought about in these situations, Dom usually made himself available in any way that Adrian preferred, by hand, anal or oral, but tonight he had been a bit reticent, waiting rather until Adrian's rash went away. What started on Adrian's face was now covering his entire body, and it itched like crazy.

Well, Adrian thought, he'd just have to get his satisfaction from Sofia, but he needed a shower first - hot water helped alleviate some of the prickly sensations. He preferred the larger shower in the main bathroom to the smaller cubicle they had en-suite; it also had two large corner mirrors. Adrian liked looking at his stiff organ when he masturbated, but his sizeable stomach proved a bit of an obstacle. The mirrors gave him an exhilarating reflection from both front and side. He snorted caustically at those who boasted about their eight or nine inches. Mostly they were exaggerating, of that he was sure. His four inches were more than adequate for any woman, and size had nothing to do with it anyway; it was all on how well you performed, and there he excelled.

The warm water was welcomed and he let it embrace his skin for a while before reaching for the shampoo. He caressed himself as fantasy images of the girls materialized in his mind. Movement became progressively more forceful, yet he just couldn't get it up, no matter how vigorously he toyed with himself. Sofia had some work to do when he was done in the shower. Stupid whore better be up to the job.

Adrian gave up his attempt to get a hard on, grabbed the shampoo and lathered his scalp. *What the fuck!* Why was he suddenly losing so much hair? Not that he had had too much to begin with, but still, this shouldn't be happening.

Concluded with his somewhat disappointing shower, Adrian dried off and went over to the medicine cabinet from which he removed his PCD prescription. He popped two of the generic pills into his mouth and dry-swallowed them.

Before he returned the bottle to its shelf, he noticed a stern warning label:

WARNING – Do not consume alcohol.

Avoid driving vehicles or operating heavy machinery.

Do not take if you have an ulcer, gastro-intestinal disease, lupus, liver, thyroid or kidney problems; asthma, heart disease, before or after heart surgery; are dehydrated, pregnant or nursing; have diabetes, chronic breathing problems, high blood pressure, haemophilia, glaucoma, difficulty urinating or depression.

Contra-indications: Fever; dizziness; sneezing; runny nose; constipation; congestion; headache; body aches; erectile dysfunction and in extremely rare cases, a mild facial rash and hair loss. Please read enclosed leaflet carefully.

Mild facial rash! Shit, it was all over his body. Why didn't that fucking pharmacist warn him about this? *Chronic breathing problems*? This is exactly the reason he was on the medication, and the label is telling him not to use it. What the hell is wrong with these fucking doctors? And how could the FDA sanction such meds?

Scratching himself, he stormed naked through to the bedroom.

"Sofia?"

No answer.

He turned on the light. Why was the bed still made up? He looked into the guest room.

Nobody.

Back in the bathroom, he wrapped a towel around himself and marched into the lounge. "Sofia, where are you? Stop fooling around." He continued into the kitchen and flipped the light switch.

Empty.

Angrily, he walked towards the dining room. "I'm warning you!"

Adrian spotted her phone on the dining room table. There was an envelope underneath. She must be here somewhere. He picked up her phone, then the envelope which he looked at front and back with curiosity. He took out the single sheet of paper and unfolded it.

"Goodbye, Adrian."

What? "Is this some stupid game?" he shouted. All he heard was the echo of his own voice. Losing his towel along the way, he rushed back into the bedroom and tore open her closet.

Except for two dresses and a pair of high-heels that he'd purchased for her last year, the cupboard was completely bare. The same with her dresser and bedside drawers.

What game was she playing? She had no family in the city, and as far as he knew, no close friends. She also didn't have any money, other than a few hundred in a savings account that she thought he didn't know about.

Bank account! "Crap." Adrian hurried to his small office space and flipped open the lid to his laptop. He moved the mouse rapidly back and forth, coxing the computer out of sleep mode.

"Come on, come on..."

As soon as it was active, he logged into his online banking portal. Fucking bitch probably cleaned me out, he thought with foreboding uneasiness. "Why are computers always so fucking slow," he muttered to himself.

Finally.

He opened up their joint account and clicked to the transactions page. The latest from her credit card was a withdrawal for organic groceries a few days ago. Nothing else. The balance was as expected. Adrian breathed a sudden sigh of relief.

As the primary account holder, he was able to lock out her credit card, which he did. With nowhere to go and no money, she'd be back in a day or so, he convinced himself. Then there'd be hell to pay. Fucking bitch!

His phone, lying on one of the corner tables in their lounge, vibrated.

Ha, that will be her now, phoning to apologise and beg forgiveness, he thought with satisfaction. Probably has to use a pay phone. Adrian walked over, picked up the phone, and without looking at the display, answered the call. "Get back home now," he commanded.

"Adrian?"

"Dom?" Adrian was momentarily baffled. "Sorry, I thought it was..."

Dominique Garcia interrupted. "Adrian, you need to get here now. I'm in the sacristy. Come through the back door."

"What's up?" Adrian asked. "You sound distraught."

"Just get here." Dominique ended the call.

Adrian disconnected and looked at his phone with confusion.

***

Emily backed away, gently reached for Ryan's wrists and lowered his hands. "Ryan, I'm so sorry. I just can't do this."

Ryan too, backed off a little and looked at her.

"There are too many conflicting things going on right now and I'm just frightened to add any more complications to my life." She saw a glint of understanding in his eyes. "I feel terrible. The evening was perfect. Great food and you've been excellent company, but I cannot give myself to anyone just yet."

After an awkward pause, Ryan spoke softly. "Emily, I too had a wonderful evening, but honestly, I didn't expect anything from you in return. It's okay." He gently reached for her hands. "I hope that your troubles don't weigh too heavily on you. You deserve more out of life than being a single mom."

Emily smiled shamefacedly. "Thank you for being so understanding."

They got up and walked slowly to the door.

"Will you stay in touch?" she asked, and meant it.

"I'd like that, Emily."

She kissed him on the cheek, forcing a faint smile to his dismayed expression.

Emily grabbed his hand just as he reached for the doorknob. "Ryan," she said with urgency. "Don't trust Adrian Bowers."

He looked at her, tilting his head.

"I mean it, Ryan. He's not what you think he is. Just be very careful."

***

"Adrian," Dominique said in agitation, as his ally entered through the sacristy's back door. "Thank God you got here so fast."

The Reverend Dominique Garcia's computer screen clearly showed what was so troubling. All the explicit child porno images had been replaced by selfies of Adrian's exploits in Bangkok. The soundtrack of Adrian and Dominique getting off on each other looped continuously in the background.

"What the...?" Adrian exclaimed, totally puzzled.

Dominique Garcia was irate. "Adrian, why did you post all these selfies on my site?"

"Jesus Christ, Dom! You think I did this?"

"What about the background sound? Have you been recording us?"

"No! Honestly Dom, it wasn't me. There must be a bug in here somewhere." Adrian looked frantically around the small room.

Dominique was hysterical. "Who would do something like that? This is a church, for God's sake."

Adrian grabbed Dominique's shoulder. "Can't you get rid of the images and sound?"

"That's the thing, Adrian," Dominique said with frustration. "The site is completely locked out to me. It's no longer accepting my admin username and password." "When the hell did this happen?" Adrian demanded.

"About an hour ago. But look at this." Dominique pointed to the counter at the top of the page. "It's clocking up thousands of hits every minute."

"Shit! Can't you stop it or kill the site in any way?" Adrian asked irritably. His continuous itching was driving him insane.

"Whoever got in, also blasted the website address all over social media," Dominique said, almost in tears.

Adrian was terrified. "Dom, there must be something you can do? How the fuck could you let this happen?"

Chapter Thirty-Two

Emily Hurst draped her light suede jacket on the office coat rack. Her brisk walk from the subway was a little demoralizing, since the seasonal westerly winds were a bit cooler than usual. Mondays were bad enough without the weather also turning colder, she thought, and East 72nd Street felt to her like she was in a wind tunnel. She should have put on something warmer before she left her apartment.

"Morning, Emily," Monica said with a smile, walking out of James's office with a bunch of papers in her hand.

"Hi, Monica. How was your weekend?"

"Would have preferred yesterday to be a bit warmer," Monica responded.

"I know what you mean. It's awful how the weather turned so suddenly."

James walked out of his office a minute later. "Morning, Em."

"Morning, James," Emily said. "Good weekend?"

"I had a chat with Warren. There's a suggestion I put forward, but I'll tell you all about it shortly. I'm on my way to the media room. Join us as soon as you can, but grab yourself some coffee first."

"More like hot chocolate," she said. "I'll be there in a moment."

Emily walked over to facilities, prepared her beverage and made her way into the war room. Halfway through the door, she turned, remembering to place her phone in the basket outside. She dropped it amongst the three others already there.

"Hey, Em," Nathan said looking up from his monitor with a warm smile.

"Morning, Em," Sven said almost automatically without taking his eyes off the screen, or his fingers off the keyboard.

James was sitting off to one side in a comfortable easy chair. Emily walked over to her usual spot next to Nathan and sat down.

"I've asked Monica to take some papers down to legal," James said. "I want to know from their perspective if what Magentis is doing is in any way criminal. It's a bit of a hypothetical situation that I've documented. I don't want to reveal too much to our lawyers of what we know."

"Of course it's criminal," Nathan blurted out. "How can it not be?"

"Provided that you're not evading taxes, free enterprise is a remarkably flexible system," James said. "As far as I'm aware, there's no law stating that you can't screw everyone out of everything."

"Point taken," Nathan said, nodding his head. "The government does it all the time."

Emily noticed a subtle grin on Sven's face from what Nate had just said. She turned to James. "How's Monica doing?"

"I'm impressed with her. She still needs to get her bearings, and has much to learn, but I'm thinking of putting her on the payroll full-time. She may still need your help at times."

"No problem," Emily said. "I'm glad she's working out okay. I like her." She stirred her chocolate drink, a little annoyed that it always separated. She hated getting to the bottom of the cup and finding all the good stuff sitting there.

James spoke to the team about an idea he had bounced off Warren over the weekend. "From what I asked, Warren believes that he can change Med-Bot's data to favour produce harvested by Magentis' competitors. He'll let me know by Friday."

"Great idea," Nathan said.

"Sven, what's new since last week?" James asked.

"Bowers' wife Sofia is now a very wealthy young lady," Sven said.

"What? Did you rip off his bank account?" Nathan asked.

"Not his current one, no. I transferred all the money from his bogus inheritance fund in Hamburg to a small savings account Sofia has here in Manhattan."

"Nice move," said Emily.

"Also," Sven continued, "Chase Manhattan has specific instructions to ensure that Bowers cannot claim any of his wife's money under any circumstances. According to the Bundesbank, the account in Hamburg was closed by Bowers, with the money being transferred to an independent beneficiary with Chase Manhattan. Under the German federal privacy laws, the Bundesbank is not obliged to disclose who terminated the account or to where the money was transferred."

"Any chance they could trace it to Sofia's savings account?" Emily asked Sven.

"With some digging, possibly, but that account no longer exists. According to the bank's records, Sofia Bowers never had an account with Chase Manhattan. Sofia however, has already spoken to some advisors on how best to invest the money registered under Sofia Balasco, her maiden name."

"How did you manage to do that, Sven?" she asked.

"Let's just say that banking is a speciality of mine," he replied.

"How much did she end up with?" James asked out of curiosity. "The IRS is very liberal when taking from people's inheritance."

"Over twenty million," Sven said. "She'll survive quite comfortably for a very long time. She's also moved out of Bowers' house without any hint of where she went. He's really pissed."

"He'll be even more pissed when he finds that he no longer has any money invested in Germany. I take it, then, that we're still monitoring his phone," James said.

"We are indeed," Nathan said. "Listen to this." He played back the heated conversation between Adrian Bowers and Dominique Garcia.

"Good," James said, when he'd heard enough. "I'm glad some pressure has finally fallen on that damned priest."

"Today, I'm sending Garcia's website address to homeland security," Sven said. "They'll have that priest's little 'cesspool of forbidden lust' internet site down within minutes."

"Isn't that sort of stuff usually handled by the FBI?" Emily asked.

"It's going to get there anyway, but I stay as far away from them as possible," Sven said. "As far as I'm concerned, the FBI and CIA, another operation I avoid, spend far too much effort trying to control or embarrass each other."

"That I understand," she said. "Kind of like who has the most classified or restricted data about the other."

"Here's something else," Nathan interrupted. He played back the conversations Bowers had had on Saturday morning with his doctor and pharmacist.

"You guys are so mean," Emily laughed. "An irritating rash, hair loss, *and* erectile dysfunction. He didn't have that much hair to begin with."

"He should learn to read the label before taking prescription meds," James said, with some satisfaction.

Sven snorted. "He deserves it."

"Nate, how's that plan of yours coming along to remove all evidence of Bowers' phone tracking scam from our systems?" James asked.

"I already have the process in place. It will totally obliterate everything," Nathan answered. "The whole procedure will take only a few minutes. Just let me know when."

"Do it today," James instructed.

"Am I the only one who didn't spend the entire weekend working?" Emily asked, looking around. "I feel guilty."

Nathan faced her with a shrewd grin. "Why should you feel bad? This is what us geeks get off on."

She nudged him gently in the ribs with her elbow.

They spent the next hour devising a plan to transfer some of Magentis' immorally earned wealth to the Children's Rights Foundation of Thailand, and the feasibility of having Hung Sin Escorts shut down. Various other lines of attack against Bowers were discussed and agreed on.

"Let's take a five-minute bio-break," James suggested. "We'll continue when we get back."

Emily didn't need the washroom, but stood and stretched her legs a bit while the men went about their business. *And women get accused of going to the washroom in packs*, she thought with a smile. She finished the last of her chocolate, now cold, and tossed the empty cup and plastic spoon into the recycle bin.

James was first through the door, followed closely by Sven and Nathan. After they were all seated again, Emily spoke of her Friday night dinner with Ryan.

"He's accepted a position as Director of Operations at the seed farm," she said. "I didn't give anything away, but he really doesn't know what it is that Magentis actually does. He's never been to the estate before, and certainly knows nothing about their underground production facility. He firmly believes that they're going to solve the global food crisis."

"Yeah, reduce the population by starving everyone to death," Sven said heatedly. "That will do it."

"He wasn't intent on prying any more information out of me about SkyTech," Emily continued. "He genuinely just wanted someone with whom he could share some good news - nothing more than a simple dinner celebration."

Next to her, Nathan shuffled uncomfortably.

"Ryan was a perfect gentleman all evening," she said. "I've never seen such a drastic change in anyone. I think that he's finally found what he's been looking for career-wise."

"A career that may be very short-lived," Sven commented.

"He spoke about a global seed vault on some island off the Norwegian coast," she said. "I didn't know such places existed."

"Probably the one on the Svalbard Archipelago," James said. "There are hundreds of similar gene crypts all over the planet. They call them doomsday vaults."

Emily felt a slight shiver at the thought of such an ominous name.

"You really think Ryan has no idea of what's going on?" James asked.

"None," she said. "It's as we all suspected. He's being played, or set up." She dropped her head in silence for a moment. "James, I actually felt very sorry for him, and I may have done something stupid."

Nathan slouched into his seat, saying nothing. James looked at her.

"I warned him about Bowers," she admitted. "Not by revealing anything, but by simply telling him that Adrian cannot be trusted. I was adamant that he understood what I was saying."

"That was actually good thinking, Em," James said. "Another point of resistance Bowers will need to contend with."

She breathed a quiet sigh of relief. "Thanks, James."

Chapter Thirty-Three

By the end of the following day, various strategies had been put into motion. The team assembled in the war room.

"Nate, let's start with you," James said.

"As far as Bowers' phone scam is concerned, all modifications made to the National Security Agency's process stream have been completely eliminated. There is no evidence that this ever existed anywhere within SkyTech's domain."

"And the actual data we've been siphoning off?" James asked.

"Also wiped out," Nathan answered, "and that includes everything transferred automatically to our off-site backup and disaster recovery sites."

"Well done, Nate," James said. "Sven, how did it go with Bowers' internet drop-box?"

"Cleaned out," Sven said. "As soon as Nate confirmed that the data feed had been successfully turned off, I removed everything."

"Great," James said.

"Another thing," Sven continued. "Payments from the FDA's slush fund for Bowers' scam were controlled by an automated process on their server. I modified it so that instead of transferring the next payment to SkyTech, which is due this Friday, it will go directly into the accounts of those three pharmacists and the doctor who pulled out of Bowers' scam. I figure they deserved a nice little bonus for their integrity. Historical transactions were also modified."

"Won't an audit of those past transactions lead to some questions?" Nathan asked.

"To Bowers, yes," Sven said, facing Nathan. "But he won't be able to explain it. The money somehow just miraculously disappeared from the FDA's slush fund. JW already pointed out that we get payments from the FDA for the official contract we have with them, but SkyTech has no accountability on that. As long as we get paid for the legitimate service we provide, it makes no difference to us from which of their accounts that money comes from."

Emily laughed. "Even if Bowers did manage to pull off a scam like that against the FDA, they wouldn't believe him if he told the truth."

"One last thing," Sven said.

Emily looked at him and smiled. Sven always seemed to have just one more thing to add.

"What, Em?" Sven asked.

"Nothing... You were saying," she said.

"All development work, as well as the processes to route data through multiple global anonymous providers, has been wiped from my home computer. Even if they do catch up with me for some of my other 'questionable' endeavors, SkyTech remains in the clear."

James gave him an appreciative nod of thanks.

"Oh, and you'll be pleased to hear that Dominique Garcia's kiddie-porn website had been shut down. He should be getting a visit from the NSA or FBI real soon," Sven said, with some relish.

"Incidentally," Nathan said. "Bowers checks his internet drop-box every morning at about nine o'clock."

James looked at each of the others in turn. "Are you all confident that everything is in place before we move forward? There will be no turning back."

They nodded.

"Good," James said. "Let's flip the dynamics. Adrian Bowers is about to be turned from predator to prey."

"And Sven, you have everything in place to modify his drop-box?" James asked. "You will need to move fast."

"Just say when," Sven replied.

"We've also set Bowers' phone back to its default state," Nathan said. "We'll no longer be able to listen in on him or track his GPS location. The clone has also been cleared."

None of them had any notion that resetting the phones, Adrian's and the clone, would ultimately lead to catastrophic consequences.

***

At the start of business, the next day, the team were comfortably seated on the Chesterfield in James's closed office. Sven, laptop open in front of him, was nearest the cookies as usual, half already consumed. Emily stirred her hot chocolate and sipped at it. Nathan was quietly tapping his fingers on the armrest.

James sat in his executive chair, elbows on his desk with hands clasped. The grandfather clock chimed nine a.m.

"Now we wait," he said. "Let's see how well we've read Bowers."

Within two minutes, James's phone sounded with the traditional telephone ring-tone. He looked at the display. *Bowers, Adrian.* He nodded at the team and accepted the call. "James Clark," he said.

"James. It's Adrian."

"Good morning, Adrian," James responded, with a cool tone.

"There's a problem with my internet drop-box."

"What drop-box?" James asked.

A moment of stunned silence.

"Don't play games with me, Clark," Adrian said. "Why is it empty? Perhaps you've forgotten about our agreement."

"I don't recall any such agreement," James said smoothly.

"I'm warning you, Clark."

"Go on, then," James countered.

"What?" Adrian said with confusion.

"Warn me." James ended the call and nodded to Sven, whose fingers immediately started flying over his keyboard.

"Hello... Hello?" Adrian looked at his phone. What the fuck was Clark playing at?

He re-dialed. No answer.

Adrian logged out from his internet account, cleared his computer's cached memory and tried logging in again.

Username: Adrian.Bowers69
Password: SeXmAcHiNe

Adrian jolted at the sight of the contents. Thumbnails of all the selfies he had taken in Bangkok. Not the limited number on Dominique Garcia's site, but all of them; literally hundreds. He clicked on one of them. The full-sized image immediately exploded across his screen.

He promptly closed it, hand shaking uncontrollably.

There were numerous sound files. He clicked on each in turn.

Multiple recordings of Dominique giving him blow-jobs; a compilation of his verbal and physical abuses of his wife Sofia, who had left no indication where she had disappeared to after running out on him; the initial conversation he had with Clark at Andersen's statue in Central Park, but only Adrian's side of the dialogue; and, most unnerving of all, a digital recording of Adrian's discussion with Davis Eldridge in the Magentis underground lab.

Adrian paled, but not so much that it shrouded his facial rash.

He selected all contents and hit the 'Delete' key.

"You are not authorized to modify or delete site contents. Please contact your local system administrator or service provider for assistance."

"Fuck...!" Adrian dropped to his knees and clasped his hands together tightly. "Heavenly Father..."

***

Bangkok, reputedly the hottest city on the planet, traces its roots back to a fifteenth-century trading post in the Chao Phraya River delta in Central Thailand. Over the next three hundred years, it became the center of modernization for the region then known as Siam. Today, with a population of over fourteen-million, a quarter of Thailand's total inhabitants, Bangkok significantly dwarfs the country's other urban centers in terms of political and economic significance.

After numerous coups and several uprisings during the twentieth century, the city grew rapidly as the country abolished absolute monarchy. During the 1980s and nineties, the Asian investment boom led to many multinational corporations establishing regional headquarters in Bangkok, making the city a major player in global business and finance. Technology and fashion were in the forefront with comparable cities throughout Europe - higher than usual platform shoes and boots being particularly popular among the locals - the reason becoming obvious to tourists after one of Bangkok's many flash storms, typical during the monsoon season.

Bangkok, well known for its Buddhist temples, culturally significant landmarks, vibrant night-life, and infamous red-light districts, draws millions of tourists every year. The Patpong quarter, located between Silom and Surawong streets, is the nucleus of the city's sex industry. In walking distance from the Bangkok Transit Service's Sala Daeng SkyTrain station, it is situated in one of the most affluent areas of the capital.

Hung Sin Escorts attracts over seventy thousand visitors annually, primarily from Japan and the United States. Clientele, mostly heterosexual businessmen, are ushered to the lounge or bar area, depending on preference, where they're seated comfortably and can order from a variety of over two hundred alcoholic beverages. Drinks are served with a discrete voucher from which clients can mark off their choice of boy or girl, along with the preferred age and length of time, in thirty-minute intervals, for which they intend to indulge themselves. Prices vary accordingly, with payment in cash or credit card up front.

Most of the child 'escorts' are available immediately, but the servers are under strict rule to keep the customers waiting as long as possible. This ensured a steady order for over-priced, watered-down drinks as well as an increased level of sexual appetite. Clients who anticipate being with their escort for an hour are usually done in less than ten minutes. There are no refunds for early withdrawals. The price per half-hour is somewhere in the region of five thousand Thai baht; about one hundred and fifty US dollars.

Most of the children sold to Hung Sin come from destitute families who live in the slums and can no longer afford the cost of food. A few are taken off the streets, and some are illegally smuggled in from Bangladesh, Russia and Uganda. The imports are the most popular, and secure the highest prices.

Hung Sin's most lucrative business hours are between one a.m. and four a.m., after which most of the customers are back in their hotel rooms or in bed with their wives - and with their wallets emptied out. The children didn't bother hiding money they ripped off customers, because the bosses would eventually find it anyway, and usually the body searches, internal and external, were more painful than what was inflicted on them by over-zealous clients.

Chapter Thirty-Four

For its large population and diversity, Bangkok has a remarkably low crime rate. Its police force, per-capita, is surprisingly small, and to an extent, ineffectual, being largely hampered by financial constraints. To get anything done usually requires a significant monetary contribution to the open hands of the local jurisdiction's police chief.

The raid on Hung Sin took place on Saturday morning at five o'clock. With temperatures already exceeding ninety degrees Fahrenheit, the pre-dawn hours ensured another swelteringly hot day in the city. Devoid of blaring sirens or flashing lights, twenty police officers arrived within seconds of each other and swarmed through the suggestively stylized front entrance, sealing it behind them. Another twelve police covered the windows and two exits in the back alley.

Minutes later, several large cube vans operated by the World Health Organization and the Children's Rights Foundation of Thailand, lined up outside the entrance. A support vehicle, provisioned with clothes, food and soft drinks, along with two ambulances operated by Red Cross and local paramedics, parked on the opposite side of the street.

Without the need for police to draw their weapons, four pimp bosses and seventeen customers, still engaged in nefarious activities in private parlours, were shackled in handcuffs and lined up in the main lounge. The customers would be taken into custody immediately and charged with child exploitation, Thailand having no clear laws specifying a minimum age for consensual sex. The pimps would be locked up and forgotten about for a few months.

Terrified children, mostly naked, scampered out of every room imaginable, hiding in narrow corridors or trying unsuccessfully to escape through the doors and windows leading into the back alley. Many of the children, mostly girls, were badly bruised from mistreatment and some were dreadfully undernourished.

The entire raid, remarkably well coordinated between the police, World Health Organization, Children's Rights Foundation and local medics, was over in less than twenty minutes. The children, putting up fearful resistance, were immediately robed in light coveralls, spurred out through the front doors and into the cube vans, for transit to the Foundation's youth hostels.

Madam Lawan Dao, owner-operator of the escort service, fled the country before police managed to locate and arrest her.

Although the doors of Hung Sin were now permanently closed, the impact on Bangkok's child sex trade was minimal, with over twenty other such services still active and available to local and foreign clients.

***

Mid-morning on the following Monday, Geoffrey Townsend, chief administrator of Magentis, stormed into the executive boardroom of the company's head office in New York. All local members of the board of directors were already seated, having been summoned just fifteen minutes before. Townsend was in a dark mood. Bowers was nowhere to be found, his personal assistant had called in sick, and now this letter explaining a huge expense was highlighted in bold on his daily profit and loss report.

He waved the sheet of paper in his hand aggressively. "I want to know who authorized a fifty-million-dollar payment to some children's foundation in Thailand?"

Sent through express post and dropped into his personal mailbox, Townsend looked at the letter for the third time today.

Dear Mr. Townsend,

Thank you so much for your most generous contribution to the Children's Rights Foundation of Thailand. With the successful police raid and subsequent closure of the escort service, over eighty children can now look forward to a brighter future. Unfortunately, not all the children enslaved by the service were mustered, but we estimate that no more than ten managed to hide or escape. Even though the police tried to calm the children, they were suspicious and very frightened, not knowing that we were there to rescue them from this life of prostitution.

Although we will not be able to find foster homes for all the children, those that remain will be cared for in one of our privately funded hostels. Your donation will be invested in education, clothing, accommodation and nutrition. Many of the children will also require medical and psychiatric care, something that would never have been possible without such a substantial donation to our charitable cause.

I would ask that you also extend our sincere gratitude to Mr. Adrian Bowers, a representative of the Food and Drug Administration, and a close associate of yours.

Annabelle Rosenfield, British Volunteer Services, International Red Cross, Bangkok, Thailand.

***

Sitting with his back to the window, Adrian Bowers drummed his fingers on the kitchen table and looked at his bottle of Bourbon, now almost empty. His phone started vibrating again. As with most of the other calls that morning, Geoffrey Townsend's name appeared on the display. Adrian had no intention of talking to that pompous ass today. He had already been grilled earlier by the deputy director of the FDA on some discrepancies in the general revenue fund. How was Adrian supposed to know? Why didn't the director ask the fucking accountants? Worst of all, Dominique wasn't taking any of his calls and Sofia, his wife, was nowhere to be found. What the hell was the matter with everyone?

Having to justify his rash to all and sundry was also wearing a bit thin. Although improving almost immediately after heatedly discarding the generic prescription drugs for his PCD condition down the toilet, he wished the continuous itching would go away. Very little remained of his hair, but at least he wasn't losing any more. His penis was red from continuously toying with himself. He still couldn't get a hard-on, no matter what he tried.

He was certain that James Clark was responsible for all the shit that was going on in his life. The problem was that he couldn't figure out how. Too much of his personal information had ended up where it shouldn't have gone. Initially, he was convinced that they'd somehow tapped into his phone, but he had had it checked out by one of his expert friends in the FDA's tech department. He was assured that it was specified according to factory default, and that none of his apps had been corrupted.

If evidence of his blackmailing scheme against SkyTech were exposed, Adrian would not only be without a job, but likely end up in prison. He wasn't too concerned about the job, having made healthy deposits over the years into various overseas accounts; the most lucrative in Hamburg. Adrian acknowledged to himself that he was a very wealthy man.

Or so he believed.

Adrian mulled over all that had transpired in the last few days, and a plan formulated in his mind.

James Worthington Clark was about to discover the extent of Adrian Bowers' tenacity.

Chapter Thirty-Five

"Finally," Nathan said to himself with a satisfied smile. His fourth-generation micro-bot fly wasn't walking off the table or into walls anymore. He had also tweaked its erratic behaviour to be more life-like. Unlike the previous model, which relied solely on remote control, his latest creation had a miniaturized GPS system that could be programmed to send the fly wherever he wanted. Once it reached its destination, it could record video and sound for up to two hours, and then make its way home again.

The micro-bot relied mostly on natural or artificial light to keep its batteries charged, but could also regenerate from the weak electro-magnetic fields given off by any standard power source in its vicinity. If none was found and no light was available, it would simply park until daylight, and then continue on its pre-programmed mission.

Nathan was glad the week was finally over. He had no plans for the next two days other than to perfect his micro-bot. He still needed to increase its GPS sensitivity and recording capacity, along with improving video and sound quality. JW had given him some great tips on better image compression without loss of resolution. Nathan also intended to add face recognition, where possible.

He considered what he should do next with his interest in micro-bots. Was there room for improvement, or had he reached the limits of capability with this current state of miniaturization? He often thought of developing nano-machines, but that was way beyond artificial or mimicked intelligence; more like artificial *life*. The concept of millions of machines, each less than a thousandth the diameter of a human hair, all working in unison fascinated him.

Much like an ant colony or the individual cells of a human heart – nano-machines were futile on their own, but, combined, were able to serve a mutually beneficial purpose. And most intriguing of all, the ability to learn and adapt to changing conditions. Certainly not a project he could accomplish on his small workshop table. He didn't know where to start, or how to even create such machines. It was a little daunting that there were government funded labs throughout the world already developing artificial life. For the benefit of humanity? He seriously doubted it.

This past week had seen some strides in their retaliation against Adrian Bowers. Hung Sin Escorts was closed for good, as was Dominique Garcia's kiddie-porn website, and Warren Ellison had successfully altered Med-Bot's database in favor of Magentis' competitors. The War Room had also reverted back to its previous functional state as a media center.

Thoughts of work could wait until Monday, but he wanted to quickly tune in to the local news. He left the micro-bot to its devices, wandering around the table-top according to its own random behaviour.

Nathan walked through to his sitting room, switched on the TV, sat down and put his feet up on the coffee table. The eleven o'clock news had just started, and the top story was as expected - Magentis' plummeting stock prices.

Further to the financial state of Magentis, images and video, broadcast over the voice of the commentator, included technicians in hazmat suits, along with clear pictures of the radioactive warning signs on the gamma pulse units. The announcer speculated that this was indeed a seed sterilization operation and not a Genetically Modified Produce manufacturing plant. Evidence was also presented that farms producing natural foodstuffs were being systematically shut down by Magentis.

With the help of Sven, JW had compiled the video, along with incriminating evidence, and had sent it anonymously to all major news networks.

After a few other news items and sports announcements of no interest, Nathan got up and turned off the TV. Just then his phone vibrated.

"Hello, Nate McIntosh."

"Mr. McIntosh, it's Mark Johnson." Mark operated the nightshift security desk in SkyTech Tower's main atrium.

"Hi, Mark," Nathan said.

"I'm sorry to bother you at this time, and I hope it's just an abnormality, but I had Phil Roberts clock in about half an hour ago. I noticed the final entry on my display just after I came back from my rounds."

"Yeah, Phil tends to work some fairly odd hours," Nathan said. "It's probably nothing to worry about."

Phil Roberts, one of Nathan's programmers, was largely responsible for developing and administering security protocols within SkyTech's network and integrated computer systems. Working at night gave him the opportunity of making software configuration changes without interfering with computing resources and services offered during normal working hours.

"Thing is, Mr. McIntosh, the log shows that Mr. Roberts clocked in just after nine thirty this morning, but there's no entry that he clocked out. Also, some of the surveillance cameras on the thirty-first floor appear to be out of commission."

That didn't sound good, Nathan thought. "Mark, can you go up to the top floor and have a look around? I'll try and reach Phil on his phone. Get back to me as soon as you can." Nathan ended the call and punched in Phil Roberts's number.

It went to voice mail immediately. "Phil Roberts. At the tone, you know what to do."

Nathan tried again. Same result.

Nathan quickly paced back to his small office and workshop, flipped open his laptop and connected through his virtual private network into SkyTech's domain. Networks, servers, and, most importantly, the IBM Sequoia all seemed to be operating normally. Maybe it was just an irregularity, as Mark Johnson had suggested, he thought.

His phone vibrated. "Mark?"

"Yes, Mr. McIntosh. I have no access to your reception area, and the glass doors were secure as expected, but there are some lights on and from what I could see in the distance, your server room door is open."

Shit! "Thanks, Mark, I'm on my way."

Nathan slipped on his shoes and fall-jacket and was out the door. It took him just under twenty minutes to get to SkyTech. He used JW's reserved parking bay in the basement and took the elevator up to the thirty-first floor.

Mark Johnson would not be of much help. Close to retirement, he had been with the company for many years, operating the nightshift desk the entire time. Neither James nor Nathan ever considered that there might be need of a more dynamic security team for the tower.

Nathan swiped his security card across the scanner, releasing the glass entrance's magnetic lock. He cautiously walked through the foyer, passing Emily's desk, and continued on towards Info Tech's door. It was held open with a piece of cardboard wedged underneath. All lights were on.

The silence was ominous.

"What the..." The elevator door had been forced open revealing a black void - the car evidently positioned at random on one of the lower floors. Someone was trying to get to the IBM in the basement. A huge crowbar rested against the wall. It appeared to have blood on it.

He walked swiftly into the developer's office. Phil was lying face down on the floor in a pool of blood. Nathan knelt down and felt along Phil's carotid artery for a pulse. He was alive, but unconscious. Nathan immediately dialled 911 for police and ambulance.

Nathan looked around in horror at the devastation. All workstations, including the one in his personal office and open-plan area, had been trashed. Surveillance cameras suspended from the ceiling were destroyed, and office phone lines had been ripped out of the walls.

Forewarning Mark that emergency services were on the way, Nathan walked towards the elevator shaft scratching his head in confusion. Suddenly, without any awareness of what was happening, he felt himself being forcibly pushed from behind into the dark abyss.

Nathan screamed. His final conscious thought was of Emily.

***

Tony De Luca raced through Info Tech, passed reception and out the main entrance. Getting caught for destruction of property was one thing; being charged with murder was something else entirely. It wasn't supposed to turn out this way.

Persistent with the elevator button, he hoped he'd get out of the building in time. The elevator arrived; he bounded in and called for the second floor. From there, he carefully made his way down the fire escape and out the back. Approaching sirens could be heard in the vicinity.

Chapter Thirty-Six

Tony De Luca, of slight build, long black greasy hair and shifty eyes, had been approached by Adrian Bowers the day before and offered fifty thousand to break into SkyTech's thirty-first floor. He had no idea how Bowers got his contact information, but didn't care. He hadn't done a job in a while, and money was desperately needed. The task was straightforward – get past security, go to the top floor, into Info Tech and trash as much computer equipment as possible. Bowers had even given him an administrator's key-card. It was registered to Phil Roberts, some guy from SkyTech's information technology department.

He didn't ask how Bowers had managed to get hold of that, but regardless of all the resourceful skills Tony De Luca had at his disposal, the card would certainly make the job a lot easier.

Phil Roberts' key-card was the one which Adrian Bowers had found surreptitiously in SkyTech's washroom during his first meeting with James Clark and Nathan McIntosh. Adrian explained to De Luca that it would give him access to Info Tech as well as the elevator to SkyTech's supercomputer in the basement. De Luca was under strict instruction to demolish that as well.

Observing patiently from his beat-up Toyota Corolla on the opposite side of the street, De Luca waited until the security guard went on his rounds. Armed with the key-card, heavy crowbar and rubber gloves, the only tools he needed, De Luca pulled his hoodie over, to cover as much of his face as possible, and got out the car.

He crossed the street and entered the building. Ensuring that nobody was in sight, De Luca clocked himself in as Phil Roberts and called for the elevator. This was going to be quick and easy.

Or so he thought.

Walking confidently through Info Tech's door into the main developer's area, Tony De Luca immediately noticed someone busy at a workstation.

Phil Roberts turned from his monitor in surprise.

They both looked at each other in astonishment.

"Who the hell are you?" Phil asked.

De Luca recovered quickly. Without thinking, he leapt forward and swung the crowbar.

Phil's arms and hands weren't fast enough to offer any resistance. The crowbar made contact and he dropped like a stone, blood gushing from his skull.

De Luca spun around, looking for anyone else who might be there.

Nobody. Good.

Using the crowbar, De Luca trashed the ceiling cameras, and then, with his gloved hands, yanked the internal telephone lines out of the wall. Again with the crowbar, he demolished computers, monitors and printers.

De Luca was startled by the sudden loud ringing of a smartphone lying on the desk. He quickly glanced at the display. *McIntosh, Nathan.* It stopped almost immediately. De Luca, still a little shaken by this unexpected event, hoped it was just a personal call.

It rang again.

He didn't have time to waste and didn't want to be hindered by Info Tech's security door if he had to make a dash for it. Ripping some cardboard from the side of a box holding sheets of laser-printer paper, De Luca folded it a few times, opened the security door and wedged the cardboard underneath.

He walked over to the elevator that Bowers had said would take him to the main computer in the tower's basement. It had a scanner as well as an alpha-numeric keypad. De Luca assumed that one or the other would allow access. He swiped the card.

The keypad display responded: *Please enter the 5-digit access code:*

Bowers had said nothing about an access code, but it should not prove too much of a challenge. If, as suggested by the display, only numeric digits were required and not alpha character as well, he could figure it out.

For some reason, people preferred odd numbers when creating numeric pass-codes. They also started with a number somewhere in the middle, like 5, then alternated between lower and higher values, or used an ascending or descending sequence. He had never understood why, but this typical practice served him well in the past.

De Luca reached into his pocket for the small hand-held black-light he always carried, turned it on and shone it towards the keypad. The black-light revealed fingerprints over the numbers 1, 3, 5 and 9. Five digits were required, so that meant one number was used twice.

First attempt: 5, 1, 9, 3, 5.

INVALID - Please enter the 5-digit access code:

Second attempt: 9, 5, 3, 1, 9.

INVALID - Please enter the 5-digit access code:

Third attempt: 1, 3, 5, 9, 1.

INVALID – Keypad has been locked

Shit, he thought with frustration. He would have to pry it open.

There was almost no space between the elevator's sliding door and its housing, so he kicked the door's edge as hard as possible a few times to create a dent into which to wedge the crowbar. After struggling with the door for about fifteen minutes, he finally managed to move it a few inches. He rested the crowbar against the wall and pulled the door with his hands. To his surprise, it opened all the way under its own power – but where was the elevator? He was looking directly into a dark hollow.

With sudden alarm, he heard someone walking through the reception foyer. Fuck! What was this sudden hive of activity, he thought anxiously. De Luca had been assured by Adrian Bowers that, besides an old security guard behind a monitoring station on the ground level, the building would be empty at this time of night.

De Luca quickly moved into the shadows on the left and crouched behind a filing cabinet. He watched as the silhouette of a man cautiously walked by into the developer's office. He heard something being muttered, a few moments of silence, then a call to the police.

Tony De Luca needed to get out, and fast.

Just as he was about to flee from his concealed spot, he heard footsteps coming back in his direction.

They stopped.

He peeked carefully around the corner of the cabinet. His adversary was standing with his back towards De Luca, scratching his head in apparent bewilderment and looking into the open elevator shaft. He didn't appear to be security.

This was the only opportunity De Luca was going to get. He bounded upright, took a few determined strides forward, and shoved the man as hard as he could. De Luca spun around, and to the chilling sounds of a terrified scream, made a run for it.

***

James looked at the destruction in front of him. Yellow tape declaring *Police Line, Do Not Cross*, was stretched across Info Tech's door. What a way to start a Monday, he thought with anguish.

Police and forensics teams, which had been coming and going since just after midnight on Friday, were still busy collecting evidence. They had already dusted the elevators and the entire foyer for fingerprints without any success, and had declared reception and the manager's offices safe to use.

One of the forensic technicians approached James from behind. "Excuse me, Mr. Clark."

James turned.

"I just wanted to let you know that we're done with the washrooms, facilities and storage areas, so you may use them again."

"Thank you," James said absentmindedly, and walked back to his office replaying the sequence of Friday night's events back in his mind.

James was woken from a deep sleep by Mark Johnson, shortly after the police had arrived at SkyTech. Mark quickly told James what he knew and handed the phone over to the senior officer on duty.

James was instantly wide awake.

A professional, no nonsense voice came on the line. "Mr. Clark, my name is Lieutenant Myra Cooke. There's very little that we can tell you at this stage, but we ask that for the next few days, no one comes to the thirty-first floor. It will be quite a while until we've completed our investigation. I would like to speak with you, however. Would it be possible for you to come here first thing in the morning?"

First thing in the morning, like hell, James thought. He was there in less than half an hour. He parked his Bentley outside the front entrance of SkyTech Tower just as some medics were wheeling a gurney out of the atrium doors. Whoever was lying there didn't have their head covered by the sheet, suggesting that whoever it was, was still alive. He leapt out his car and rushed over.

Chapter Thirty-Seven

James looked at the battered and bloodied face of Phil Roberts lying motionless on the gurney. "Is he unconscious?" he asked one of the paramedics.

"Yes, possibly in a coma," was the response.

"Shit. Any idea what happened?" James asked in a concerned voice.

"Struck across the head with what we think was a crowbar."

"Please, do what you can." James made his way into the building and greeted Mark Johnson, who was pacing back and forth in front of the security monitors.

"Mr. Clark," Mark acknowledged. "The police asked me to get back to my station. They said I was in the way of their investigation."

"Thanks for contacting me, Mark. How are you holding up?"

"Not so good, Mr. Clark" Mark said. "Quite frankly, I have no idea what happened. I'm sorry to say, but it's a hell of a mess up there."

"I guess I'm about to find out," James said, giving Mark's shoulder a firm grip of re-assurance before continuing towards the elevators.

"Mr. Clark?"

James stopped in his stride and turned around.

"Mr. Clark, we have no idea where Mr. McIntosh went," Mark said nervously.

"Nate was here?" James asked in surprise.

"Yes, sir."

James nodded and quickened his pace to the elevators.

"Hell of a mess" was an understatement, James thought when he walked into the chaos on the top floor. He was greeted by Lieutenant Cooke, who brought him up to speed with what they knew so far.

"Lieutenant," an urgent voice called from within Info Tech. She turned around. "Yes, what is it?"

"We found the other man."

James's thoughts were back in the present.

Emily, sitting in the Chesterfield, looked up as James walked into the office. Her eyes were red from the tears she had been shedding all weekend.

James sat down beside her and gently took her hand. "We'll find out why this happened, Em, and who was responsible."

"I think we all know who was behind this," Emily said, looking at James.

"The police have our surveillance videos from the elevators, as well as the few seconds taken before the cameras inside Info Tech were destroyed. Judging by the way he covered his face; the guy knew what he was doing. He was also wearing gloves. It's going to make the forensic department's job that much more difficult."

Emily lowered her head and wiped away another tear.

"Don't be so hard on yourself, Em," James said with compassion. "They'll catch whoever it was."

They sat in thoughtful silence for a few minutes.

Sven walked in with a gloomy expression. "Are we ready to go to the hospital and see how Phil is doing?"

Phil Roberts had been wheeled out of ER on Saturday morning, following extensive surgery, and relocated to the intensive care unit. Emily, James and Sven walked quietly into Phil's private room with solemn expressions. His head, with multiple electrodes attached, was almost fully bandaged. He had a saline drip in one arm and a series of probes in the other. Monitors displayed a steady pulse and shallow breathing.

"My God," Emily whispered.

A nurse came in behind. "He's still in a coma," she said, "but according to the surgeon, not too deep." She offered encouragement. "His heart rate and breathing have been steady since yesterday and the electrodes have detected no abnormal or erratic brain activity."

They all turned around to a clomping sound coming through the door behind them.

"Sorry I'm late - can't move around quite as fast as I'd like."

"Nate," Emily said with a smile. "We didn't expect you to come. You should be at home resting." She looked down at the cast set below the knee of his left leg and embraced him in a warm hug.

"Love to hug you back, Em, but if I let go of these crutches, I'd probably fall down."

She hugged him even tighter.

"How did you get here, Nate?" James asked.

"Stretch limo," he replied. "Hope you don't mind if I expense it back to the company."

James laughed quietly. "No problem. But you'll need to do something about your car. I want my parking spot back." Nathan's car still occupied JW's reserved bay, where he had left it on Friday night after the ill-omened call from Mark Johnson, SkyTech's night-watchman.

"How's Phil doing?" Nathan asked.

"The doctors are optimistic," James said, "but not much more can be done until he regains consciousness."

"Maybe we should leave Mr. Roberts in peace for a while," the nurse said, urging them out through the door. "We'll contact you immediately if there's any change in his condition."

"You've taken this all very personally, Em," Sven said.

"How could I not?" she replied. "It should never have come to this."

"Listen," Sven said. "We're almost sure Bowers is behind what's happened at the office, and I intend to do something about it. But I'm going to need your help."

"Anything," she said.

Walking slowly down the corridor, James turned to Nathan. "I'm just glad the elevator decided to park itself on the twenty-ninth floor, Nate. Any lower would have been far worse for you - even fatal."

"The leg is actually just a minor fracture, so not too bad. I think more damage was done to my head when the paramedics pulled me out the shaft," Nathan said, drawing attention to the large Band-Aid across his forehead.

"I doubt that," Sven joked. "Your skull seems to be quite thick."

Nathan gave him a lopsided grin. "Yeah, I guess you're right. They've put me on a mild dose of opioids to ease some of the pain, and the doc says I should be out of this cast in about two weeks."

"Just don't get addicted," Emily said seriously.

***

There was little change to Phil Roberts's condition during the week that followed. The team visited for a few minutes each day to see how he was progressing. The doctors and nurses were still very optimistic that he would be out of his coma soon.

Info Tech was still unserviceable, and James Clark had suggested to his managers, administrators and clerks working on the thirty-first floor that they should take the week off. Forensics had done all they could and renovations had begun. Most important was the elevator; the door and frame had been repaired, and the entire unit was fully operational by mid-week. On the same day, new computer equipment had been delivered, and Sven set up temporary workspaces adjoining facilities.

"At least we're close to the coffee," Nathan mentioned to Emily who was seated next to Sven. He had come to work every day, arguing that there was nothing for him to do at home except mope around. He pulled up a chair on the other side of Sven. "What are you up to?" he asked, resting his crutch against the table. He had no need for the other one anymore.

Sven explained that he and Emily came up with a plan that would hopefully get Bowers arrested very soon. Sven had already decided on his intentions, but kept Emily involved so that her mind could be taken off some of the personal guilt she was needlessly carrying.

They had sent an anonymous tip to the Food and Drug Administration concerning the fifty million transferred from Magentis to Bangkok. They made it look like Bowers had embezzled funds through a money-laundering scheme, using the FDA's slush fund as an intermediary. Their rationale was that Bowers would be getting a call from the FDA very soon, and possibly a visit from the FBI.

"Good news," James said, walking through the short passage towards them. "I've just had a call from Lieutenant Myra Cooke. Forensics identified the intruder as a certain Tony De Luca, a small-time criminal preying on the elderly who live in apartments along Park Avenue."

"How did they figure that one out?" Sven asked.

"A single strand of hair behind one of the Info Tech filing cabinets," James replied. "They put it through DNA. De Luca was in their system and came up on multiple felony charges."

"That's great," Emily said. "Has he been arrested?"

"Not yet," James said. "The lieutenant said that it won't take too long to hunt him down."

"What are we going to do about Phil?" Nathan asked with a note of concern. "It was, after all, his carelessness that gave De Luca access into our premises."

James considered for a moment. "We'll know more on how De Luca got hold of that access card once the police have caught up with him. For now, though, let's wait until Phil has fully recovered. That's the important thing."

Nathan nodded in agreement.

"After that," James said, "any disciplinary action will be up to you, Nate. I will back whatever decision you take."

"Thanks," Nathan said. That wasn't a discussion he'd be looking forward to, but JW was right. Worry about Phil's recovery first. Everything else was incidental.

Chapter Thirty-Eight

By the end of the third week following the break-in and destruction at SkyTech, the thirty-first floor was back in operation. Overall disposition among the team had been cheerful since Phil had regained consciousness. If there were any gloomy thoughts, it was with the realization that the official start of winter was slowly creeping up on them. Phil had been relocated to a private room in the general recovery ward for observation. James took care of any additional expenses, to ensure that Phil was afforded all the comforts necessary.

Nathan no longer depended on his crutch, having had his cast removed the day before. He was advised by his physician to take every care walking – hobbling, more likely. He was able to drive again, even if it meant sitting a bit awkwardly behind the wheel with his left leg stretched out, but he managed fine.

With the understanding that the worst of this fiasco with Bowers was now behind them, James invited Emily, Nathan, Sven and a few close friends over on Friday night for a little celebration at his home in Roslyn Heights, Long Island.

Not too far out of his way, Nathan offered to pick Emily up, saving her the cab fare.

Nathan turned into James Clark's wide cobble-stone driveway from the softly illuminated suburban boulevard and followed it left. He came to a halt next to an expensive European import already parked in front of the three-door garage adjoining the double-storied tan-brick house. His two-door compact appeared a little out of place.

Although not classified as a mansion, the size of James' house certainly qualified as such. On each side of the contemporary twin-columned portico, two ornate bay-windows overshadowed perennial flowerbeds, now lacking exuberance and colour since the onset of the colder weather.

Surrounding an embossed semi-circular rose window, an attic casement extended from the peaked shingled roof, providing rustic elegance to the house. Below, on either side, south-facing bedroom windows had their blinds drawn.

Recessed into the portico, the wide front entrance, embellished with Edwardian stained glass, opened into a short hallway leading to the great-room. Antoine, James's long-standing butler, welcomed them cordially and offered to take their coats.

Emily had only been to James's home once, about two years ago. The decor was much the same as she remembered - extravagantly stylish.

A baby-grand Steinway with its back-lid half open was angled near the large opulent garden window on the left. Black and brown leather armchairs with matching mahogany side tables were placed amid small Persian scatter-rugs throughout the large room. Providing cordial lighting, Emily, looking up, admired the decorative multi-faceted crystal chandelier suspended from the high coffered ceiling. Forked electrified candelabra hung unlit on each side of the large red-brick fireplace at the far end of the room. The wood fire added to the warm ambience.

Catching Nathan and Emily in the corner of his eye, James interrupted his animated conversation with a tall attractive brunette near the open bar to the left of the fireplace.

Why is everyone around me always so tall and appealing, Emily thought with mild amusement? What happened to all the short, unadorned people?

James acknowledged Nathan and Emily and beckoned them over. Emily noted a new addition to the tasteful modern art mounted within hand-carved wooden frames adorning the wall on the right.

"Welcome," James said, with a friendly smile. He grasped Emily's shoulders and kissed her lightly on the cheek. "Nate, glad you're reasonably mobile again." They shook hands. He made the introductions. "Emily, Nathan, I'd like you to meet a long-time friend of mine, Brenda Barrett."

"Hi, Brenda," Nathan said. "Most people just call me Nate."

"Nate, then," Brenda consented with a friendly smile.

"Brenda," Emily said, greeting her.

"Nate manages our software engineering department," James said to Brenda, "and Emily, our soon to be graphics designer."

"Most people call me Em, and I loathe it," she said, with a satirical smile aimed at Nathan and James.

Both looked at Emily, startled.

"I think Emily suits you far better," Brenda remarked with candour. "James speaks very highly about both of you."

"Well, we do try to keep him out of trouble," Nathan said.

James smiled. "Emily, can I get you some wine?" he asked. "How about you, Brenda, ready for a refill?"

James catches on fast, Emily thought, hearing him use her full name.

Nathan looked at Emily. "You really don't like Em?"

"Never liked it," she said, "but I've gotten used to it."

James returned from the bar with a bottle of white wine, filled a glass for Emily and refreshed Brenda's. "I'll be right back with your beer, Nate," he said. "Ale, Pilsner or Lager?"

"A nice cold Lager will be perfect, thanks, and don't worry about a glass."

Warren Ellison came up from behind. "Em, Nate, great to see you both again."

Emily and Nathan turned.

"Warren," Emily said, smiling. "You're looking very handsome tonight."

Warren leaned down and kissed Emily on the cheek. "And you look very fetching yourself."

Nathan reached out and shook Warren's hand. "Good to see you, Warren. Did you fly in today?"

"No, yesterday," he responded. "Can't say I particularly like this weather. I've suggested on numerous occasions that James relocate to the west coast."

James, returning from the bar, overheard the exchange. "Let's not start that again," he said, looking at Warren and laughing. He handed Nathan the beer.

"Cheers," Nathan said, twisting off the cap.

Emily's attention was drawn to Sven walking through the front door. Clutched tightly to his left hand was the cutest little seven-year-old girl Emily had ever seen. There was no doubt as to whose genes she shared. She had long and wavy ash blonde hair with big blue eyes that tried to absorb everything at once. Glancing briefly up at Sven for reassurance, they made their way towards the group. Although not prissy in any way, she looked almost like a little princess in her partially frilled white dress with matching knitted ankle-socks and soft-soled shoes.

Emily turned to Nathan. "I didn't know Sven had a little sister," she said out the corner of her mouth.

"It's his daughter," Nathan said.

"Oh," Emily responded in surprise.

"I'll leave it for Sven to tell you," Nathan said, carefully avoiding anything else Emily might want to ask.

Emily knelt down as they approached. "And who are you?"

The girl looked up at Sven, then back to Emily.

"This is my daughter," Sven said. "Kayla, this is Emily."

"Hi, Kayla," Emily said. "You are so cute. Can I have a hug?"

After a short moment of uncertainty, Kayla sprang into Emily's open arms.

"Sven, she's adorable," Emily said, with a gleaming smile. "How old are you, Kayla?"

"Six," she said, letting go of Emily.

"You're so tall," Emily said in wonder.

Kayla looked up at Nathan. "Hi, Uncle Nate."

"Hi, sweetie. Aren't you looking enchanting tonight in that lovely dress?"

Kayla smiled and dropped her eyes.

"Come," Nathan said, taking her by the hand. "Uncle Jay has some new activities in the playroom." They disappeared down the corridor leading to the back of the house.

Emily looked at Sven. "James has a playroom?"

"Many of the guests invited to his annual fundraising events have kids," Sven explained.

So typically thoughtful of James, Emily reflected. She was aware of his charitable donations, many to child welfare organizations, orphanages and youth hostels. It was no wonder he readily agreed to have Sven siphon off fifty million from Magentis to the Children's Rights Foundation in Bangkok.

James, Brenda and Warren walked towards the bar, discussing their individual plans for the holiday season.

"Come, Sven. Sit with me and tell me all about Kayla," Emily said, urging him towards a two-seater leather divan.

"I'm very lucky to have her," Sven said. "You probably wonder why I'm out of the office at the same time every day. She's the reason."

"Do you manage okay?" Emily asked. She knew that he wasn't married.

"Kayla's at school now, but spends the afternoon with my mom. I pay for an in-house day-care provider so that mom isn't burdened too much."

"I'd forgotten the energy of six-year-olds," Emily said. "Elle wasn't too bad, but Matt. He just never stopped with his demands and his perpetual 'watch me' every time he did something."

Sven smiled in understanding. "Yes, I've heard that boys are far worse than girls."

"Were you married?" Emily asked. "Sorry, Sven, probably none of my business."

"No, that's okay," He replied, eyes sinking with poignant memories. "Her name was Elena."

There was a moment of thoughtful silence. Emily sensed that he wanted to say more.

"An infection from eating genetically modified fruit that had gone wrong initiated a perilous intestinal inflammation," Sven said. "She was thirty weeks into her pregnancy and there was little else the surgeons could do except keep her as comfortable as possible. The inflammation had poisoned her entire body. For over a week, she was in such terrible pain, but I've never known anyone so desperate to hang on to life. I was standing by the bed, holding her hand when I felt her strength wane away - and that horrific sound of the heart monitor emitting its continuous beep. It's a sound you never forget. The finality of something you knew would come, but hoped it never would."

Emily was emotionally shaken by what Sven was telling her.

"How the infection never got into her womb is still a miracle," he said, almost to himself.

Emily let his thoughts slowly unfold.

"We were both religious people, and went to church regularly, but after losing her, I lost all faith. I spend far too much time cursing God and dwelling on myself."

Emily bowed her head and stared blindly at the floor.

"The baby was saved, but spent several weeks in an incubator under intensive care and observation," Sven said. "Elena never saw her baby, and Kayla was never held by her mother."

Emily rested her hand lightly on his knee. "I'm so sorry Sven."

"We already knew after twelve weeks that Elena was carrying a girl, and agreed on a name there and then. If nothing else, at least Elena died knowing she was carrying a little girl named Kayla."

Emily couldn't imagine Sven's grief. They sat in silence for a few moments.

"JW and Nate already know what I've just told you," he said, "but a much bigger burden has been weighing heavily on me for the past few years - stuff that I've never mentioned to anyone."

Emily looked Sven in the eyes.

"I've always felt a deep sense of integrity and trust in you Em, and it's about time I told someone the full story. It will also explain a few things."

"If you feel there's something you need to share, by all means." She took a sip of wine. It didn't ease the lump in her throat.

Chapter Thirty-Nine

Reluctant at first, and unsure of where to start, Sven, sitting with Emily in the two-seater leather divan, confided in her.

"I traced the bad fruit that poisoned Elena back through its various distributors to Magentis," Sven began. "I was aware of their GMP operation, but never expected it to hit quite so close to home, nor quite so hard. It took a few days for everything to be recalled, but by that time it was already too late. Besides my wife, the contaminated fruit left quite a few other fatalities in its wake. Magentis, of course, denied having anything to do with it and conclusive results from FDA's testing were never made public."

"Big surprise," Emily said.

"I was consumed with hatred," he continued. "Creating genetically modified food is not a crime, and, being what it is, food will deteriorate over time. Elena's death was a result of an experiment gone wrong. Having it covered up by the Food and Drug Administration was the real crime."

Sven was speaking freely now, but Emily could sense a deep-seated anger surfacing.

"Magentis and the FDA have no doubt been in collusion for a long time," she said.

"I also found out the hard way that trying to expose this was a complete waste of time," Sven confessed. "You cannot fight a government department and hope to win."

"So, what happened?" Emily asked.

"I formulated a plan to expose Magentis for a scheme that would be so despicable, in the eyes of public opinion, that they would either change their operation into something more ethical, or close down completely. It took me two years of research to come up with a completely viable and profitable stratagem to convert their operation from genetic modification of foodstuffs to total sterilization."

"You mean that whole scheme of theirs was entirely your idea?" she asked.

"Yes," he nodded, with modesty. "The final document was a detailed schematic of intake chutes, seed conveyors, sorting machinery, gamma units and despatch, all with precise parameters for successful operation. I also provided scientific proof that sterilization was achievable by modifying the seeds, and that you didn't have to wait for the crop to reach maturity."

"Nate and I discussed that entire plot and we were both convinced that it couldn't possibly have been conceived by just one person," she said.

"I sent it anonymously to Geoffrey Townsend, Magentis' CEO, figuring that the FDA would eventually get involved, but my fight wasn't really with them, it was solely revenge against Magentis. You may remember the scandal about them and the FDA a few years ago."

"Yes, we spoke about it in one of our group meetings," she said.

"That was the result of the document's being mysteriously leaked to the press."

"I take it you had something to do with that."

"Of course," he said. "That was the whole idea. Their stock prices took a serious nose-dive and they ended up with a real fiscal crisis on their hands."

Emily looked up at him with a mocking smile. "You're scary, you know that."

"Well, I did finally get over my blind hatred. I had something far more important to keep me occupied – Kayla. She is the reason I didn't go completely insane after losing Elena."

"She is so adorable," Emily said, "and takes after you."

"Only her height, blonde hair and eyes. The rest is her mother, especially her wonderful temperament."

"She seems very loving," Emily concurred.

"That she is."

"What happened after that? With Magentis I mean," Emily asked, getting back on topic.

"I didn't figure on Townsend's determination," Sven said. "I also didn't think for one minute that he'd actually go ahead with the scheme. In that, you and Nate were right, it did take more than one person. I think Davis Eldridge had a lot to contribute and I have no doubt there were others."

"Who is Davis Eldridge?" Emily asked.

"He's the vice-president of operations at Magentis' Missouri location. You've actually seen him."

"I have?"

Sven looked at her with a sly grin. "He's the guy we dubbed Stan Laurel."

Emily laughed.

"Geoffrey Townsend and Davis Eldridge planned very carefully," Sven said.

"But you planted the seed," she said, intending no pun.

"Thing is," he said, "it started taking on a life of its own. I didn't give much thought to the deal JW reached with the FDA until Adrian Bowers and Magentis started showing up on various blogs. You know, those conspiracy blogs everyone mocks me about." Sven smiled sardonically. "It didn't take me long to conclude that something very suspicious was going on. I had to put a stop to SkyTech's involvement."

"That's when you approached me," she said.

"Yes, and I'm glad you offered to help."

"I nearly didn't," she admitted. "I was horrified at what you were asking me to do, sending intrusions into James's computer."

"This is far from over, and I'm not so sure I want to revisit haunting memories from the past. We've been so intent on pursuing Bowers, we may have lost sight of the bigger picture," Sven speculated.

"Most important is that, whichever way things turn for Magentis, SkyTech is now clear of any illegal or immoral involvement," Emily pointed out.

"Magentis are certainly getting a lot of bad publicity again, and I will gladly help add some extra momentum to that, but this time I'll do it for the right reasons, not out of blind hatred." Sven paused in thought. "It's that hatred that could have caused SkyTech to close down, and, worst of all, put JW behind bars."

"Well, it's behind us now without any serious consequences to SkyTech, but if you need some more help..." Emily left the rest unsaid.

"You wouldn't have believed my shock when I saw the entire underground manufacturing plant in operation after we tapped into the seed farm's security system," Sven said, laughing. "It was exactly to my specification, to the very last detail."

Antoine came by with a tray holding a fresh glass of wine for Emily. She hadn't realized her glass was already empty.

"Thank you," she said, looking up and replacing her empty glass with the full one.

"I'd actually like some wine as well," Sven said to Antoine. "Red, preferably."

"Certainly sir," the butler affirmed, walking towards the bar. "Em, please don't say a word of what I've just told you to anyone," Sven asked almost pleadingly. "I've learned a hard lesson over the years getting anger confused with passion."

"Of course," she replied, intent on keeping her word. "It won't go any further, I promise."

Antoine returned with Sven's wine - Cabernet Sauvignon.

"Thanks, Antoine." Sven turned back to Emily. "I probably don't want to know what JW pays for this stuff, but I'm going to appreciate every mouthful regardless."

"Food will be ready shortly," James announced from the bar, "so make sure your glasses are full, and get yourselves comfortable in the dining room."

"Did *you* cook all this, James?" Emily asked; savouring the aroma of the various dishes spread across the long oval dining table, around which ten people could be comfortably seated.

"Warren, mostly," James said, pulling up the captain's seat at the head of the table. "You didn't think I invited him all the way from California just for his good looks, did you?"

Emily sat on the left between James and Sven, with Brenda Barrett on James' right. Opposite Emily, Nathan and Warren were exchanging recipes. Kayla, comfortable at the far end of the table, kept herself occupied with half a dozen Smurf figurines she'd brought in from the playroom.

For the appetizer, Emily helped herself to a few battered oysters, which she dipped in a spicy cocktail sauce. Next, she sampled a small portion of steamed mussels, dusted with finely shredded roasted garlic flakes. The creamy potato-bacon soup with cheddar biscuits that followed was much to her liking.

The entrée included two generously stacked platters of crispy golden shrimp, bay scallops, clam strips and flounder. Another platter comprised of thinly- sliced roast beef smothered in pepper sauce and layered on top of seasoned greens and potatoes.

Two large bowls of salad were prepared: classic Caesar and Greek.

Emily tried a bit of everything.

"Warren, you and Nate have something in common," she said, swallowing the last of her scallops.

"And that is?" Warren asked.

"You are both magnificent cooks."

"Glad you're enjoying the food," Warren said, accepting the compliment.

Emily noticed that Nate only had soup, beef and potatoes – lots of each. Obviously he was not a seafood person, which she thought unusual for someone who showed such talent in the kitchen.

James turned to Emily. "I didn't invite all of you over tonight to discuss the situation with Adrian Bowers," he said, "but I specifically wanted you to meet Brenda. She's in the legal profession, and her tactics, although somewhat unconventional, are very successful."

Brenda smiled.

"I've been thinking," James continued. "There's no way Bowers was involved with the fabrication of the sterilization scheme. Excluding his other deviant interests, his agenda is simply one of greed, but his association with the FDA proved useful among the top echelon of Magentis. This is a very ingenious plan that must have taken a group of very smart opportunists quite some time to formulate."

If only you knew, Emily thought, hoping her face wasn't giving anything away. Sven appeared not to be taking any interest in the conversation, but she had no doubt he was listening carefully to every word.

"From what I understand of Ryan, your ex, he's a bit of an under-achiever and lazy enough to be content with it," James said. "Sorry, not trying to demean him in any way, it's just my perception."

"I actually agree with you, James," Emily said.

"If exposed, the risks to Magentis are enormous," James said, "and they're going to need a fall-guy. Unless I'm seriously mistaken, this could all land on Ryan. I can think of no other reason he was placed into such a senior position at the seed farms. It's far beyond his measure."

Emily nodded in agreement.

James went on. "I don't think anyone should go to prison for ignorance or stupidity, but if that's what's in store for him, I've asked Brenda to be his legal counsel."

Emily took James' hand and squeezed it. "That's very thoughtful of you, James." She looked at Brenda and tilted her head with an appreciative smile. "I'm really touched."

Emily turned her head to the sound of Antoine wheeling a dessert cart through the swing doors leading from the kitchen.

"Ah, you're about to experience one of Antoine's many culinary delights," James said with glee.

Emily marvelled at the considerable selection of finely crafted pastries assembled imaginatively on the cart's top tray. "I'd almost feel guilty eating any of those," she said. "Almost."

Antoine gestured with his head in acknowledgement.

"They look absolutely delicious," Emily said.

Kayla was already engrossed in her own plate of small cookies, a variety of candy and a hot chocolate drink which Antoine had brought through just moments earlier.

While everyone sampled the pastries, Antoine prepared the Irish coffee. They watched in admiration as he sugar-frosted the rims of the delicate glass mugs, heated them and put them to one side. In a separate glass, also pre-heated, he poured in just the right measure of whisky, held it over the burner and applied more heat, being cautious not to bring the liquor to boiling point. He then swirled the contents and tilted the rim of the glass over the flame, causing the vapour to ignite.

Watching the alcohol-fuelled yellow-blue flame cascading between mugs, was a floor-show on its own. After the final decant, he added strong, dark-roasted coffee, freshly whipped sweetened cream, and a sprinkle of cocoa powder.

Antoine smiled diffidently at the applause given by James and his guests.

Emily looked to James. "I didn't know you drank alcohol."

"I don't, but that's the whole point of preparing Irish coffee correctly," he explained. "Most of the alcohol evaporates, and, as it burns, gives the whisky that distinct flavor."

"The way Antoine held the glasses over the flame, I'm surprised none cracked," she said.

"Oh, he's had a few mishaps in the past."

Sven, immersed in the pastries, joined the conversation. "You know, it doesn't get its name because people use Irish whisky. In fact, it never started that way. Regular single-malt was preferred, and because there is no alcohol left after burning it off, they made fun of it and called it Irish. The name just stuck and people started using Irish whisky simply because it offers a smoother flavor."

While they savored their coffee, James reached into his jacket pocket and took out three envelopes. He handed one each to Emily, Sven and Nathan.

Emily faced him with a puzzled expression. James gestured to the envelopes in answer.

Emily opened hers, fumbled inside with her fingers and pulled out a personal cheque from James. She did a double take, looking at him, then back to the cheque. She counted the zeros again.

Three hundred thousand dollars. "James?"

Sven and Nathan, dumbfounded, were also looking at James.

He briefly glanced at each of them in turn. "Call it an early Christmas bonus," he said, smiling.

"Some bonus," Nathan said, still in awe. "To what do we owe this unexpected gift?"

"Both your undivided support and getting me out of a huge mess," James replied.

"But we did it as a team," Emily said.

"Still," James responded, "I feel indebted to all of you."

Emily reached over and hugged him tightly. "You have no idea what this means to me and my family, James."

Sven stood up, walked over and took James's hand with both of his. "Thank you so much, JW. This also means a lot to me."

When Sven moved back to his seat, Nathan stretched out his arm behind Brenda, grabbed James' hand and saying nothing, expressed his gratitude with a sincere nod.

"What started as a horror story could actually turn into a situation with a silver lining," James said. "I'm thinking of diversifying."

They all looked at James with curious expressions, expecting him to say more.

He left it at that.

Chapter Forty

It was an uneventful drive home along Interstate 495. Emily looked at Nathan, whose eyes were focused on the road ahead.

"Sven told me about Kayla and his wife Elena," she said. "What a depressing story. He almost had me in tears."

"It's not something he easily talks about," Nathan said. "Sven had a really rough time with it."

"It explains some of his arrogant behaviour in the past, and also goes to show how badly I've misjudged him," she said. "You never really know all the stories people have to tell."

"And we all have them," Nathan agreed, "yet Sven has never expected any sympathy from anyone. In retrospect, he probably has the best gift left to him."

"You mean Kayla? She's such an adorable little girl," she said. "I can see Sven's devotion to her."

"Have you ever wondered why he still carries around that old smartphone?" he asked.

"I guess he just likes it," she answered.

"It's his connection to Elena. It has her last voice message to him."

"Oh, the poor guy," she said. "I really feel for him." Emily was left with a lump in her throat, realizing with acute understanding what Nathan had just said.

They drove in silence for a few minutes, both deeply engrossed in their own private thoughts. Emily's feelings were trading off between the sorrow of Sven's loss and the euphoria of James' generosity. That amount of money would really break through her budget constraints and give Matt and Elle some well-deserved spending power. It was going to be a wonderful Christmas.

Nathan briefly took his eyes off the road and looked at Emily. He spoke with gentle determination. "Emily, will you come home with me and spend the night?"

Before he had the chance to apologize or second guess himself, Emily put her hand on his leg. "I've been hoping you'd ask me that for a very long time, Nate." It wasn't the wine talking.

Emily reached into her clutch-bag and pulled out her phone.

This was going to be awkward, she thought. It was just after eleven p.m., and her kids would still be out with their friends. She dialled Elle, expecting it to go directly to voicemail.

It didn't.

"Hey mom, 'sup?" Elle's jovial voice answered.

"Hi Elle." How was Emily going to put this? "Listen, I um... I won't be coming home tonight."

Elle's response was a total surprise. "It's about time, mom. We've been wondering how long it was going to take you to finally get a life. I hope it's with Mr. McIntosh. He's cool."

Emily blushed. Her kids obviously had more presence of mind than she thought. "Er, well yes, it is."

"That's great," Elle replied. "Don't worry about us. We'll see you some time tomorrow." She ended the call.

***

They walked hand in hand through the front door of Nate's condo. He kicked it shut with his foot. In the passageway to the lounge, he turned Emily towards him, and put his right arm around her waist drawing her nearer. With his left hand, he gently lifted her chin and gazed deeply into her eyes. He lowered his head, and kissed her tenderly on the lips. She responded enthusiastically and without reserve.

Firmly locking arms around each other, their body hug grew more forceful with each demanding kiss. Neither wanted this moment to end, both aware that each had wanted this for a long time.

"Oh, Nate," she said passionately, after their lips reluctantly parted. "You have no idea how I've longed for that."

"Em, I've thought about holding and kissing you for longer than I remember. I've so often wanted to confront you with my feelings."

"You have?" she said with incredulity. "You've never shown any interest."

"For fear of losing a friend," he admitted.

"And I always thought it was because of my being a twice divorced mother of two."

"What does that have to do with it?" he asked, chuckling.

"I don't know. Just a guess I suppose," she said, shrugging her shoulders.

"Emily, do you have any idea just how cute and sexy you are?"

"Well, let me show you just how sexy I can be," she said with a mischievous twinkle in her eyes.

Emily undid the top button of her blouse and slowly pulled it over her head. Kicking off her shoes, she undid the side zipper of her skirt and let it drop to the floor.

Nathan was already stripped down to his jocks. "In my wildest dreams, I never thought I'd see you in a bra and panties."

"You're about to see me fully nude," she teased, stepping out of her panties, undoing her bra and letting it fall. Regardless of what happened tonight, she had no intention of holding back with any of her past uncertainties.

Nathan eagerly pulled off his underpants and picked her up, marginally aware that his leg had not entirely healed yet.

With her arms around his neck and legs tightly wrapped around him, their lips embraced. She felt the cool passage wall on her back as Nathan pressed himself vehemently against her naked, eager body, his hands clutched firmly onto her buttocks.

Oh my God, she thought. He's solid - and huge. Emily felt herself swelling. She wanted him inside her.

He carried her to the bedroom, mindful of his leg, and, like a prized possession, laid her gently on the bed.

Emily lost all caution. The more selfish and demanding she became, the more Nathan's sexual appetite intensified. The physical release and emotional fulfillment was like nothing she had ever experienced or imagined. Both were eager to give and take. No words were necessary. They contorted themselves into positions she had never thought possible, and she felt no indignity in whatever Nathan wanted to do with his hands, fingers or mouth. This was the first time in her life she had felt pure sexual freedom.

They made love three times that night, the third being the most prolonged and without doubt, the most passionate. Emily had never before experienced multiple orgasms within what seemed like seconds of each other.

Nathan lay on his back and drew Emily closer, delighting in the pressure of her breast against his side. "Emily, that has got to be the best experience I've ever had."

She tilted her head up and kissed his cheek.

"If I'd known your sexual appetite was this remarkable, I would have made advances to you years ago," Nathan said. "You're incredible, you know that?"

"I've never let myself go like that, Nate. I think you had a lot to do with it as well," she said, in a mellow husky voice. "You've left me more than satisfied and totally exhausted." She kissed him again.

"Do you know how often I've fantasized about you, Emily?"

She was furtively delighted both at the compliment and at the fact that he used her full name. "Been giving yourself lots of exercise, have you?" A brief image of him masturbating flitted through her mind.

"More than I'd care to admit. But yes," he said, with a slight touch of embarrassment.

She shifted her hand and tightened her fingers around his partially erect penis, elated at feeling an instant involuntary twitch.

"And all these years, I've been holding back for fear of being judged," she said. "I think you've just released the devil in me."

"No, I think you've released it in yourself by freeing your mind."

"Oh, don't get all scientific on me," she rebuked.

"I just hope I don't wake up in the morning and find this was all a dream," he said earnestly.

She doubled over and gently bit his penis.

"Ow! That hurt," he said, smiling inwardly. "But in a nice way."

"At least now you know you're not dreaming," she said.

Nathan's grin grew broader. With all his erotic notions about Emily over the years, he had never thought that making love to her could be so utterly mind-blowing.

She prodded him in the ribs. "You want to tell me about some of your fantasies?"

"About you?"

"Duh! Of course," she said, with amusement.

"Maybe I will, but not today. I'd hate you to run out of here in horror."

"That bad, hey?"

"No, that good." He hugged her a little tighter.

Any dreams that either of them had were forgotten by the time they woke up mid-morning. Emily, lying on her back with the sheet halfway up, turned her head.

Nathan was lying on his side, elbow in his pillow and head resting on his hand.

"What?" she said, her face breaking into an inquisitive smile.

"I just like looking at you." He gently stroked her breasts and tummy.

"Mm, that's nice," she crooned. "Careful, you might get me started again."

"And that would be a problem because..."

"Mm," she murmured with an enticing smile.

"Would you like to take a shower?" he offered.

"No, but I'd love to try your bath," she answered.

"Then let me get it ready for you."

Lying in the warm water, Emily's thoughts drifted back to some of the truths they shared last night. She couldn't believe that they'd been skirting around each other for so many years, both with mutual desires cautiously concealed. Emily's admitting to her fear of being judged and Nate's confession that he was simply afraid of rejection seemed silly, now that she gave it some serious thought. She still couldn't believe the years wasted with all her trepidations of what people might think of her words or actions.

Both played the game very well, neither showing any signs of wanting an intimate relationship with the other, yet here she was taking thought in what she considered the best night of her life as a result of letting down her guard. She would no longer be introverted and detached from her true feelings. She was finally free from all her reservations and insecurities. Nate made her feel like a million dollars. She had also discovered the understated difference between having sex and making love. All her notions of another serious relationship evaporated. This was the man she was going to spend the rest of her life with.

Shutting out the enticing aroma of toast, bacon and coffee drifting from the kitchen, Emily laid further back, closed her eyes and let herself slide beneath the surface of the deep water. Fully stretched, her toes weren't able to reach the far side of the sizeable tub. She felt wonderful, enveloped in the comfortable weightlessness. Totally at peace with her inner thoughts, she was oblivious of Nathan walking through the open bathroom door.

After a few moments, she opened her eyes and noticed his shimmering silhouette looking down at her from an angle. Exhaling, she pushed herself up into a sitting position and faced him with a playful smile.

"Having fun?" she asked, breathlessly.

"Did I ever tell you what great legs you have?" he said.

"You did mention it a few times last night," she answered.

"I'm glad to hear you say it again today, and that it wasn't your insatiable lust talking."

"Insatiable is an understatement," he said with a thoughtful expression. *Living the dream* had taken on a whole new meaning for him.

Nathan leaned over and kissed her. "No rush, but when you're done, breakfast will be served." He turned and walked back towards the kitchen.

"It smells fabulous," she said loudly after him. "Give me five minutes." Damn, she was just about to pull him into the tub with her, clothes and all.

Wearing nothing but one of Nathan's oversized shirts, Emily sat opposite him at the counter between the kitchenette and lounge. "Hope you don't mind my borrowing one of your shirts," she said, adjusting the stool, resting her feet on the stool's cross-beam and wiggling her toes into place.

"I didn't know that shirt was quite so transparent," he said. "It looks much better on you than it does on me."

Emily would never have considered walking around as exposed as she was now, even when she was married. Since last night though, she was adamant in her resolve; if she wanted to do something and felt good about it, she was going to do it. Nathan had helped her see that it was okay to be who she wanted - without having to justify herself.

She wasn't wearing any undergarments and felt at ease having her naked body partially revealed through Nate's shirt. She could see from his approving glances that he had absolutely no objections either.

"Good coffee," she said, after taking a sip.

Nathan served up the eggs, bacon, breakfast sausages and toast.

"Here's butter," he said, sliding the dish over, "and if you want jam for afterwards, I can get that. I also have a small bowl of diced mixed fruit in the refrigerator."

"This all looks delicious Nate. Didn't realize just how hungry I was."

Both tucked in with gusto.

"I still can't get over James's generosity," she said. "Any plans about what you're going to do with your bonus?"

"Last night I knew exactly what I was going to do," he said. "This morning I'm not so sure anymore."

"And what *were* you going to do?"

"Spend a week by myself on Easter Island. I've never been there and have always had a fascination about the place."

"That sounds great," she said. "And somewhere between last night and this morning, you changed you mind?"

"Yes. Now I'm seriously thinking of renting one of those self-contained private islands in the Aegean, off the Greek coast."

She looked at him. "Oh yes?"

"And taking you with me," he finished.

"I should certainly hope so," she admonished with a smile.

"You would have found out anyway," he said. "I came to the conclusion years ago that all women are mind-readers."

"No, we're not."

"Then you must have mental telepathy, or some other mystic power known only amongst yourselves."

She was laughing. "No, we don't."

"Okay," he challenged. "Answer me this. How did you know I was standing over you when you were lying underwater in the bath with your eyes closed? You couldn't have heard me."

"I just knew," she answered, as if it were obvious.

"Okay, how about this? As soon as a man goes to the furthest geographical location in the house to where his wife or partner is, she immediately starts calling him?"

Emily looked at Nate sideways.

"Ha! See... You do have supernatural abilities."

"Oh, all right," she joked. "But don't let on. It's a secret known only to us women."

"When I first bought my car, I felt great driving around in it," he said, remembering an amusing story. "Back in the day, it was considered one of the most sought-after affordable sports coupes."

"That's the car you still have now?"

"Yup," he said. "And I still love driving it."

"It's a great little car," she said.

"Anyhow, I was waiting at a red light when two really hot young women walked in my direction. Both looked at the car with admiration and I felt a bit of a thrill, so I looked back at them. As soon as they saw that it wasn't some muscle-bound stud behind the wheel, but rather this greying old man - well, old in their eyes – and without any visible hint of communication between the two, they instantly gave me 'the look' and turned away. It took them literally a millisecond to simultaneously react. I swear, not a single word or other form of body language passed between them."

Emily burst out laughing.

"But you know that look projected by young women who consider themselves entitled - making it obvious that I'm disrespecting them simply because I exist."

"And I thought Sven was paranoid," she said. Now they were both laughing.

For the next hour, conversation was a mix of the thrill of discovery which they had had the previous night and regret that they had been so evasive towards each other for so long.

After they had tidied up a bit and washed a few dishes, Nathan offered to take Emily home. She slipped into her blouse and skirt, not bothering with either the bra or panties. She felt liberated, and a little naughty.

Pulling up outside her apartment, Emily faced him. "You can take you hand off my leg now," she teased.

"Must I?" He gave her leg a gentle squeeze.

"Why don't you come over for dinner tomorrow night, Nate?" she offered.

"I'd like that very much."

She leaned over and kissed him lovingly on the lips. "See you then. Come over late afternoon if you like," she said, stepping out the car. "You can give me some cooking tips."

Chapter Forty-One

New York County Supreme Court – day three. Judge Harrington Abercrombie presiding.

Brenda Barrett, appointed lawyer to Ryan Hurst and close friend of James Clark, reviewed her list of key witnesses.

Geoffrey Townsend – CEO, Magentis, NY

Davis Eldridge – VP, Magentis Seed Farms, Missouri

Adrian Bowers – Director, Food and Drug Administration, NY

She looked over her shoulder towards the witness stand, where Townsend, Eldridge and Bowers were seated like the Three Stooges with smug expressions on their faces. She suppressed a smile, thinking of Davis Eldridge and Adrian Bowers being referred to by James as Laurel and Hardy.

Geoffrey Townsend noticed Brenda Barrett looking towards them. Geoffrey knew exactly the approach his own lawyer was taking. It concerned the manuscript and fraud for which Ryan Hurst was being charged. The document, brought into evidence at the start of the trial, provided schematics and detailed instructions on how to successfully sterilize seed. Furthermore, it delivered viable options on removing all opposition.

The document had turned up in Townsend's personal mailbox some years back, and he had had absolutely no idea where it came from, but it was perfect. Their entire operation in Missouri was now based on this technical specification. Townsend had of course lied when questioned about how long it had been in his possession.

He had planned carefully, knowing that success ensured personal wealth beyond measure, but public knowledge or exposure meant failure, and that required flunkies. Davis Eldridge had treacherous ambition, Adrian Bowers, an unplanned added extra, was greedy, and Ryan Hurst was gullible. All three were perfect pawns to take the fall now that the entire operation was in jeopardy due to bad publicity.

It was essential that Geoffrey Townsend take Magentis GMP out of the media spotlight. In a desperate attempt at misdirection, he laid criminal charges against Ryan Hurst for a deliberate scheme to overturn the farm's 'ethical' GMP operation into one of seed sterilization.

So far, it had worked out perfectly. Ryan Hurst had been arrested; Geoffrey Townsend, Davis Eldridge and Adrian Bowers had been subpoenaed by a messenger of the courts as witnesses. Still, Geoffrey Townsend had to play this very carefully.

Sebastian S. Sedgwick, Magentis' lawyer, rose from his chair with self-assurance and buttoned his jacket.

"Your Honour," Sebastian Sedgwick said with smooth confidence. "I would like to review the document that was entered as evidence against Mr. Ryan Hurst. These are copies of the original that council for the defence has already seen."

He handed one copy to the judge, then walked with measured poise towards Ryan and handed him a second copy.

Briefly facing the jury, Sebastian Sedgwick raised a third copy of the document for dramatic effect, and then turned back to Ryan. "This document," Sedgwick continued, "clearly details a plan formulated by you, Mr. Hurst, to exploit the production of sterile seed with extensive financial reward to yourself." He presented the evidence. "Mr. Hurst, for absolute confirmation, is that your signature on page 23 of the document?"

Ryan looked at the bottom of the page referred to by Sedgwick. It was the last sheet of the NDA he had signed in the office of Geoffrey Townsend, the administrator, on the day of his promotion to Director of Operations. "Er, yes, it is," Ryan said nervously. Why was he being asked this again? He had already explained it on the first day of the trial. His palms were sweating profusely.

"Sorry, could you please speak up, Mr. Hurst," Sedgwick said.

"Yes, it is," Ryan repeated, a little louder.

"And you have already admitted that your platinum credit card is that linked directly to Magentis' corporate expense account."

Ryan cleared his throat. "Yes."

"But somehow you have no recollection of two million dollars mysteriously being transferred through your credit card to an account in the Cayman Islands?"

"I've... I've never been to the Cayman Islands," Ryan stammered.

"Come now, Mr. Hurst," Sedgwick incited. "You honestly expect us to believe such a claim holds substance, in today's world of online banking?"

Ryan was at a loss for words.

Sebastian Sedgwick had made his point. "No further questions, your Honour. Cross-examine?" he asked, looking at Brenda Barrett with a challenging leer.

Brenda stood up. At the same time, Emily Hurst rushed into the courtroom, walked swiftly over to Brenda and handed her some documents. She gave Emily a curt nod and an almost imperceptible smile.

Brenda walked up to Ryan. "According to the evidence submitted by Mr. Sedgwick on behalf of Magentis, you signed and dated the document two years ago. Is that correct Mr. Hurst?"

Ryan was confused. "I signed it just recently, but it's a non-disclosure agreement. I explained all of this the day before yesterday."

"Just answer the questions," Judge Abercrombie said to Ryan. "And the date?" Brenda asked.

"There was no place to enter a date," Ryan said, "so I didn't put one in, but you already know this."

Brenda seemed to ignore his reply. "Yet there it is, right beside your signature. Did you even read the document before signing?"

"No, I wasn't given the opportunity." Ryan was having difficulty justifying himself. He was getting angry and his chest felt tight.

"Mr. Hurst," Brenda continued, "I have here copies of the employment contract you signed when accepting your current position as Director of Operations."

She handed a copy to Judge Abercrombie, Sebastian Sedgwick and Ryan. "Amongst other things, I see that you were offered an increase in salary, a car, housing, and a new credit card. Is that correct?"

"Yes," Ryan said, after looking at the contract. What did this have to do with anything, he thought?

"And the credit card, which is still in your possession, is the one linked to Magentis' corporate expense account?"

"Yes, I believe so," Ryan said.

"Is that your signature on the contract?" Brenda asked.

Ryan looked at the paper again. "Yes."

"What about the date? Is that your writing?"

"Yes," Ryan replied.

Sebastian Sedgwick was on his feet. "Relevance, your Honour - what has the accused's contract of employment got to do with the elaborate scheme he's being charged with?"

Judge Abercrombie looked at Brenda. "I have to agree with Mr. Sedgwick. Is there a point to this line of questioning, Miss Barrett?"

"Yes, your Honour," Brenda said. "Please bear with me for just another minute."

"Move it along, then," the judge said sternly.

"And that's the same date when you received all the benefits that came with the contract - new car, increased salary and so on?"

"Yes," Ryan stated more forcefully.

Sebastian Sedgwick was still on his feet. "Your Honour..."

"Miss Barrett?" the judge asked testily.

"Yes, your Honour," Brenda said. "You'll see the relevance now." Sebastian sat down and unbuttoned his jacket.

"Mr. Hurst," Brenda said. "The charges against you are based on a highly detailed stratagem with a questionable date as to exactly when you signed it, and evidence that a substantial amount of money was transferred through your credit card. Yet you appear unable to provide adequate responses in your defence. The only thing that you seem to be clear about is signing this contract."

Ryan's mind was in a spin. The lawyer appointed to him wasn't putting up much of an argument against Sedgwick. She seemed to be making things worse.

"Are you absolutely sure about all your facts, Mr. Hurst?" Brenda asked. "Mr. Townsend, the administrator to Magentis, has already stated under oath that the document was dropped anonymously into his internal mailbox some months before you claim to have signed it. He also stated, under oath, that it was most likely deposited by a disgruntled employee. Mr. Townsend didn't take the document seriously until the recent inquiry by the FBI. Doesn't that seem a little odd?"

Ryan looked pleadingly at the judge, then to Brenda. "I, ...I don't know." Why was his lawyer being so hard on him?

"It is odd," Brenda stated. "Your Honour, new evidence has just been handed to me." She offered a copy of Emily's documents to the judge and another to Sebastian Sedgwick who glanced at it and immediately rose to his feet, almost knocking his chair over backwards.

"Objection," Sedgwick shouted, buttoning his jacket. "We knew nothing of this. It's inadmissible."

"Sit down, Mr. Sedgwick," the judge said calmly. "I will allow it." He turned to Brenda, inviting her to continue.

"Very odd indeed," Brenda said, facing the jury. "Mr. Hurst has admitted to signing the manuscript in question, yet the date exactly matches that when Mr. Hurst was overseeing seed delivery during his first or second trip to the Svalbard Global Seed Vault two years ago."

Brenda turned and faced Sebastian Sedgwick. "The documents you are looking at show the departure and return flights as well as confirmation by the airline that Mr. Hurst was indeed on those flights."

Sebastian Sedgwick was starting to get nervous.

"On the next page," Brenda went on, as the judge and Sedgwick flipped to the second page, "you will see the approved reservation for his overnight stay at the Oslo-Lufthavn hotel in Norway, as well as the payment settled in full by Magentis. You will also notice a small expense for alcoholic beverages incurred by Mr. Hurst."

The judge and jury's attention was piqued, and they were now listening to what Brenda was saying with deep interest.

"Seems to be a rather unusual time and place to sign such an incriminating document. And what of his signature? Who was Mr. Hurst signing it for, himself? That seems a bit of a peculiar and impractical thing to do, wouldn't you agree?"

Sebastian Sedgwick was on his feet again fumbling with his jacket. "Your Honour, I strongly object. How is any of this relevant? Mr. Hurst clearly signed the document. What does it matter where he did it?"

"Mr. Sedgwick," Judge Abercrombie said, as calmly as before. "One more outburst from you and I will have you in contempt. Now sit down."

Brenda continued. "And what of the administrator's claim that such a significant document somehow made its way into the hands of a disgruntled employee, who then decided on a whim to become a snitch?"

The jury were all nodding in agreement.

"Please turn to the last page," Brenda said, looking at the Judge, then at Sedgwick with a knowing smile. "It's the transaction record of the two million transferred through Mr. Hurst's credit account. It's dated the day before Mr. Hurst signed his contract. The day before Mr. Hurst actually received the credit card."

"Hurst obviously made a mistake with the date," Sedgwick bellowed, without bothering to stand up.

"The same mistake he made when he signed a technical manuscript over to himself?" Brenda asked Sedgwick sarcastically.

The courtroom erupted. The Three Stooges were muttering heatedly amongst themselves.

The judge slammed his gavel. "Order, please."

"None of this adds up," Brenda Barrett said, shaking her head.

"Your Honour, ladies and gentlemen of the jury. It's obvious that the money transfer, and this so called plot, is a complete fabrication by Magentis itself and that Mr. Hurst was coerced into signing it under completely false pretenses. If Mr. Hurst is guilty of anything, it's signing something he didn't read or fully understand. That is not a crime. I move that all charges against my client be dropped immediately."

Sebastian Sedgwick was on his feet again. "This is preposterous," he shouted, shaking his fist.

"Bailiff, please have Mr. Sedgwick removed from this courthouse." The judge pounded his gavel. "Case dismissed - and have Mr. Townsend, Mr. Eldridge and Mr. Bowers detained for further questioning. I want to see all three in my chambers in the next five minutes."

Chapter Forty-Two

Judge Harrington Abercrombie walked around the desk of his chambers and sat down, without removing his black gown. He recalled a scandal some years ago involving Magentis and the FDA, and wondered if these three had anything to do with that. From what the judge remembered, no charges were laid as it was more of an internal dispute than a legal case, but it did receive considerable attention from the media. It sounded like the accusations against Ryan Hurst might well be a comparable situation.

The bailiff knocked on the chamber door and ushered in Geoffrey Townsend, Davis Eldridge and Adrian Bowers. The judge regarded his audience and hoped these three clowns weren't going to add to the headache he already had. "Would any of you care to explain what's really going on here?"

All three started talking at once.

"Quiet!" the judge exclaimed. "Mr. Townsend, let's start with you."

Geoffrey Townsend cleared his throat. "Your Honour, I can only comment on the document that came into my hands. If Mr. Hurst is not to blame, then I would conclude that it was Davis Eldridge who concocted this scheme."

The other two looked at him with abhorrence.

"How so, Mr. Townsend?" the judge asked.

"In his position at the seed farms, he has full control and the most to gain. My primary function within Magentis is overall administration of the company and keeping our investors happy. I'm not physically located at the farms, and don't know everything that's going on with operations," Townsend asserted. "I hire senior staff to do that."

"And in your opinion, what exactly does Mr. Eldridge do regarding operations oversight at the farms?" the judge asked.

"The objective of Magentis is the research and manufacture of seeds that produce higher yielding crops. It's our aim to eradicate global famine and Mr. Eldridge's job is to realize that undertaking."

"According to the media, you are more concerned with producing seeds that are sterile, making farmers one hundred per cent reliant on you."

"No, your Honour, the press has been misinformed," Townsend said quickly. "Sterility is just part of natural selection. It does happen, but in the case of our seed farms, on a very small scale. If more than acceptable levels of sterile seed are being manufactured, Mr. Eldridge is ultimately accountable."

The judge faced Davis Eldridge. "Your comment?"

"I still believe that this plot was instigated by Ryan Hurst in collusion with Mr. Townsend and Mr. Bowers," Eldridge said, shifting the blame.

"You're questioning my final ruling?" the judge challenged.

"Er, no, your Honour."

Judge Abercrombie's brow furled. He looked menacingly into Davis Eldridge's eyes. "Then what exactly are you saying?"

Eldridge back-tracked. "It's just that whoever is to blame, I had absolutely nothing to do with any of this. The first I heard was when I was subpoenaed for this trial."

"Go on," the judge said.

Eldridge's mouth was now moving faster than his thought process. "If Mr. Hurst is truly as ignorant about all of this as I am, I can only think that Mr. Townsend positioned Ryan Hurst as Director of Ops at the seed farm so that this scheme could succeed."

Christ, Davis Eldridge thought, this would not sit well with Geoffrey Townsend, but it was time that this cigar-smoking slob was replaced by someone more competent, like himself. For now, though, Davis needed to rephrase his statement.

"What I mean," Davis Eldridge stammered, "is that maybe Mr. Townsend was simply acting on a suggestion brought forward to him."

"Oh," the judge said. "So now there's someone else that's to blame."

Eldridge was cringing. "Maybe it was Adrian Bowers. I don't know, your Honour."

"What?" Adrian Bowers blurted.

Geoffrey Townsend gave Davis Eldridge an enraged look.

"You're fired," he whispered with venom.

A few moments of uncomfortable silence passed. This blame game was going nowhere, the judge thought.

"Mr. Townsend," Judge Abercrombie said, looking at Geoffrey and ignoring the other two. "My conclusion is that internal operations and the mismanagement of corporate funds by yourself and Mr. Eldridge is of no legal concern. As far as I'm concerned, the way Magentis runs its business and the way payments and bonuses are disbursed should be resolved internally. It is not for the courts to decide. That also includes any plots and power struggles amongst senior executives."

Geoffrey Townsend shuffled uneasily under the judge's scrutiny.

Abercrombie continued. "I also believe that your company made a substantial donation to a charitable organization in Thailand. As commendable as that may be, this again, has no legal consequences. But I will remind you, Mr. Townsend; contributions to foreign charities cannot be claimed as tax deductions, so I do not want to hear of any creative accounting going on at Magentis."

"Yes, er, no, your Honour," Townsend said.

"You and Mr. Eldridge can go," the judge said. "Mr. Bowers, you will remain."

Geoffrey Townsend and Davis Eldridge were escorted from the judge's chamber, leaving no doubt as to their mutual hostility towards each other.

The judge looked at Adrian Bowers. "I have a few questions concerning an associate of yours – Tony De Luca."

Bowers swallowed nervously.

The judge went on. "De Luca was arrested recently on charges of burglary, altercation and destruction of property at SkyTech Tower. He had quite a few interesting things to say."

Bowers started sweating.

***

Adrian Bowers woke up with a blinding headache. He had passed out on his living room sofa some time in the early hours of the morning. Two bottles of Bourbon, both empty, lay on the carpet by his feet. Another, still half full, stood on the coffee table next to the letter which he had received in the post the previous afternoon. He picked it up and read it again, through blurry, bloodshot eyes.

DEUTSCHE BUNDESBANK

"Providing Maximum Investment Security"

Dear Mr. Bowers,

We thank you for your business over the last three years and hope that we have provided favorable returns on your investments during that time. We pride ourselves in offering total privacy and security for all our valued customers and are assured that you were satisfied with all the advantages our bank has had to offer in this regard.

We hope that we can be of service to you again in the near future.

Yours sincerely, Gunther Oberhausen

International Investments

Deutsche Bundesbank - Hamburg

The FDA had handed him his dismissal papers the day before, and now this. Various phone calls to Hamburg proved futile. As far as the Bundesbank was concerned, he had closed the account, and had had the money transferred to Chase Manhattan, but Chase had no record of any such transfer into his account.

He was broke.

How had his life turned to such a living hell? Was God testing him? Had God forsaken him completely? Surely his righteous and moral existence should offer some rewards? Not this.

Things certainly couldn't get any worse for Adrian Bowers.

***

After a week of extensive investigations by National Security and the FBI, Adrian Bowers was arrested and charged with embezzlement, child porn and tax evasion on multiple counts over many years. A spokesperson for the Food and Drug Administration denied all knowledge, claiming that the first hint of any such activity by Bowers only became evident after some very large and unaccountable discrepancies were detected in their general revenue fund.

Adrian Bowers' final sentence: twelve years for embezzlement, with a chance of parole after ten years, four years for possession of child pornography, and thirty-five years for tax evasion, without parole. He was in for life.

Geoffrey Townsend walked out as Chief Administrator for Magentis, and took up a new post as CEO of Lifespan Pharmaceuticals Inc.

The Deputy Director of the FDA resigned, apparently for personal reasons, awarding himself five million dollars as a tax-free exit bonus. Media speculation implied that his resignation was due to concerns with his health. No comment was available.

Chapter Forty-Three

Obadiah Brown was a mountain of a man – six foot six in height and over three hundred and fifty pounds of solid muscle, a product of working in construction his entire adult life. The pay wasn't bad, and, with no family, Obadiah had very few expenses. Most of his weekly paycheck went into a high-interest savings account.

Obadiah avoided social interactions and had no ambitions in life except to retire at fifty, at which point he would buy a small cabin near a mountain lake and live out the rest of his days fishing. That, at least, had been his plan. Now he was serving the last few days of his prison term for a crime he considered well worth the cost.

Obadiah was a very gentle and soft-spoken man, avoiding unnecessary confrontation wherever possible. One of the few real joys he had were the weekly dinners with his sister Louetta and her ten-year-old daughter Jasmine. He loved his niece, giving her all the attention she demanded, trying as best as possible to fill in the gap for a father she had never known.

Jasmine was considered by friends and family as lucky to be alive. Theodore Coleman, a child molester prowling their neighbourhood two years previously, had snatched her from the school playground, pretending to be a friend of her mother's and had driven her to a quiet suburban street. Muffling her screams with one hand, he used the other to fondle and probe into the most private parts of Jasmine's terrified young body. If it had not been for a passing cyclist, she would, in all probability, never have been heard from again.

Obadiah took time off work without pay to attend all the court proceedings. His sister, but more so Jasmine, needed all the moral support he could muster. The final ruling was that Theodore had experienced a momentary lapse in judgement, and, this being his first minor offence, he was not considered a menace to society. His name, address and social security details were recorded in the offender's registry; he was fined two thousand dollars, and given six months community service.

Obadiah felt an anger he had never before experienced. Louetta burst into uncontrollable tears.

Jasmine was scarred for life.

According to sources in the neighbourhood, this was not the first time Theodore Coleman had misbehaved. The complaints of a few children that he had flashed at them had been discounted as kids just looking for attention. No children had ever gone missing and nothing had ever been proven.

In his youth, Obadiah Brown typically had withdrawn in the face of controversy, and had shied away from confrontation, especially during his last years at high school, where bullies felt they had something to prove against the 'big guy'.

But not this time.

Two months later, Obadiah, intent on justice, paid Theodore Coleman a late-night visit. He barged through the door, said nothing, and pushed Theodore through to the kitchen. Ripping Theodore's denims off his spindly white legs, and grabbing a large meat cleaver from the counter, Obadiah chopped Theodore's penis off and shoved it down his throat.

The immediate neighbours, hearing the commotion and anguished screams, dialed 911. Within ten minutes, sirens blaring, the police arrived. Pistols drawn, they cautiously walked through the open front door and into the kitchen. Obadiah stood up slowly from the chair where he had been waiting patiently and handed the cleaver over to a confused officer.

"He's alive," said Obadiah looking at Theodore lying on the floor with his crotch bleeding profusely. "But you should call an ambulance."

Obadiah Brown was arrested and thrown into prison. During the trial, at which Obadiah pleaded guilty, many of his sister's neighbours testified that Theodore Coleman was a known child molester, and that his sentence was ridiculous and totally insulting to the local community.

There were no contradictions that Obadiah had finally served real justice, but Obadiah's actions seemed very harsh to the judge. Theodore Coleman was left with his balls still intact, and, subsequently, all his natural desires. Having been forced to swallow his only means of sexual pleasure, he would live the remainder of his life with urges he could do nothing about.

The jury agreed with the community that something needed to be done about creeps like Coleman, but they had Obadiah's felony and the law to consider, not the motives. A verdict of guilty was reluctantly passed.

The Honourable Theophilus Adelbert Chauncey, recently reassigned from South Carolina, looked Obadiah sternly in the face. "This is the most heinous of crimes, Mr. Brown. One the justice system cannot take lightly."

Obadiah stood proud.

"Based on the verdict of this jury and in the eyes of the law," the judge stated, "you will be punished according to the maximum prison term required by the State of New York's criminal justice system."

Judge Chauncey struck his gavel ruthlessly against the sound block. "Taking all things into due consideration, you are hereby sentenced to two years in the federal penitentiary, minimum security, on the charge of altercation with the intent of causing severe bodily harm."

Obadiah was stunned at the light sentence, as were Louetta and the witnesses. Many applauded the sentence, regardless of the fact that they were holding the court in contempt.

Judge Chauncey, grandfather of three young girls, left the courtroom with a barely noticeable smile.

Obadiah Brown's prison term went by without incident - to himself at least. He ate his meals alone and sat quietly by himself during the two hours allowed in the exercise yard. With his intimidating size, the other inmates tended to leave him alone. Louetta and Jasmine visited for an hour each week, and, being minimum security, were allowed contact in the guarded common room. Although not strictly permitted, and one to which the guards turned a blind eye, Jasmine always brought a small homemade cake for Obadiah.

Books were freely available from the prison library, and Obadiah consumed these with passion alone in his cell before lights out at ten p.m. He did not currently have a cell-mate and there were unlikely to be any volunteers. The other inmates knew precisely what Obadiah did to some of them in the shower block. More for their pain than his pleasure, Obadiah occasionally grabbed one of the pathetic wife-beaters or child-molesters in his block and ensured that they couldn't sit for a week. Most times they couldn't even have a good shit for at least a month without crying in agony.

Obadiah was affectionately nicknamed *Alice*.

Shortly before release, a guard approached Obadiah's cell and unlocked it. "Alice, I found you a temporary room-mate," he said. "It seems like we have a slight problem with available accommodations in maximum security."

The guard yanked the new prisoner into Obadiah's view. "He likes little girls and boys."

Obadiah Brown smiled sadistically.

Adrian Bowers wet himself.

***

"In today's business news," the CNN reporter announced, "share prices of Magentis GMP are climbing rapidly from an all-time low, following the recent scandal of the produce giant's unethical sterilization of food crops. In a surprising turn of events, SkyTech Aeronautics acquired 51% of their stock last week, giving them full control of Magentis' future business practices. In an exclusive interview with CNN, a spokesperson stated that SkyTech intends to destroy the entire crop of modified seeds stored at the Missouri gene banks, and replace it with natural seed that will be imported from vaults across the globe. SkyTech has also cancelled the merger between Magentis and a major European pharmaceutical company.

"In our local news segment, we now cross live to CNN's Bob Montgomery, on location outside the federal penitentiary, where some sort of riot seems to be going on. Bob, over to you."

"Thanks, Gary," the anchor said over the noise of the crowd. "As you can see behind me, it's not a riot at all, but more like a welcoming committee. You may recall CNN's exclusive coverage two years ago of the vigilante who decided to take matters into his own hands concerning a local paedophile. They are just about to release him. Yes, the gate has just opened."

The crown erupted into enthusiastic applause.

"There are a woman and a young girl rushing over to embrace him. I will get closer and see if I can get a few comments." Bob threaded his way through the crowd. "Mr. Brown. Bob Montgomery, CNN. Welcome back."

Obadiah, still hugging Louetta and Jasmine tightly, looked towards the news anchor.

"What are your plans, now that your sentence is behind you?" Bob prompted with the microphone.

"Er, I've been offered a job in security at SkyTech Tower," Obadiah responded self-consciously.

"Oh, leave my brother alone," said Louetta, angrily pushing the microphone out of the way. "Can't you see that he doesn't want to talk to you people from the press?"

"Thank you, Mr. Brown. Good luck for the future."

Bob moved away from the crowd. "Well, it seems like SkyTech is really diversifying, Gary."

"It certainly does," Gary agreed back in the studio.

"From aeronautics and communications to farming, and now they are hiring ex-convicts. They must have good reason."

"We certainly do," Emily commented, as she, James, Nathan and Sven listened to further speculation from the CNN reporter on James' TV.

"Wonderful job tracking down Adrian Bowers's unfortunate transfer to Obadiah's cell block," James said, looking over to Sven. "I don't even want to know how you hacked into the federal pen's database and modified it to indicate that the maximum-security wing was over-crowded when it's almost empty."

Sven smiled but said nothing.

"Also glad you were able to research Obadiah's history, Em," James said.

"I'm glad we're able to give him a break," she said. "He has strong moral backbone and will eventually make an excellent head of security for this building. Timing is also great for when Mark Johnson retires in a few months."

"What are you going to do with Magentis' sterilization operation?" Nathan asked James. "There's billions of dollars of equipment there."

"Their entire operation is already fully automated from the silos to despatch," James said. "We leave it exactly as is, but turn off the gamma pulse generators. In time they'll be dismantled and sold."

"Who would buy them?" Emily asked.

"The steel industry," James answered. "Foundries use very similar equipment in their furnaces and spectrometers."

"On the international news front," Gary continued, "The Vatican has appointed Dominique Garcia as chamberlain to the Pope at Castel Gandolfo, His Holiness' summer retreat north of Rome. Reverend Garcia recently served the congregation at a local Baptist-Catholic church in Jersey, New York State. Appointments such as these are normally reserved for priests and cardinals who have performed exceptional services to their communities or to the Catholic Church."

***

Info Tech had been completely refurbished. Old computer equipment was dismantled for removal, as scrap and the developer workstation cubicles had been remodelled into a spacious, open-plan environment. Nathan's office was refitted with modern furniture, along with the latest in computer hardware, featuring dual monitor, Bluetooth keyboard and wireless mouse.

By way of a small perk, James presented each member of the software development team with a tablet for both personal and office use.

Emily was getting used to the hushed surroundings preferred by the developers - a sharp contrast to the perpetual activity of the reception area, now managed full-time by Monica.

Phil Roberts, now fully recovered and back at work, was taking his duties very seriously. He had presented his resignation to Nathan on the day he had come out of hospital, but Nathan hadn't accepted it. Phil, however, was given a serious talking to about taking security seriously.

James agreed that Nathan had made the right decision, figuring that Phil was a good developer and had years of experience with SkyTech, expertise that would be arduous and costly to replace.

Emily was called into James's office.

"Won't keep you long, Emily," James said. "I wanted you to know that we've reached out to Ryan and offered him back his old job in logistics if he wants it."

"That's very kind of you James," she said. "As bad as it was, Ryan got a good wake-up call from this debacle with Bowers and Magentis. I doubt he'll be quite so ignorant about his choices in the future."

"I'll have Monica draw up a new contract for him," James said.

"He can keep his present salary, but without the yearly bonus. He can also keep the car, but I want that corporate credit card back."

"Something tells me he doesn't want anything more to do with company credit cards."

They both laughed.

"How is it going with you and Nate?" he asked.

"I couldn't be happier," she said, trying unsuccessfully to suppress a smile. They had attempted to keep their relationship a secret at work, which, of course, meant that everyone knew about it.

"Matt and Elle absolutely adore him," she said. "The discussions Nate and Matt have during dinners at my apartment suggest that Matt wants to study for a new career in micro-robotics."

"That's excellent news," James said, with a broad smile. "I'm surprised it took the two of you so long to get together. Your feelings for each other have been obvious for a long time."

"Unfortunately, not obvious to us," she said with a slight hint of regret.

"Well, I'm not going to keep you any longer. Looks like most of the admin departments have already packed up for the holiday season."

SkyTech closed business between Christmas and New Year, but James always let everyone off work a few days earlier, so that they could enjoy some extra well-deserved time with friends and family.

"I hope you have a great Christmas, James," she said. "Will you be spending it with your parents again?"

"Yes. They'll be coming to me this year," he said. "I take it that you and Nate will be spending most of your time together?"

"As much as possible," she said. "Matt and Elle are getting used to my weekend sleep-overs at Nate's condo."

"Glad to hear it."

"I know this is unprofessional of me in the workplace, James, but..." She walked around his desk and gave him the biggest hug she could. "Thanks for everything, James. Merry Christmas."

"And a Merry Christmas to you too, Emily." He returned the hug. "Give my best to the kids."

Chapter Forty-Four

Fate had certainly played a large part in Ryan Hurst's life over the past few months. Ryan's winter, both metaphorically and physically, was behind him. He was quite content to be out of the rat-race of the big cities, and had settled quite comfortably in his Kirksville home. What started out as a typical bachelor pad now had all the subtle finesse that followed from a woman's touch.

Yet another twist of fate, he thought with fondness, as he drove his BMW out of the Magentis Seed Farms complex in Missouri.

The new love of his life, whom he would be picking up on his way home, had opened up a small and very successful deli in the New Year, choosing Kirksville as being suitably far from her depressive existence in New York.

They had connected almost immediately, their chemistry bonding at first sight of each other. She moved in with Ryan a month later, and they were engaged shortly afterwards, having to wait until her previous marriage was annulled by the courts. Their relationship was one of undeniable love and suitability – she didn't want children, and he was infertile.

Ryan was thankful that Mr. Clark had offered him the opportunity to work as Logistics Manager from his office at the farm's administrative complex. He still found it difficult to believe that, after all his years with Magentis, he had absolutely no idea that their underground sterilization facility even existed. He was so convinced that Magentis was all about improving life for humanity.

A new Director of Operations had been hired to oversee dismantling of the gamma pulse generators, now deactivated.

Modifications to the intake chutes, conveyors and seed-sorting to improve delivery to the despatch area were under way.

Davis Eldridge, the previous head of operations, whom Ryan had only seen for the first time in court, was rumoured to have been fired by Geoffrey Townsend in the judge's chambers shortly after Ryan's verdict was ruled. Eldridge's underground office was temporarily converted into a contractor's station while the operation was being overhauled.

A new CEO in the New York offices had still to be appointed.

Ryan parked outside the entrance of the deli and waited for a few minutes. Through the open glass doors, he could see her finalising a few things with the manager who would be running the shop for the next few hours. The success of the deli was largely due to the volumes of food students from Truman State could consume. It also helped that her business was located opposite to the university on Franklin Street.

How ironic, he thought, that two perfect strangers would meet in such a small community, each previously connected in their own way to the same person, namely Adrian Bowers.

He looked up at the colourful sign above the entrance and smiled – *Balasco Organics and Deli.*

Sofia's creativity in dressing the sidewalk-facing windows with delicious pastries almost made Ryan's mouth water.

***

Emily and Nathan were lying naked on the over-sized bed in their secluded cabin. The night was warm with a cool Mediterranean breeze blowing gently through the open window. The soft sound of waves lapping leisurely against the shoreline added tranquility to the blissful moonlit night.

Emily's energy was pleasurably depleted. She was relaxed and completely at peace with the world. She had never snorkelled in the nude before, and making love in the ocean was also a first. Nate had admitted to that being one of his erotic fantasies about her.

Nathan cast his mind back to five months ago. Had time really gone by so fast? He interrupted her dreamy thoughts. "You know what was really absurd about that whole Magentis fiasco?" he said, turning to face her. "If it hadn't been for Bowers's greed, and that senseless blackmailing stunt of his, their scheme would have actually worked."

"Mmm..." Emily drifted to sleep, snuggling into him a little tighter to the sound of his heartbeat against her ear.

***

In the silent darkness of its secure basement domain, SkyTech's IBM, void of opinion or self-awareness, was faithfully processing data at the rate of terabytes every second. It redirected all of its computing and memory resources in an attempt - so far, with no success - to decode a communications bit-stream for which there was no recognisable encoding.

The data originated from somewhere in the Mojave Wastelands south of Nevada.